T0318855

An Earth ravaged by an environmental catastrophe now faces its greatest threat—from space. And only the woman known as H124 can harness a lost technology to save it from absolute destruction.

The Skyfire Saga

As a deadly asteroid careens towards Earth, H124 and her Badlander companions race against time to piece together the ancient ruins of a spaceship that can intercept it. But this is not their only mission. In case their plan is not successful, they must warn the residents of Delta City of the impending impact, giving them a chance to seek shelter.

Aligned against a power-hungry media empire that feeds off an apathetic and unsuspecting populace, H124 knows that knowledge is her greatest weapon. And as news of the incoming asteroid spreads, the citizens begin to turn away from those who have kept them shackled in ignorance. Backed into a corner, Earth's corrupt rulers will do anything to stop H124, even if it means sacrificing the planet itself . . .

Visit us at www.kensingtonbooks.com

The Skyfire Saga by Alice Henderson

Shattered Roads
Shattered Lands
Shattered Skies

SHATTERED SKIES

The Skyfire Saga

Alice Henderson

REBEL BASE BOOKS
Kensington Publishing Corp.
www.kensingtonbooks.com

Rebel Base Books are published by

Kensington Publishing Corp. 119 West 40th Street New York, NY 10018

Copyright © 2019 by Alice Henderson

All Kensington titles, imprints, and distributed lines are available at special quantity discounts for bulk purchases for sales promotion, premiums, fundraising, and educational or institutional use.

To the extent that the image or images on the cover of this book depict a person or persons, such person or persons are merely models, and are not intended to portray any character or characters featured in the book.

Special book excerpts or customized printings can also be created to fit specific needs. For details, write or phone the office of the Kensington Special Sales Manager:
Kensington Publishing Corp.
119 West 40th Street
New York, NY 10018
Attn. Special Sales Department. Phone: 1-800-221-2647.

Kensington Reg. U.S. Pat. & TM Off
REBEL BASE Reg. U.S. Pat. & TM Off.
The RB logo is a trademark of Kensington Publishing Corp.

First Electronic Edition: October 2019
eISBN-13: 978-1-63573-048-7
eISBN-10: 1-63573-048-1

First Print Edition: October 2019
ISBN-13: 978-1-63573-051-7
ISBN-10: 1-63573-051-1

Printed in the United States of America

To everyone out there who is fighting to preserve this amazing planet and all the species we share it with. Forge ahead and we will prevail.

Chapter 1

The submarine lurched sickeningly to the right, the klaxon blaring above H124's head. Flashing red light filled the tiny space as she grabbed onto one of the bunks to steady herself.

"Captain to the conn! Battle stations!" someone cried from the command deck. The captain squeezed through the doorway from the next chamber and pressed by her, hurrying to his station.

"What is it?" H124 called to Raven, grabbing onto the bunk edges to move forward to the next compartment. Raven stood in the doorway to the command deck, his long black hair falling into his eyes as he struggled to keep his balance. "I don't know!"

She moved next to him, peering toward the command deck, and heard the sonar tech shout, "Torpedo incoming bearing 150!"

The captain was quick to respond. "All ahead full, come left to 240, depth twenty meters!"

The sub lurched to the side and she caught herself against the fuselage. They waited in a tense ensuing silence, then once again the command deck burst into action.

"Torpedo incoming bearing 170!" the sonar tech shouted from her station.

"All ahead full, come left to 260, depth thirty meters!" the captain yelled.

"Aye!" the helmsman called back.

Once again the sub swayed to one side with a sudden burst of speed. But the enemy craft had been too close to them when it launched its projectile. She heard something clang dully against the sub, and seconds later a violent explosion wracked the submarine. The sea around them erupted into a tempest of bubbles.

"Glancing blow, sir," the weapons officer reported.

"Is there a breach?"

"Doesn't look like it, sir," the officer responded.

"We need to neutralize that thing now! Fire torpedo tube one!" shouted the captain.

"Fire torpedo tube one, aye," shouted the weapons officer.

H124 could hear the clanking of boots on metal as crew members hurried back to the torpedo bay. Moments later she heard a dull *thunk* as a torpedo left one of the bays.

"We're too damn close. Brace for the shockwave!" the captain called, and H124 grabbed onto a metal handle. But an impact didn't come.

"Missed the target, sir," said the weapons officer.

"Damn!" cursed the captain. "Fire torpedo tube two!"

"Aye!" called the weapons officer, relaying the order to the crew in the torpedo bay.

Much quicker this time, she heard the dull *thunk* of a torpedo leaving the bay.

"Direct hit!" called the weapons officer.

"Brace for the shockwave!" shouted the captain. H124 gripped the handle and Raven held onto the door frames to either side of her. His dark brown eyes met hers in the red flashing gloom of the submarine, and then the entire vessel rocked violently to one side, tossed in the concussive wave from the explosion. She struggled to remain standing. He grabbed her arm. They steadied each other as the sub shuddered and fell still again.

"Enemy craft disabled, captain," reported the weapons officer.

Raven turned and approached the command deck.

They'd connected with this group of ocean-going Rovers in the hopes of finding the next piece of equipment for their mission.

An asteroid was careening toward the earth on a collision course. It had fragmented into four pieces in antiquity. Two pieces were still on the way: a smaller fragment soon to hit the Pacific Ocean, and the main asteroid, which was heading for a devastating land strike. Though they had a blast deflection craft to deliver a nuclear detonation and throw it off course, they still had no nuclear weapon and no way of launching the craft into space. But they hoped with this Rover crew journey, that this would soon change.

A few weeks before, Onyx and Orion had finished recovering much of the data from the disks and drives that H124 had picked up at the university under New Atlantic, along with the drives they'd recovered from the various aeronautic facilities where they'd found pieces of the blast deflection craft.

One of the monumental tasks before them had been building a rocket that could deliver the blast deflection craft into space. Then they'd lucked out. On one of the disks, they'd found plans for a launch vehicle that could take off from the ground and fly directly into space, no rocket needed. It was the craft designed to replace something called "the shuttle program." But the new program hadn't gotten far. One had been built, and then all the funds from the project had been diverted into military spending.

The vehicle, named the A14, had been built and housed in a facility that was a mere ten feet above sea level on what had then been the east coast. But as the temperatures had risen due to anthropogenic warming, so too had sea levels risen to disastrous heights, inundating coastal cities and flooding facilities like this one.

The vehicle they searched for now might have been more than two hundred feet below the waves, lying there for so many years it felt futile to even hope that it was still down there and still reparable, even if they'd have to salvage parts to rebuild it. But they had to try.

They'd been lucky that a group of Rovers lived in the area, people Raven had met as a kid when he'd traveled around with his parents, checking on the experimental forests that the Rovers had planted, trying to restore some areas to what they'd been before.

He'd contacted them, and they'd agreed to help.

"What was that thing?" Raven asked the captain, an older, sharply dressed man with a mane of white hair that spilled down his shoulders. In the gloom, his pale face hovered above a thick black woolen turtleneck sweater and black woolen jacket. H124 didn't know how he wasn't sweating to death. Even his pants were wool, and he wore knee-high boots and a fancy hat with a gold emblem on its brow depicting a porpoise cavorting between two curling waves. "Ancient nuclear AUV. Autonomous underwater vehicle," the man said. "A long time ago, they were designed to patrol these waters and disable any enemy ships in the area."

"And they think we're an enemy ship?" H124 asked.

He nodded. "Back when they were built, friendlies were tagged with an old identify friend-or-foe system so the AUVs knew who was supposed to be there. If you don't have a tag, you're a hostile."

"And these things are still operational?" Raven asked, his voice wavering. "After all this time?"

"They're nuclear-powered, like this sub. They'll go and go until their fuel gives out. This area's full of them, probably put in place to guard this very facility you want to break into." He glanced thoughtfully toward the sonar station. "This place used to be a heavily guarded base full of top secret projects in development. They employed hundreds of these AUVs to patrol the water. We've disabled quite a few over the years, but countless others are probably still out there. We've got to be careful unless we want to end up in a watery grave."

"What the hell was that?" came an out-of-breath voice behind them. H124 turned to see Dirk framed in the doorway, a collection of wires in one hand and a multitool in the other. Perspiration beaded on his sepia skin, soaking into his long purple and black dreadlocks.

"Apparently ancient tech that wants us dead," Raven told him.

Dirk wiped the sweat off his forehead with his sleeve. "That was a hell of a blow. Tell me there aren't more."

"Lots more, unfortunately," the captain answered.

"Captain," said the helmsman, looking at his screen. "We're here."

H124 took a deep breath. It was time to dive.

The dive master appeared in the doorway and gestured for them to follow him back to the lockout trunk. It was a chamber where divers entered, and water filled to match the outside water pressure. Then the door would open, and divers could swim out from there.

The dive master had already gone over all the diving equipment, and now she, Raven, and Dirk climbed into the bulky diving suits with full-face helmets. Each helmet had been fitted with transducers that converted their voices to ultrasound, and receivers that converted those ultrasonic signals back to audible sound. This would allow them to communicate with each other and the sub while underwater. Exterior lights on the helmets would allow them to see in the murky depths. She felt the heavy weight of oxygen tanks being placed on her back as she secured the seal on her helmet. Other crew members buzzed around Raven and Dirk, securing them. Dirk looked distant and sad, just as he had every day since he'd woken up from his coma. She'd never forget his reaction when he'd learned about his twin Astoria's fate.

That day, she'd heard Dirk's scream from the far end of the hall. He'd staggered out of the med lab, gripping the doorframe, swaying there in the open doorway. Byron had reached out to steady him, but he'd shoved his friend away, bringing his hands up to the sides of his head. His mouth had opened in a silent scream, his eyes squeezed shut, as if begging his brain to take back the horror. Byron had reached out again, steadying his friend, who'd nearly crumpled to the floor. He'd gripped his elbow, steering him to a nearby bench. Dirk had shaken his head, teeth clenched. "It can't be. I don't believe you!"

H124 had felt frozen to the spot. She'd told her legs to move toward him, but they wouldn't. She'd been with Astoria when it happened. And though she didn't know how, she'd felt she should have saved her, felt she could have done something, anything, to have returned to Sanctuary City with her alive. Though logically she knew that Astoria had forced her hand, had shoved her off that rooftop and run shouting into the tangle of soldiers, H124 couldn't help but feel she'd let Dirk down, that she was somehow responsible for the gaping hole that had yawned open in his life.

Now in the gloom of the submarine, Dirk's eyes looked hollow, and though he'd never been incredibly talkative before, he definitely wasn't now. He'd been the first to volunteer to go on this mission, insisting that he come along because he knew his way around old tech, and while that was certainly true, she knew that mostly he just didn't want to be left alone with his thoughts. She'd noticed that he'd been working with Orion nonstop since emerging from the med bay. He'd barely slept, and kept busy constantly. Now he stared vacantly off into the distance as a crew member secured the seal on his helmet.

"It's going to be dangerous down there," the dive master warned them for the twelfth time. "Doorways, hallways, narrow passages, a million places where you could get hung up or trapped and run out of air. You're going to be at a dangerous depth, more than two hundred and ten feet, so don't screw around down there." He checked them all over, making sure the suits were secure. It was old tech his crew had retrofitted, and they'd only have an hour of air. "We've mixed other gases with your O_2, sort of an updated version of the old gas Trimix."

"What's that?" Raven asked.

"It'll let you go deeper than a regular O_2 mix and will protect you from the narcotic effects of nitrogen. Still, this is a fool's mission. There's no way that ship is still down there."

H124 peered through the opening into the cavernous lockout trunk. A sudden fear squeezed her stomach.

"It's our only lead," Raven told him. "We have to do this." Now fully suited up, he stepped into the lockout chamber with H124 and Dirk.

The only way the sub crew had agreed to take them out to the facility was if they didn't have to risk any of their own crew by diving.

"We lost a man last year," the dive master had told them when they'd first met him. H124 had only learned later that it had been his son, that he'd become hung up when a rusted wall had collapsed on him, damaging his air tanks. Though he'd had a diving partner, the other man hadn't been able to lift the debris off, and he'd died in a matter of minutes.

Now the dive master locked eyes with H124. "It's dangerous diving. The most dangerous kind, entering a structure. This could well be a suicide mission."

"We don't have a choice, unfortunately," Raven told him. "Not if we're going to divert this thing. It's either risk our lives here, or die when the asteroid hits."

"It's your funeral," the dive master said with finality, giving a sterling vote of confidence. He shut them inside the lockout trunk and flooded it with water.

Once the water pressure equalized, the hatch opened with a groan. H124 peered into the dark depths of water beyond. She'd never been in salt water before, never been in such depths. The most she'd ever done was swim in rivers and, once, a small, sapphire-blue lake up by Sanctuary City. The water there had been bitterly cold. Here, though the surface temperature wasn't so bad, she knew they'd be experiencing severe cold at this depth.

She pushed off the lip of the sub. The dark water yawned beneath her. This was a crazy crapshoot. If the craft was even still down there, it would be rusted and...

She pushed the hopeless thoughts away.

Dirk and Raven swam out of the chamber, joining her in the water. Raven nodded to her, and all three switched on their helmet lights. Brilliant beams cut through the water. All three swam deeper. They'd each been fitted with special PRD displays that could operate down there, adjusting for the magnification of the water. She turned hers on and it shimmered, showing a schematic of the old building, the way to the hangar that had historically held the A14.

The cold water pressed against her body, and she could feel the added pressure on her chest as she descended, allowing the weight belt around her waist to pull her downward.

"Everyone okay?" Raven asked. His voice, reassuring in the dark cold, came across clearly. She gave him a thumbs-up. "Remember we only have sixty minutes of air, so we have to make this quick."

As she slid into the dark, she turned on the lights mounted on her helmet. The others did the same, and she glided down through the water until a shape loomed up beneath her. Strange white fingers covered it, and as she drew lower, she could make out more detail. A long, flat surface lay beneath a myriad of small tangled white shapes, some indeed shaped like fingers, others like small trees.

Raven drew up beside her. "It's coral."

She'd heard the captain use the term. It was something the Rovers in this area were trying to save, a living organism that formed reefs, which provided habitat for a number of marine species. She'd read about how warming oceans and unsustainable fishing practices had destroyed the reefs in antiquity, how warming seas had caused them to bleach and die. Slowly these coastal Rovers were trying to fix that, planting coral where it had once thrived.

H124 took in the expanse of the flat surface, stretching away into the gloom in both directions. She peered down at her feet, where the shape extended into the darkness in that direction as well. It was the roof of the building, covered in coral.

"All this coral is bleached and dead," Raven breathed. "The sea here is too warm for it to survive." From what they'd told her, the sea had been too warm for so many years that no one even remembered when the coral had thrived here.

As she drew closer and could make out the ocean floor, she saw that the coral wasn't just bleached and white here. Much of it was broken and shattered, the original shape of the reef destroyed. "What broke all of this up?"

"Bottom trawlers," Raven told her. "Back before the oceans were overfished and fishing was still economically viable, these seas were full of life. To dredge up bottom-dwelling fish, they dragged massive weighted nets along the sea floor, grinding up everything in their wake."

She stared at him through her faceplate. "What?"

"They weren't too good at considering the consequences. Just the immediate profit."

Raven turned away, staring down at the destroyed reefs.

H124 touched down on the roof of the building, finding an old rooftop door leading down. It stood open, rusted solid on its hinges.

She took the lead, lowering herself into the building. She followed the schematics down a long hall to a stairwell. Everything inside the underwater structure was covered with white corals and dead sea creatures she recognized from books as barnacles. She reached an open elevator shaft and peered down into the darkness. If the elevator car still existed, it was at the bottom of the shaft.

She pulled herself facedown into the dark passage and kicked her legs, descending into the black. Her helmet beam shined over more bleached coral and barnacles. The water was murky with floating debris, and she was starting to really feel the cold through her suit. Light flashed on the walls around her, and she looked up to see Raven and Dirk following her into the elevator opening.

She reached what would have been the first subbasement of the building and paused at a closed elevator door.

Dirk floated down next to her and picked up a piece of rebar lying on a small ledge. Together they levered the door open, revealing a vast room filled with ancient office equipment. Chairs and desks lay around the room, all in states of extreme decay. Sand had sifted in through a broken window, creating a drift by one of the far walls.

Together they swam across the room. She looked at her PRD. The warehouse space where the A14 had been stored was just past this room. They arrived at a heavy set of double doors. Dirk still had the rebar, so they tried to lever it open, but it wouldn't budge.

Raven swam up behind them, pulling a pocket pyro out of his dive bag. He went to work cutting a hole big enough for them to slip through.

He'd only cut through one foot of the metal when a deafening *whump* sounded behind them. H124 spun in time to see an AUV in the elevator opening, firing an explosive at them as bubbles filled the room.

Chapter 2

Kicking away from the door, H124 barely dodged the small projectile. It smashed against the door with incredible force, setting off a blinding explosion that rocked the entire room. The concussive wave threw her backward into a jumbled pile of old rusted metal. She felt a searing pain in her thigh, and sucked in a sharp breath as the freezing cold sea made direct contact with her skin. Crimson blood billowed outward. The bubbles around her dissipated.

Wincing against the pain, she stared out as the water started to clear. One section of the room remained a turbulent mess of water. She realized it was Dirk, physically engaging with the AUV, his suit giving off a torrent of bubbles. He had both hands wrapped around the craft, but it was too big to get a good hold on it. Raven joined him, and together they pushed the thing back into the elevator shaft.

H124 swam to the elevator quickly, her thigh screaming in protest. As they wrestled the AUV into the elevator shaft, Dirk started to swim upward with it.

"Get the door shut!" he cried.

H124 and Raven went to work sliding the doors closed, leaving just enough room for Dirk to slip back through.

Then he shoved the AUV toward the top of the shaft and turned around, kicking against the wall to propel himself downward. H124 grabbed his hand as he neared and pulled him through. Then all three desperately shoved at the door, finally managing to slide it shut.

"It won't take long for that thing to turn around and start blasting at this elevator door," Dirk said. He noticed the blood pouring out of her leg. She clamped her gloved hand over it. "Is it bad?"

"I don't think so," she answered, though she really wasn't sure. They turned back toward the door that led to the warehouse. The blast from the explosive had crumpled it inward, closing off the little cut that Raven had managed to make. But small spaces had torn open at the top and bottom of the door now, and H124 could see through to the other side. It was too gloomy to make out any details, and they still couldn't fit through.

Raven went to work again with the pocket pyro, cutting two feet before they heard another explosion on the other side of the elevator door. "Hurry!" Dirk urged him, not that he needed to. Raven cut quickly, opting for a small hole just big enough for them to get their shoulders through, though not enough to accommodate the AUV.

The metal glowed red, and soon the cut was almost complete. H124 heard another explosion on the far side of the elevator door; it groaned and shot outward, the metal bent and forced. One more blast and the thing would be through.

Raven completed the circle and leaned back, kicking the metal with his foot. Dirk did the same, and it fell away. H124 looked down at her leg, pressing on the wound until it clotted. At least that was looking up. Quickly they filed through the small hole, Raven first, followed by H124 and Dirk.

Raven lifted up the cut away section of door and placed it back inside the hole, hoping the thing wouldn't be able to see them on the other side of it. Dirk borrowed the pocket pyro and welded it in a couple places to keep it in place.

They turned, their helmet lights flooding the warehouse. H124's spirits fell. The space was empty.

At the far end of the room stood another door. They swam toward it, finding it rusted open, and moved into the next room, touring it slowly. H124 gently kicked her flippered feet behind her. Her thigh stung, but the bleeding had definitely stopped.

This room had been more protected from the sea than the others. It was still flooded, but not as covered with sediment. A few objects lay about the room, so largely disintegrated she couldn't tell what they had been. Now they were just corroded lumps on the floor. She could guess that some of them might have been old computers. A tall, rusted rectangle might have been an ancient filing cabinet or maybe even an old server. But it was damaged now beyond repair. Her heart started to sink further.

Dirk checked the schematics. "This was an old records room." Bubbles rose from his suit, fanning out above his head.

Raven turned slowly, taking in the space. "It's so empty. Maybe most things were moved before the building was inundated."

"Moved to where?" H124 asked.

Raven met her eyes, his brow creased in worry. "I don't know." He swam in a slow circle around the room. "Maybe we could find some other records among the things we gathered at the aeronautic facilities." He was trying to sound hopeful, but she could hear the note of despair in his voice. They'd been through those records countless times, scouring for any additional information they could find that would tell them how to stop the asteroid. If there was something in there on the location of the A14, they'd have found it by now.

"Didn't you go through all of that?" Dirk asked, uttering the words that she didn't have the heart to say aloud.

Raven turned to him. "Maybe it's on some of the corroded parts of the data. We're still repairing some of the disks."

She looked behind them, to where several large rectangles had been mounted onto the wall. Sediment coated them. She thought of the similarly large objects she'd found in the university under New Atlantic. They'd been accounts of the past. Framed articles from newspapers. Posters that held information. When she'd been staying at the Rover camp just after the airship crash, she'd gone through the Rover books and discovered things like the "Periodic Chart of the Elements," and knew that at least one of the rectangles in the university had been just that. Maybe the ones here held information.

She swam to the first one and dusted it off, the sediment momentarily clouding the water as it billowed out from under her glove. When it settled, she saw that it was an image printed on some kind of lightweight metal. Parts of it were corroded now.

The picture showed two massive brown tubes with fire blasting out from beneath them. Mounted on them was a small white object with wings. She recognized it from the data they'd scoured through. It was a space shuttle. The photo depicted the rockets blasting off, billows of smoke pouring out. "Look at this!"

They swam to her, staring at the image.

She moved to the next one and dusted it off. As the water cleared, she could make out an image of a metal pod of sorts floating in the ocean, a white parachute spread out on the blue waves next to it. On the pod's side she saw an emblem of red and white stripes, and an arrangement of stars set against a blue background in the upper left.

Kicking her feet, she maneuvered to the next rectangle, clearing it off. This one showed a photo of a barren red landscape, rocks covering the ground into the distance.

The last image on the wall depicted scientists in white suits gathered around a probe covered in places by gold foil.

She spun slowly in a circle, taking in the whole room. More frames had been mounted to the opposite wall, so she swam toward them. Dusting off the first one, her heart suddenly soared. It showed a grey metal craft taking off from a runway, its front wheel already lifted off the ground. She instantly recognized it from the schematics they'd recovered from the disks. It was the A14. "Here it is!" she said.

The others swam over, examining the picture. A long silence engulfed them. "If only we had more than a picture," Dirk said quietly.

Undeterred, she swam to the next rectangle, and the next, until she'd uncovered them all. The next showed a photo of a four-legged craft in a warehouse. Another showed the close-up of a man in a bulky white suit descending a ladder from the same vehicle, against the blackest sky she'd ever seen.

The next one shocked her. It depicted the same four-legged craft on a barren grey surface. Hanging in the sky was an incredible blue and white swirled moon. It was the most stirring, mysterious image she'd ever seen. She glanced back at the image of the four-legged craft inside a warehouse, and then at the one on the barren surface. She gasped. The blue marble wasn't a moon. It was the earth, taken *from* the moon.

"What is it?" Raven asked, responding to her gasp of astonishment.

"Take a look at this!" she called out. "This is unbelievable." They all stared as realization dawned.

"It's our planet. Taken from space," Dirk breathed.

"They were really up there," H124 said, her voice almost a whisper.

Raven pushed off a corroded filing cabinet to take in all the pictures. "But we're no closer to finding the A14." He couldn't disguise the sheer disappointment in his voice now.

She swam back to the photo of the A14 taking off from the runway. She saw white scratchings at the bottom of the photo, partially covered by corrosion. She noticed they all had the marks. She peered more closely at the one of the man descending the ladder and saw there was writing. "Neil Arms…" it said. She could also make out a few other words: "Eagle" and "Apollo XI."

She moved back to the image of the A14, gently brushing off corrosion with her gloved finger. More words appeared. She couldn't make out the name of the craft, but she already knew it was the A14. The rest of the words read "Museum," "air," and "Aviation Wing."

Making a slow circuit of the room, she read as much of the writing as she could discern on the other images. At the bottom of the shuttle image, she read "housed in," and again "Museum" and "air." On the photo depicting the pod floating in the ocean, she read "Mercury," "Museum," and "Innovation Hall."

She recognized the word "museum" from the Rover books she'd perused. They'd had one book about something called the "Smithsonian," which had stood in "Washington, D.C." and had held countless collections of cultural and scientific interest. She'd seen photographs of the bones of ancient creatures who had roamed the earth, paintings of important people, ceremonial and sacred objects belonging to various cultures. The museum had long since been inundated by rising sea levels, but the collections might have been moved to other areas of the country.

"I think all these vehicles were moved to a museum," she told them.

Raven met her gaze. "Even the A14?"

She glanced at its photo and nodded. "Even the A14."

"So now we just have to find out where they moved the A14 to," Raven said, scrutinizing the pictures.

H124 turned toward the door, catching Dirk floating near the doorframe with a distant look on his face. His chin trembled, then he caught her gaze. Tears brimmed on his lower lids but hadn't fallen. She wanted to reach out and squeeze his arm, but felt like she didn't have the right. Astoria had died on her watch. She still felt she could have done something to prevent it.

Dirk blinked and averted his gaze.

Raven crossed to another door on the opposite side of the room. "Can't go up the way we came down," he said, wrenching this second door open. "That thing's probably still in the elevator shaft. We'll have to go this way." He checked his schematics and pulled himself through the doorway. H124 followed.

Dirk took up the rear as they propelled themselves down a corridor on the right, looking for holes in the structure that led to the open sea.

The corridor led past numerous doors, some open, some still closed. They searched other warehouse spaces, hoping the A14 might be there. But all of the spaces were empty. It made H124 believe more in her theory about the vehicles being moved to another facility. They had to have gone somewhere.

As they swam, they paused in the open doorways, looking for breaches in the walls beyond, hoping for a different way out. Rusted metal lay twisted and covered with sediment and corrosion. At the end of a corridor, they came to a thick metal docking door. Crusted handles protruded from the base.

H124 checked her schematics. According to them, open ocean lay on the other side of the docking door. She examined their oxygen levels. They only had twenty-four minutes of air left. She stifled the nervous pang that rose inside her. "Twenty-four minutes," she told them.

At first she and Raven tugged on the handle of the docking door, but it had been corroded shut for too many years to budge. Raven pulled out his pocket pyro again, and started to cut a hole in the metal. The progress was agonizingly slow.

"Seventeen minutes," she said quietly.

Dirk had swum up next to the door, where he floated listlessly, that faraway look on his face. She could hear his uneven breathing, holding back emotion. She couldn't imagine what it must be like for him, to lose someone he'd known his whole life, who'd always had his back.

She looked back at Raven's progress. He was almost there. Eleven more minutes.

He finished cutting the hole and punched the metal circle out of the door. Beyond, the dark blue of the ocean awaited them. "Let's go!" He signaled for H124 to go through first, and she kicked over to the hole, then pulled herself through. Raven emerged next. Above them the bright surface of the ocean looked too far away.

Six minutes.

Dirk's gloved hands appeared as he started to pull himself through the hole. She had just begun kicking for the surface when a dark, bullet-shaped body sped toward them through the water. An AUV. It launched a projectile, and an eruption of bubbles sprang forth from its nose cone. The mini torpedo barely missed her, screaming by in the water, pushing her back with its concussive wave. Raven was far off to one side, so it sailed past him. But Dirk was just fully emerging from the hole, right into the line of fire.

It connected with his body, propelling him backward. He slammed into the side of the building, the projectile lodging itself into the building wall beside him. H124 kicked away quickly. Sharp spikes dug into the building's exterior. Dirk kicked away from it, but he was still too close. The torpedo detonated, sending them all reeling through the water. H124's ears rang as she somersaulted backward in the water, being driven not up toward the surface, but down toward the seabed. When the bubbles cleared, she saw Dirk struggling in the water near the hole they'd cut. Crimson clouds streamed out around him. She kicked away from the sea floor, angling up toward him. Raven, who'd been blown far to the right, also propelled himself toward Dirk.

When she got close enough, she saw a jagged piece of metal had run clear through his stomach. Another piece had sunk into his shoulder, a two-foot piece of rusted rebar that had pierced above his lung. He gasped, gritting his teeth. They had to get him up, and fast. His eyes went wide as he looked behind them. Two more AUVs joined the first, hovering in the water a few dozen feet away. Another discharge of bubbles streamed out from the closest one, sending a projectile tearing through the water.

She grabbed Dirk's arm and kicked upward, barely clearing the building as the second explosive *thunked* into its side. Seconds later it detonated, sending them tumbling through the water. She lost her bearings, and for a second couldn't figure out which way was up. Then she saw the bright surface of the water and started to kick toward it. But the third AUV maneuvered itself between them and the surface, angling itself down to fire. Raven was suddenly beside them, taking Dirk's other arm.

She glanced at her O_2 meter. Three minutes left. They weren't going to make it.

Dirk started struggling against them, shoving them away. She watched, confused as he grabbed something off Raven and kicked toward the hole in the docking door. Then she saw a jet of fire stream out from him. He'd grabbed the pocket pyro and cranked it all the way up. The AUVs maneuvered in the water, angling toward the heat signature. He swam furiously, blood streaming out from his stomach and shoulder in waves. He made it to the hole and pulled himself through.

"Dirk, what are you doing?" H124 shouted.

"Get to the surface!" he shouted.

She looked at her oxygen gauge. Two minutes.

"We're not going without you!" She started kicking toward the hole just as the first AUV reached it.

"They're programmed to protect the facility!" Dirk shouted. "They're not going to bother with you if I'm in here with a jet of fire."

Sure enough, the AUVs sped toward him, all three disappearing through the hole behind him.

"Dirk!" she shouted.

"Come back out!" Raven pleaded over the comm.

"Astoria wouldn't want this. She died to save you!" H124 yelled.

"I know," he gasped through the pain. She heard him swallow hard. "So let it count for something. Get that launch vehicle and save the planet. Go!"

They heard two explosions and a stream of bubbles erupted from the hole as fiery light streamed out.

"Damn it!" she cursed. Raven grabbed her arm and started kicking them toward the surface. "We can't leave him!"

And then she ran out of air. She gasped, her lungs rebelling. She felt her stomach tremble, as her mouth opened and shut in vain. She kept kicking, sensing that her whole body was about to burst. Raven's body kicked and convulsed; for a moment her eyes met his in the dark water, and in them she saw terror. Up and up they kicked, clawing for the surface. Her vision tunneled, and her brain felt like it was about to explode. The world grew tiny, narrow, and black-and-white. But the white parts got brighter, and suddenly she was breaking through the surface. She tore off her mask. Raven emerged next to her, his body flopping. She tore off his face mask, and he gasped in a ragged breath of air.

About a hundred yards away, they saw the conning tower of the submarine. "We're here!" she said over the comm, waving. "But give the facility a wide berth. There are three more of those things down there."

A watchman spotted them and climbed back into the sub. It motored toward them, skirting on the surface around the outside edge of the facility.

Her heart thudded in her chest. Her mind struggled to understand what had just happened, that they'd lost Dirk. She could hear the dull thrumming of the sub's engines in the water as it motored toward them, but it felt like it was a million miles away.

When they'd almost reached her and Raven, she heard the weapons officer call out over the comm. "Sir! Coming up beneath us! Another AUV!"

"All ahead full! Right to 160!" shouted the captain.

The sub wheeled to the side, and she and Raven started to swim backward. A dark shape sped up through the water below. But it didn't pause to take aim at the sub. It careened toward the surface, bursting into the air with explosive force. Immediately she saw that something was attached to it, which slid off into the water, floating on the surface. "Dirk!" she shouted, kicking over to him. The AUV sank back down into the depths as Dirk struggled to stay afloat.

She and Raven reached him, treading water with him between them, ripping off his mask. He drew in a harsh breath. His head bobbed, but a wry smile came to his face. "Astoria always said there wasn't anything I couldn't rewire." He coughed. "The other two are destroyed."

H124 grinned, then said over the comm, "It's okay to pick us up. The AUVs have been neutralized."

And they floated there, their friend between them. Blood seeped out around Dirk, and already he was losing consciousness. They'd have to get him to a medpod fast, but he was alive.

She gazed up at the blue sky. A storm was brewing to the southeast. Looked like it was going to be a doozy. She thought of the hurricane she and Raven had braved. As the sub drew closer, she looked out at strange skeletal platforms dotting the horizon. She'd learned people had once lived on these massive platforms, stations that had once drilled deep down into the seabed to extract oil. It had been a dangerous place to live back then, with violent explosions that killed workers, and accidents that spewed millions of gallons of oil out into pristine waters, destroying wildlife.

She'd seen similar rigs out in the distance when Raven had taken her up to the northernmost extent of the continent above Sanctuary City. He'd told her that both locations had once been wildly diverse places full of myriad marine wildlife, but that after several disasters on the oil rigs, millions of gallons of oil had washed up on shore, killing countless birds and other flora and fauna besides.

Now she tried to imagine what it had been like, teeming with creatures, vibrant coral communities with colorful fish. Next to her, Dirk bled into the ocean, and they all held on to each other, bobbing with the waves.

Chapter 3

H124 gazed out over a flat, dry brown landscape. Orion and Onyx had dug around in the Rover archives, poring over ancient historical documents, and finally found a probable location for the A14. When low-lying areas in the east had flooded, museums had moved priceless collections westward to the interior of the continent. A lot of vehicles from the old space program had been moved to a location just east of Delta City called the Museum of Innovation and Science.

Gordon, her stalwart friend and pilot, had picked up H124, Raven, and Dirk in his Lockheed Vega, eager to see the A14, if it still existed. Dirk had healed in a medpod, but his side still bothered him. Sitting across the plane aisle from her, he winced. All three had developed the bends after surfacing so fast, and each had to spend time in a medpod.

As they approached the coordinates, H124 gazed out the plane window. Raven sat a few rows ahead in the small jet, studying the museum's layout on his PRD. Below, dirt billowed and swirled in the relentless wind, and even though the plane's climate controls hummed in the cabin, it couldn't compensate for the hot, dry air outside. Dirt devils wound away on the landscape, and in the distance, a pair of long, parallel metal tracks stretched to the horizon. She swallowed, her throat dry and scratchy. She looked at her PRD, studying the photograph of what the original entrance to the museum had looked like.

A large glass structure had stood above ground, with lush green grass and bright rows of flowers surrounding the building. They'd built most of the museum underground as a way to protect the spacecraft and to keep visitors cool and comfortable without wasting a lot of energy on climate control. It stayed cool under there, and the protection from UV radiation had been an additional preservation measure for the air and spacecraft.

The old photo showed happy patrons approaching the entrance, while others read informative signs at outdoor displays. There had been demonstration gardens with plants from all over the world, an old Thor-Delta rocket standing off to one side, and a Republic P-47 Thunderbolt plane mounted on a stand a few dozen yards away.

Gordon circled, setting down right at the coordinates. He slowed, bumping along the rough ground and coming to a stop. She gazed out. All that had endured were the rusted remains of the stand the plane had been mounted on, now lying on its side in the dirt. She could see the vague outline of the foundation of the building's aboveground portion.

A person could walk right over this area and not even know it was there.

They'd brought explosives in case they had to blast their way in, and from the looks of it, that was exactly what they'd have to do.

Raven consulted his PRD, gathering his bearings. "Looks like they probably loaded craft in through some big docking doors to the south. The public entrance was on the north side of the complex. For now, it'd be a smaller job just to blast our way through the smaller main entrance."

They piled out of the plane, loading a maglev with packs of explosives. H124 checked her toolbag. It had been growing heavier by the week. In addition to her rain gear, water bottle, multitool, and pocket pyro, she now carried the flight suit she'd used to infiltrate Delta City with Astoria. It folded up neatly in a brick-sized pack, so it was worth keeping with her.

Raven moved to the north side of the complex, and studied a location in the dirt. "The main entrance should be under here."

Gordon and Dirk set up the explosives, and they all withdrew to a safe distance. Sweat poured down her back in the sweltering heat. Gordon's white hair stood out in unruly tufts on his beige scalp, and he dabbed at the sweat with the red rag that always hung out of his back pocket. She watched Gordon work, his body spry for his eighty-plus years, his overalls hanging loosely on his bony frame. She always found his energy and enthusiasm inspiring. "Fire in the hole!" Gordon called out as a deafening explosion tore through the afternoon, sending up a massive cloud of dirt. When it settled, the resulting crater exposed two rusted doors.

Raven cut through them with a pyro, and they fell away, exposing a cavernous underground space. Stale air rasped out, cobwebs fluttering in the darkness. H124 donned her headlamp and switched it on. The beam fell on displays and dusty equipment.

She entered the quiet cool of the museum, instantly grateful for the relief from the relentless heat. They'd been smart to build it underground. Much of the museum was still intact. A wide staircase led down to a lower level.

On the ceiling hung a jet of some kind—she'd looked through numerous books on aircraft, but didn't know this exact model, though she recognized it as a combat plane.

They split up, exploring different rooms. In the first hall on the right she discovered a collection of old planes. She explored the hall, reading their placards. A silver one with a painted name was called *The Spirit of St. Louis*. Hanging from the ceiling was a yellow Beechcraft C17L Staggerwing from 1936 and a black Curtiss R3C-2 seaplane from 1925. Nearby, taking up a section of floor space, stood a delicately winged 1903 Wright Flyer.

In the next room, she stopped before a display that read, "How Do You Contribute?" Originally it had been a powered display. A cord snaked off into the wall. She pulled out the wire and hooked it up to her PRD's power cell. Light flickered from a contraption in the floor and filled the old display. H124 stepped back in wonder. Three-dimensional people suddenly stood before her, all made of light. Green grass stretched into the distance, and huge living trees shaded the area, their leaves rustling in the wind.

"What are you doing to help the planet?" the voice of an off-screen interviewer asked. A smiling man faced the camera. He wore brown shorts and a collared white-striped shirt, his hair cut short, his face red with sunburn.

"I teach my kids to respect the earth."

"And what have they done so far?"

In the background H124 could see the man's kids kicking around a black-and-white ball. One of them kicked it past the other and let out a whoop.

The man continued to beam. "Oh, well, nothing yet. But they'll teach their kids, too."

The scene shifted to show an older woman smiling into the camera. "And what do you do to help?" the interviewer asked.

She grinned. "If I can make just one person smile, I've made a difference."

The display shifted to a woman with long blonde dreadlocks, a white knitted tank top, and a flowing rainbow skirt. "And what do you do to help?" asked the off-camera interviewer.

"I figure if I can convince two people to be more green-minded, then those two people will convince four more people, and those four will convince eight, and on and on until everyone on the planet has a greener mindset."

"And why do you think that hasn't already happened?"

Her smile faltered. "What do you mean?"

"Well, conservation has been a part of the global dialogue since the days of writers and thinkers like John Muir, Henry David Thoreau, and Rachel Carson. Why didn't their thinking convince two people, who went on to convince four, who went on to convince eight? If that worked, wouldn't we already be a predominantly green-minded society?"

The woman stared into the camera, her smile now gone.

The green display turned brown and black, and in the ensuing darkness, the off-camera voice said, "And what are you doing to help?"

The display went dark, and H124 stood for a few minutes, processing what she'd just seen, thinking of the ruined landscape above her. The last person interviewed...the idea wasn't a bad one. So why hadn't it worked, this passage of ideas from one person to the next?

But H124 already knew the answer. The PPC was the last holdout from this culture that valued greed and power over the preservation of the planet. The woman's theory didn't work because for every one of her, there were millions of other people passing on the idea that personal gain was more important than a communal, earth-friendly attitude. Make money. Take what you can get. Think in the short term. That signal had been a thousand times more powerful than conservation, and in the end, even when things had become so dire with rising sea levels, megastorms causing massive damage, and CO_2 levels changing the very composition of the earth-ocean system, greed still won out.

She thought of the PPC destroying the experimental forest Raven's parents had worked so hard to maintain, all so the media execs could furnish their offices with wood. The mentality was still present, and powerfully so.

"You okay?" came Dirk's voice from across the room. She turned to him, unplugging her PRD from the display.

She turned to him. "Yeah. This place is just..."

"Haunting?"

She blinked. "Yeah. It's hitting you that way, too?"

He gazed over his shoulder. "All these amazing inventions, this dedication to learning and exploration. I feel like we're on some alien world, or that we discovered a long-lost civilization. Can't believe these were our ancestors."

He hooked his thumb to the left. "Looks like there's a whole room about airships over there." He moved past her, on to a different section of the museum.

The next room did indeed hold photographs and artifacts from a variety of early airships. And finally she knew why the PPC ships were called "*air*ships." Early ones had been filled with helium or hydrogen, the latter being highly flammable and dangerous. She stopped at a photograph depicting a huge airship on fire, anchored to a metal scaffolding of some kind. Over the years, airships had gotten sleeker and slimmer, more maneuverable. She stopped at a display showing the undercarriage of an airship prototype, instantly recognizing it as an early model of what the PPC now flew.

The base was triangular, with a sleek but small cabin, just big enough for a weapons officer, pilot, and two or three additional crew members. This particular airship had been fitted out in luxury, with a mirrored bar, comfortable sitting area, and several bedrooms at the back. The exhibit described how the airship was fitted with a flexible solar array that could create super-heated air to the give the airship lift. The original designer had gone bankrupt, unable to find backers for his new design. The military had stepped in, buying the patent and designing a series of weapons that could be mounted on the underside of the cabin, devastating discharges of energy that could destroy whole villages in a single blast.

She thought of the airship that had destroyed the Black Canyon Badlander camp, and of the one who had fired on them on the east coast when they'd been out retrieving the first piece of the blast deflection craft. The weapon was certainly effective.

She passed through to the next room, meeting Raven as he emerged from a connecting chamber. Here the room had been painted black, with constellations of stars dotting the walls, and a large depiction of the moon painted on the far side. Before the moon stood the lunar lander she'd seen in the flooded facility. A mannequin in a space suit stood in mid-descent on the ladder, one foot stepping onto a simulated grey lunar surface.

In a neighboring display stood a capsule-shaped craft called the *Mercury*. She stopped at a third display, staring in awe. The shuttle *Atlantis* stood behind long velvet ropes. It was so much bigger than she'd imagined after seeing photographs of it.

"We're getting closer," Raven said. "It's got to be here in this wing."

In a section just after the shuttle towered a gigantic metal machine. It stood on treads, like the photos she'd seen of tanks in books. It was absolutely monstrous, bigger than some of the single-story houses she'd sheltered in during her trek from New Atlantic. The exhibit sign said it was a "Shuttle Crawler Transporter." As huge as it was, she was staggered to see photos of even bigger ones that had transported gigantic rockets to lift-off areas.

Gordon joined them from an adjoining room as Raven moved off in a different direction. "This place is out of sight!" the pilot said, his eyes sparkling.

She and Gordon walked into the next exhibit hall and stopped abruptly. In the center of the room, roped off and still gleaming and silver, stood the A14. Its sleek body was not entirely unlike the shuttle, but it was narrower, and the wings were slightly sharper in shape.

Gordon gave a long, low whistle. "There she is." Together they walked around the ship, making a complete circuit. It was in remarkably good shape, and H124 closed her eyes briefly, basking in relief.

She could hear Dirk and Raven talking in the next room. "In here!" she called out.

They hurried toward her, standing in wonder. "We found it," Raven breathed. "And look at it! Looks like they just built it yesterday. It's in fantastic shape."

H124 leaned in to read the A14's placard:

"While never launched, the A14 was the first and only craft in a planned series of spacecraft that would replace the shuttle program. Designed to take off directly from the ground on its own power, it did not require the use of rocket bodies. As space junk orbiting the earth became more and more of a hazard, designs like this became more valuable, as ejected rocket bodies became the biggest orbiting debris risks to communication satellites and other craft. The A14 was designed to make the trip quickly and efficiently, and could be used to repair orbiting telescopes and make delivery runs to the International Space Station."

H124 paused at that part of the description. An international space station? Though a ceiling blocked her view of the sky, she found herself involuntarily looking up. There was a space station up there? Was it still there? How had all of this been lost? She returned her attention to the placard.

"Though this project was heralded as the next vital step in space exploration, due to numerous budget restrictions and funding cuts, ultimately the A14 project was abandoned. This is the only model that was ever built."

"It was never even launched," H124 said. She found a large stepladder on wheels in a back room, and Gordon climbed to the top to examine the A14's engine. He gave a sigh, relieved to find the engine was still in there. Some of the planes had had theirs removed to make them lighter and easier to display. Dirk and Raven stood beside her, staring up anxiously. "We'd have to do some tinkering before this thing will be able to fly," Gordon told them. "Not the least of which, we'd have to convert it to a different fuel source. Not a lot of refined jet fuel lying around these days." "Do you think you could do it?" Raven asked.

Gordon turned, his eyes sweeping over the fuselage. "Needless to say, it's pretty different from other craft I've worked with. But I think with Rivet's help, we might be able to repair it." Rivet was the Rover's top engineer, and she was currently in Sanctuary City, piecing together the blast deflection craft. H124 gripped Raven's arm happily. As Gordon climbed down, she hugged him fiercely, and he chuckled and hugged her back. "At least we can try." He took in the size of the thing. "Getting it out is going to be a challenge."

Already H124's mind pored over possibilities. They'd brought along a number of maglev sleds, figuring they might have to maneuver the A14 out of a tight spot. But they wouldn't be able to move it very far. The sheer weight of the craft meant that the sleds would only be able to labor for a few minutes before their power cells depleted. They could recharge in the sun, but it would take so many repeated cycles that it was completely impractical. And getting it to a place where there were no Death Riders, PPC, or hostile Badlander groups was essential if they were going to get it ready to go. They had to move it somewhere safe enough that Rivet and Gordon could get to work converting the fuel system. It would take teams of people coming and going, bringing supplies, and it wouldn't be long before others noticed their presence and showed up in droves to pick them clean of whatever tech they had.

Dirk turned to Gordon. "We can't just work on it here. It's too exposed with that blasted crater now. It won't be long before Death Riders notice we're here."

H124's mind flashed to the bloodthirsty marauders and a chill swept through her. *If they're not already outside now.* She brushed the thought aside.

Raven nodded. "I agree. We'd be a target for every band of scavengers once they saw activity in this area." He paced, thinking. "We do have a satellite location near the west coast. It's still across the country, but it's a lot farther south than Sanctuary City, and would get us a little closer. It's a protected location, and there's an engineering lab, some living quarters, an armory."

"We still have to get the A14 out of this museum," Dirk pointed out.

H124 thought back to the previous room. "What if we use the synced maglevs to lift it onto the Shuttle Crawler Transporter?" She glanced around at their faces. Dirk seemed to like the idea. "It's electric. The plaque said it had an enormous amount of torque. We can charge up the Crawler with the UV recharger. Then we just drive it, A14 and all, right out of the loading doors."

Dirk brought this hand to his chin, then pointed at her. "I like it."

"And then?" Gordon asked. "Once it's outside?"

"Could we lift it somehow?" H124 asked. "Fly it under a helicopter?"

"It's too heavy for what we've got," Gordon put in. "I've been mentally going through all the aircraft I know of, stashed around the country and up in Sanctuary City. We don't have anything that could carry something like this."

H124 thought of the train tracks she'd seen from the plane. They weren't far away from here, and they stretched all the way to the horizon, joining with a network of tracks that all converged in the ancient metropolis in the distance. Hadn't Byron mentioned something that first night they met? Something about the "Big Worm," a steam engine that glided along tracks just like these? "The Big Worm," she said aloud, her eyes lighting up.

Dirk spun, staring at her in disbelief. "The Big Worm?"

"Yes. Isn't that what's called? It's a steam train."

Dirk shook his head adamantly. "That's a crazy idea. They can only drive it so far before it gets too much unwanted attention. They've had to armor the whole train."

She wouldn't let the idea go. "But it's possible, isn't it?"

He looked at her skeptically. "We don't even know where it is right now. It could be anywhere along the route."

"Who operates it?"

"This Badlander Grant."

"Do you know him?"

"I've never met him, but I hear he's completely crackers. Spent too much time alone."

"But Byron knows him, doesn't he? He said he'd seen the Worm work."

Dirk pursed his lips.

Opening up her comm window, she called Byron. In case their mission was unsuccessful, he and Rowan had been moving Badlander camps into an old network of bomb shelters they'd found.

"Halo!" he said, grinning when he saw her. He'd taken to calling her by that nickname more and more often.

"Byron." She gave a little smile, though her stomach did flips at the sight of him. His long brown hair hung around his shoulders, his green eyes twinkling in his tawny face. She still hadn't figured out what she was supposed to do with her feelings for him. "Do you remember that first night we met, when you kidnapped me and stole my car, then forced me to march through a river of fecal matter and break into a hostile megacity?"

"I'll never forget it." His grin widened.

"You mentioned something that night about The Big Worm."

"I remember."

"Is it still operational?"

"Sure is, and they've cleared an even longer track."

"How long?"

"From a hundred or so miles east of where New Atlantic was, all the way to about two hundred miles shy of the west coast. Granted, it runs through some pretty desolate territory."

"Could we, say, borrow the Big Worm? We found the launch vehicle and need to move it cross country."

"You'd attract a lot of attention."

"It's our best chance."

"A lot of *hostile* attention."

"Yes."

Byron cocked an eyebrow. "So you want to load this thing onto a steam train and drive it a thousand miles across the weather-ravaged, Death Rider-infested, PPC-airship-patrolled wastelands?"

"That's about it."

"I am *so* in."

She laughed.

"Let me check with the engineer, Grant. See where he is right now, if he'd be up for this crazy adventure."

"He would have bragging rights after."

"Always important."

"Tell him we need to get the A14 as far northwest as possible, to a safe place where Rivet can work on it. There's a Rover satellite location there."

"Give me a minute," Byron told her. "And I'll contact him." He signed off.

"First step," Dirk said, moving away, "is getting these loading doors opened."

He retraced his steps through the museum entrance, the others following. Back at Gordon's Lockheed Vega, they unloaded a portable UV charger and twenty heavy-lifting maglev sleds, transporting them all back to the museum.

The loading doors had been fitted with backup hand cranks in case of power outages, but hopefully the portable UV charger would provide enough power to get it open. They still had to blast through layers of windblown dirt that had accumulated over the loading doors, but didn't want to do it until the last minute.

Unhooking the mobile UV charger, they laid it on a maglev and moved it to the Shuttle Crawler Transporter. After attaching it to the transporter's massive bank of batteries, they programmed the maglev sled to hover beside it as it moved. They dragged a few displays out of the way to clear a path to the loading doors.

H124 climbed up into the controller booth of the Crawler and started it up. Lights blinked on the instrument panel, the battery meter flickering to life. She exhaled gratefully and inched the massive machine forward, out of the area where it had stood for so long. The treads groaned and creaked, breaking free after lying immobile. Angling it down the corridor toward the A14, she found it to be surprisingly maneuverable, able to turn even when stationary. The treads below rotated and trundled forward. She stopped in front of the A14.

Raven linked all the maglevs together, and maneuvered them beneath the body and wings of the A14. Then as one, the sleds lifted the craft. She could hear their whirring propellers working desperately to get lift, the tiny motors revving high. Then the A14 was aloft, slowly rising up. Raven steered it up, passing over H124 in the controller booth, and began to position it over the transport platform on top of the Crawler. The A14's tires had gone flat long ago. He had just started to gently lower it when H124 heard the maglev rotors begin to wind down, their power depleting quickly.

They were still two feet above the Crawler when the humming of their rotors dropped to a barely perceptible thrum. Raven entered a command, and the maglevs slipped out from under the A14 just as the sleds gave out altogether. The A14 dropped the remaining two feet onto the Crawler, and the vibration shook H124 in her booth. The sleds fell to the floor, completely depleted.

Dirk climbed up the exterior of the Crawler and began strapping down the A14 with Gordon.

H124's PRD beeped, and she opened the comm window to see Byron. "It's all set," he told her. "Here's the coordinates where we'll meet you." Her map blinked, letting her know it had received the location. "See you tomorrow afternoon," he said with a grin, and signed off.

For the rest of the evening and part of the next day, they hid underground, exploring the vast museum. H124 slept in the lunar display next to the Eagle lander. They'd placed the maglev copters outside to charge in the sun, and by the next morning, they were ready to go again.

Outside in the blistering heat, H124 helped Dirk transport more explosives over to the loading door area. Countless years of dirt and windblown debris had covered it, so they set up a few explosives and moved a safe distance away.

They lay down and covered their heads.

"Fire in the hole!" Gordon called out.

Dirt rained over H124, dusting her clothes.

They stood up, brushing themselves off, and approached the exposed door. Using small folding shovels, they uncovered what little dirt was left, completely clearing the opening. The aperture was definitely big enough to get the Crawler and A14 through. Now they just needed to feed power to the door's mechanism to get it open.

They returned to the quiet cool of the museum, H124 taking a deep breath of the chilled air. It was musty and smelled mildewy, but it beat the brutal heat above.

H124 climbed back into the operator's booth on the Crawler. With the A14 still secured on top, Raven gave H124 a thumbs-up. She turned the enormous transporter, aiming for the exterior doors. The progress was tortuously slow, inching forward across the floor of the museum. Her mind began to race, worrying that Death Riders or Badlanders might see the open doors above and come to check it out.

They turned on the power to the loading doors, and they wrenched open. Sunlight poured into the subterranean museum, illuminating displays that hadn't seen light in too many years to count.

Finally she reached the bottom of the ramp and drove upward, feeling the weight of the craft pulling at the Crawler. But she managed to motor all the way to the top and out into the blinding sunlight.

She watched as the doors cranked down slowly, sealing once more, blending in with the desolate terrain. She checked her PRD. The intact railway track was close, only two miles away, but the going would be very slow. She started out, knowing the others would easily catch up to her. She'd only gone a hundred feet when they emerged from the museum entrance and walked over to her.

"How's it going up there?" Raven called up to her.

"I might break a land speed record here for slowest vehicle ever."

He chuckled and walked alongside her, the others joining him.

Above her the heat beat down, so she fished her sun goggles out of her toolbag and slipped them on. Better. Already sweat trickled down her back and her feet were starting to overheat in her boots.

Dust devils swirled by as she maneuvered around a stand of long dead trees. Just as she had outside New Atlantic, she spotted strange objects among the barren trunks. Large metal cylinders, hollow and riddled with rusted holes, lay scattered, some still upright. Metal benches, leaning and falling apart, had been situated throughout the trees. A small, crumbling footbridge spanned what was now a dry creek bed filled with sediment and dust.

They passed a dilapidated structure with the faded word "Café" barely visible above doors open to the elements.

A collapsing knee-high black fence encircled a large depression in the center of the trees. A worn metal sign read "Paddle bo...rent." A plastic contraption with a steering wheel and foot pedals, sun-damaged almost to white, sat cockeyed in the middle of the dry depression.

They passed a few more dilapidated structures. Dirk walked out front by himself, his expression distant. Below her, Raven and Gordon chatted companionably about the experimental forests the Rovers had been planting.

When the tracks came into view ahead, H124 mentally urged the Crawler to go faster. She checked her PRD. The Big Worm would be here in just a few minutes. She edged up to the tracks, the glare of the sun still dazzling even with her goggles on.

To the west, the tracks bent away out of sight, angling gently northwest. She heard the train before she saw it, a metallic singing in the tracks. Dirk bent down and touched one of rails, feeling the vibration. "Right on time."

Then she saw a column of white steam in the distance and the train came into sight, the sun glinting off its black metal sides. As it powered down the tracks toward them, she could hear the steam engine pumping away, the rhythmic chuffing as it moved the wheels.

It slowed, chugging to a hissing stop in front of them. She could see now that it was completely shielded in armor, thick iron plates covering all areas of ingress. With a clang and a hiss, a metal door covering the engine jutted out and slid upward. Inside she saw a few steps leading up to the engine compartment.

Byron appeared in the doorway, gripping a handle and leaning out. "Halo!" he called, jumping off the train. He waved up at her on top of the Crawler, and she waved back, her stomach once more doing acrobatics.

He greeted the others, then turned back to the train. The engineer stepped out, a bearded, heavy-set man with tousled brownish-black hair framing a tanned face. His brown eyes twinkled as he took them all in.

"This is Grant," Byron said. He introduced the others.

"Make no mistake," Grant said, eyeing them each in turn. "This is a crazy mission, and if my train gets messed up, I'm hunting you all to your graves."

They stood in silence for a moment, and then Grant burst out laughing, holding his generous belly and shaking with laughter.

Raven gave an uneasy chuckle.

"I have a few ground rules for riding in my train," Grant went on. "First, don't spill coffee on the control board. Second, you go to the bathroom on your own time." He scowled at them each in turn, and they all exchanged confused glances. "And lastly, and most importantly, don't go drinking so much liquor that you shoot up the place, thinking it's infested with opossums."

They glanced at each other, then nodded hesitantly.

"All right. Let's get this show on the road. Don't like to stop too long in one place." He returned to the engine and threw a few levers. In the middle of the train, one of the cars hissed. The top of it moved, parting at the top and splitting in half. It opened up and outward, unfolding into a huge metal platform.

"Load 'er up!" Grant called.

Raven checked the charging level of the maglevs. They were ready to go. He assembled them together and programmed them to work in tandem. Their power cells beeped in unison, indicating they were full.

He flew them up to the A14, angling them beneath the fuselage and wings. They lifted, their rotors working furiously, finally managing to get it aloft. He steered them over to the train's platform, the rotors starting to whir erratically, the power cells already depleting. He barely got the A14 positioned over the platform when they gave out, slamming the A14 down onto the train.

"Hey!" shouted Grant. "You be careful up there. Not a scratch, remember? Not a scratch!" He rubbed his beard thoughtfully. "Forgot to mention that rule. Rule #4: Not a scratch!" He emerged from the engine compartment and climbed up onto the platform, bringing out tow ropes with hooks. Dirk helped him fasten these around the A14, securing it to the train.

In the cargo car, they loaded up the remaining explosives.

Then Grant hopped down to the ground, moving back toward the engine. "Let's get movin'! There's a turn around a few miles ahead. Hop aboard."

Gordon stepped back. "I'll leave you to your journey. I'm going to fly the plane back. I can help Rivet set up for converting the A14."

Raven approached Gordon, then typed into the pilot's PRD. "Here are the coordinates for the satellite location. I'll tell her to meet you there."

H124 started to climb down from the Crawler, then thought better of it. It was an amazing piece of engineering. She didn't want it sitting out like this. It had helped them, and could be useful in the future, if not for her, then maybe someone else on a future mission. She remained in the control booth. "You guys go on ahead. I'm going to drive this back and stash it. Then I'll meet you along the track after you turn around."

Gordon looked up at her. "I'll ride with you." He grabbed a handle on the lower side of the Crawler and hopped up onto a small ledge.

"Here, you'll need this," Raven said, handing over the portable UV charger. Gordon grabbed it and hauled it up onto the Crawler.

Raven said goodbye to Gordon, shaking his hand, then looked up to H124. "See you in a few," he called up. He climbed the stairs into the engine room. Byron joined him, leaning out again, hanging onto the handle. He gave her a small wave as the shielded doors came down. The train began to pull out, steam billowing from the chimney mounted on front of the engine.

H124 turned the Crawler around, and they made the creeping journey back to the museum. Gordon hopped off as they got close, carrying the portable UV charger. He made his way to the main museum entrance, where he disappeared. Moments later, the huge loading door screeched open. H124 drove the Crawler down the ramp into the welcoming cool and dark. She parked it back at its original display, then climbed down. They shut the loading doors again and made their way through the dark museum to the main entrance.

"This was an amazing place," Gordon said as they paused at the door. "Must have been incredible to live back then. So much innovation. Exploration."

She nodded. "To have been to the moon!"

"I know! Can you imagine?"

H124 could.

Outside, she accompanied him for the mile back to the plane. They loaded the UV charger into the plane, then she hugged him tightly.

"I'll get everything set up with Rivet," he told her, double-checking that he had the coordinates of the Rover satellite site.

She pulled away. "Good luck. Take care of yourself."

He turned and boarded the plane.

She looked after him, watching him disappear through the door. Then he stuck his head back out. "About Dirk…you keep an eye on him. Everyone says time heals all wounds," Gordon said quietly, "but I've always found that to be a complete dung pile of rubbish." Then he climbed into the plane and pulled up the ladder.

She watched until he taxied off and the plane climbed into the sky. Then she squinted in the direction of the train tracks, wondering if they'd make it all the way to the satellite location.

Chapter 4

H124 trudged back toward the train tracks in the blistering heat, past the fallen trees again. Wind whistled through holes in one of the rusted barrels. In the distance she spotted the train chugging back in her direction. It pulled up alongside her, and the shield door opened. She climbed into the engine compartment, purple floor and ceiling lights giving the space a slightly spooky feel. Several view screens showed the dusty world scrolling by.

As soon as the armored doors slammed shut, H124 realized with a grateful sigh that the interior was climate controlled. Coolness spread over her body. Grant hooked a thumb behind him. "The others are in the back compartments." As her eyes adjusted to the gloom, she noticed a door leading to the back cars. She stepped up to it and pushed a button. It slid open.

The door admitted her into an elaborately decorated train car. Red velvet sofas and recliners, linen-covered tables, and a decorative bar filled the space. Byron sprawled on a red chaise-lounge, holding a glass with some kind of amber liquid in it.

Raven sat at one of the tables, going over the A14's schematics on his PRD. Like in the engine compartment, this room showed displays projected from outside. They glowed from within wooden window frames, and after a few moments, she forgot they actually weren't windows.

"Welcome!" Byron said. "Have a seat. Can I get you a drink?"

H124's mouth was parched. "Definitely." She made a circuit of the room, taking in the furnishings appreciatively. "Where's Dirk?"

Byron mouth turned down at the sides. "He found a bed to lie down in. I'm worried about him."

"Me, too," she said.

They drank in companionable silence, watching the scenery scroll by. Later, they ate MREs and played cards with Raven. Dirk still hadn't emerged when night fell. She snuck into the sleeping car to check on him, found him curled up on one of the bunks, face toward the wall, his breathing even and steady. She slipped back out.

* * * *

The next day, H124 woke refreshed, finding that the gentle rocking of the train had led to the deepest sleep she'd had in a while. She dressed, watching the terrain scroll by on the wall displays. Heat shimmered off vast dry plains. The landscape was the flattest she'd ever seen, without a hill in sight.

Exploring the train, she passed from car to car, completely taken aback by the sheer opulence of it. More red and purple velvet seats, antique wooden bars, landscape paintings with rich patinas. In one car, she even found a contraption similar to one she'd seen in an old photograph. In the image, a woman had been seated in front of a large machine of some sort with black and white levers and brass foot pedals.

H124 approached the contraption.

She pressed one of the white levers and a tone sounded. She pressed another to the right, and a higher tone rang out. She pressed two at the same time, feeling a vibration through the machine as the tones sounded and faded away. A bench stood before it. There she sat down, tinkering with the levers.

The door behind her whooshed open, and Byron came through. Lights from the screens passed over his face, the golden afternoon sunrays shining from the displays.

She paused, her fingers lightly touching the levers. He walked over to the bench, sliding in beside her. She could feel the warmth of his body, their sides touching. She swallowed. "What is this?"

"Isn't it amazing?" He stroked the levers affectionately. "It's a musical instrument, a piano." He smiled, his expression faraway. "When I was a kid, on one of our scouting expeditions with my folks, we came across this old woman who lived in a huge underground bunker. She'd hoarded all kinds of things down there, including this piano. At first she was scared of us, offered to give us things if we left. But my parents were kind to her, intrigued. She painted like my dad, and they got to talking. After that, we went back to see her again and again. She taught me a little." He ran his hands over the wood. "When she passed away, I was in my teens. It was a real blow. She was so eccentric—knew so much about the world that had come before, and if you were quiet and listened, she taught you things. I couldn't bear to let the piano go to some Death Rider camp to be destroyed, so I took it. Gave it to Grant. Figured if it were on a moving target, it would have a better chance of survival."

H124 looked down at the instrument. "So this is it? The same piano?"

"The only piano, as far as I know."

"Can you play something?"

Byron looked a little shy, then straightened his back and flexed his fingers. He played two notes, then eased into a wonderful melody with rich bass notes intermingled with melodic higher notes that sang out. She'd never heard music before, not like this. She'd heard some strange sounds piped into the citizens' quarters in New Atlantic, but they were somehow artificial and rigid.

This melody cascaded, and he worked the pedals, making the music deep and resonant. H124's heart started to beat faster. Her mouth came open a little as he continued, moving his body with feeling as the piece grew more intense until it came to a crashing finish. He took a deep breath then, and slowly brought his fingers away from the levers.

He rested his hands on his legs and looked at her out of the corner of his eye, a bit sheepish.

"That was…amazing…" she breathed. "I've never heard anything like it."

He turned to face her, swinging one leg over the bench. The pull to him was magnetic. She did the same, swinging her leg over to face him. They sat there for a moment, his green eyes intense with emotion. Then he reached out, touching her hand, pulling her closer. She moved on top of him, straddling his body, crossing her ankles behind his back.

They faced each other, his eyes smoldering in a way that robbed her of breath. His hand came up on her back, and he pulled her into a kiss. She pressed her lips to his, their bodies clasped together, and he groaned with pleasure.

His hands moved up her back, fingers navigating through her hair. She felt a fire building in her down below, a desire to devour him and have him devour her. She bent her head down, kissing him deeply, but suddenly the train lurched, throwing Byron off the bench, toppling her over with him. It lurched again, braking hard, and they went sliding across the room, Byron still holding onto her.

They sat up, peering outside. H124 sucked in a sharp breath. She snapped her head toward the other window, Byron leaping up beside her.

Dune buggies roared into sight on both sides of the train, drivers pulling up flush with them. Their faces painted with blood, teeth bared, the marauders brandished battle axes and shotguns, screaming with fury in the thrill of attack. Each buggy was jammed with attackers. Spikes mounted on the back of each vehicle held human heads, bloody hair streaming in the wind from broken skulls.

The Death Riders had found them.

Chapter 5

The train passed by more and more Death Riders, some on foot, pumping spears in the air, others roaring toward them in jeeps and buggies. She didn't see any of the heavy trucks they used. The train slowed and the Death Riders started banging against the sides. It ground to a halt. Then the engine chugged again, harder and faster, growing louder, and the train began to move backward.

The Death Riders pursued, running and pounding on the sides of the train with staffs and spears. Others tried to leap onto the train from vehicles, but couldn't find purchase. A few fired guns point-blank into the armored sides. She heard bullets pinging off the metal. Their combustible engines roared alongside the train.

H124 and Byron raced through the door, running toward the engine control booth. They reached it just behind Raven.

Grant stood in the booth, his face sweaty, his eyes wide. "They've built a barricade on the tracks. Some hulking metal wreck of a thing. We can't get through."

"So what do we do?" Byron asked.

"We have to go back. We have no choice."

"Won't they just follow us?" H124 asked.

Grant's face had completely drained of blood, and he looked gaunt through his layer of sweat. She thought of the time she and the others been taken by them, fighting in the arena, barely escaping with their lives.

"This took some planning," Grant said through gritted teeth. "They knew the route. There are tons of disused tracks up here. But they knew we'd be using this one."

Raven looked nervously out of the window toward the back of the train. "What if they *want* us to go back? What if they've set up a larger war party farther back along the track?" H124 grabbed a pair of diginocs off the control board and looked out at the obstruction. Grant was right—it was huge. Some sort of amalgamated, welded monstrosity, a joining of two or more semi-trucks with mounted spikes. It would take an airship to blow that thing off the tracks. She paused then, thinking of the explosives they had. "Wait a minute." She ran back to the cargo car. Digging through a box, she pulled out the remaining explosives from blasting their way into the museum. They didn't have any remotely detonating explosives left, but they had plenty of self-igniting ones. If she used enough of them...

But she'd have to travel the distance between the train and the obstruction, and she'd have to be fast. No way she could do it on foot. Her eyes moved around the room, settling on the maglev sleds. They'd recharged their power cores on the platform next to the A14, then stored them away down here.

Just then the door whooshed open to the cargo car. Byron stood framed there with Raven. "What is it?"

She held up one of the explosives. "I've got an idea." She grabbed a maglev, unfurling its transparent surface sheet and calibrating the four copters beneath it. Then she paired it with her PRD. "How fast can these things go?"

Raven stepped forward. "Fast."

Byron moved past her, uncurling a second maglev. "I like where you're going with this."

"Wait a minute," Raven said, holding up a hand. "You're not thinking of...*riding* that thing?"

"We used it to top the shield wall in Murder City."

"That was a little different. It doesn't even have handles."

She started stuffing explosives into a munitions satchel, then strapped it across her body. "Keep backing up the train, distracting them, luring them along with you." She just hoped a group of them hadn't waited at the barricade.

She ran to the front of the train. Grant frantically looked out of the windows. Most of the Death Riders were keeping pace with the train. There were a few on foot that had been left behind, but all of the buggies and jeeps bounced alongside the locomotive, Death Riders screaming with the thrill of pursuit.

Except for the few stragglers on foot, the track to the obstruction was clear. "As soon as you see the explosion," she told Grant, "start coming back this way." She glanced up. "Is there a top hatch?"

He nodded, pointing above his head. "You want me to open it?"

Byron ran up, a satchel full of explosives slung over his shoulder. She looked to him and he nodded.

"Open it."

Grant threw a lever on the control console, and the hatch clicked and slid to one side. She climbed onto the maglev and steered it up through the hatch. Behind her, Byron did the same. On top of the train, the wind blasted her back, throwing strands of her hair into her eyes. She lowered her center of gravity, crouching on the maglev, and ordered it to take off at top speed toward the barricade. She startled at how fast it jolted ahead, and had to grip the edges of the thin sheet to keep from tumbling off. It flew over the front of the train, speeding down the tracks, the wind streaming into her eyes.

The few Death Riders on foot shouted and roared, pointing her out, taking off back toward the blocked track.

She glanced over her shoulder, seeing Byron grinning, holding on to the maglev at a half crouch, raising his fist at one of the Death Riders. He shouted something at one of them, but the wind carried away his words.

She approached the obstruction and dug into the munitions bag, pulling out one of the tubular explosives. It had a self-igniting cap, so she struck it, sending a spark to the fuse. As she flew over the pile of debris, she let it drop. It clinked onto the mass of joined metal and seconds later a blinding flash of fire and light shook the mound. But it wasn't nearly enough. Only a small part of the front blew off. They'd have to drop a number of the explosives at once in a coordinated attack. As she swung around the back side of the obstruction, she saw that two Death Riders had remained at the pile of debris. One pointed a nasty-looking weapon at her, a long gleaming tube with a barbed spear loaded into it. He raised it and she banked away, almost coming off the sled. It wasn't built for something like this.

She opened up a comm window to Byron. "We have to drop the explosives at the same time!"

On her vid screen, he gritted his teeth as his maglev veered to one side, narrowly missing a shot from one of the Death Riders. The gleaming barbed spear flew out, attached to a rope, narrowly missing Byron as he careened by. Instantly the Death Rider began reeling the spear back. He shoved it into the weapon and readied to aim again.

She flew down the far side of the tracks, beyond the barricade. She couldn't see any Death Riders this far down the tracks. They hadn't expected them to make it past the obstruction. She hovered above the tracks about five hundred yards away, and Byron pulled up beside her. Her hands hurt from gripping the maglev sled, and she flexed her fingers.

"Exactly how long are these fuses?" she asked.

Byron pulled one out of his pack and eyed it. "About fifteen seconds, I'd say."

"Think we can light them all at once? This has to be perfect."

He unslung his satchel and set it down in front of himself on the maglev, slinging his legs on either side of the sled. Stacking the explosives neatly together, he practiced the action of setting them all off by leaning on them with his hands and arms.

She did the same, arranging them in a straight line inside the satchel.

Ahead of them, the two Death Riders with the spear guns lifted their weapons, readying to defend the barricade.

She pulled up a counter on her PRD. "Ready?"

"As ever," he said, grinning way too much.

"Okay." She positioned her hands and arms, making contact with the tops of each explosive while keeping them in the weapons bag. Byron did the same.

"Okay. Light 'em!" She pressed down just as he did. She heard the spark and hiss of the fuses igniting. They raced forward, speeding toward the barricade. The two Death Riders took aim, firing both spears. One sailed between them, but the other one glanced Byron. She saw him flinch and cry out, but he kept going. They sailed over the Death Riders' heads and dropped the explosives onto the obstruction. The Death Riders on foot had almost caught back up to the debris pile, and they lifted their guns as they flew past.

A deafening boom erupted behind them. H124 saw Death Riders consumed in flames, flying up into the air just as a concussive wave hit her maglev. The copters whirred into high RPMs and began plunging down toward the ground.

To her left, Byron's sled went out of control. He crashed to the ground hard, and she could see now where the spear had torn through his thigh, his pants ragged and bloody. He stumbled to his feet, limping, grabbing the maglev parts and waving frantically through its controls on his PRD.

As H124's maglev sailed past several Death Riders on foot, she kicked one in the head, grabbing his shotgun as he fell. But she went off balance. Her maglev crashed all the way to the dirt and the rotors stopped. Two Death

Riders ran forward, closing in, only a hundred feet away. She struggled to restart the maglev. The copters recalibrated themselves, moving into position, and she jumped on again just as the Death Riders raised their guns. They fired as she veered off toward Byron.

As she approached him, she saw the train had once again reversed direction; it was powering toward them now. Two Death Riders approached Byron, carrying chains and closing in on him. One held a revolver, the other a blood-encrusted trident. H124 flew in over them, lowering the shotgun and blasting the man with the revolver. His head erupted in a crimson geyser, and his body slumped to the ground. The one with the trident took off, dropping the chains, and she gave pursuit, seeing that two more Death Riders were homing in, one with a flash burster and another with a chainsaw.

Behind her, Byron struggled to get his maglev functional again. He picked up one of the copters and shook it, surveying the ground for something. It had broken. He wasn't going to be able to get airborne again. The chainsaw-wielding Death Rider was almost on top of him, and Byron took off, limping, but the one with the flash burster closed in and aimed. Chainsaw shouted at his friend, his eyes wild with delight, and raised the chainsaw over his head, ready to bring it down onto Byron.

H124 swooped low, brought the shotgun to bear, and flew past, blasting a hole through Chainsaw's neck. She cocked the shotgun, banked around, and hit Flash Burster point blank in the chest. Blood erupted from his shirt.

Six more Death Riders approached from the east. H124 lowered the maglev, holding a hand out to Byron. He gripped it, his hand hot in hers, and swung up onto the maglev beside her. She veered around and took off for the train, hearing the loud boom of a gun to their rear. She weaved and banked wildly, trying to make a difficult target. She approached the train at a dangerous clip, but she couldn't risk going any slower. Behind her Byron groaned, grasping his leg, blood seeping out at an alarming rate.

As the train readied to pass beneath them, she saw the roof hatch slide open. She slowed, hovering just above it. Then she lowered the maglev into the cool of the engine control booth.

Grant sealed the hatch above them.

They were almost on the area where the barricade had been. "I hope the track is intact!" he shouted as they sailed over it, gaining speed. A jarring vibration shuddered through the train as she hopped off the sled. She almost lost her footing, but Raven caught her. He then helped Byron down off the sled.

Grant picked up speed, the buggies no longer able to keep up as the train powered west. He glanced over at Byron, seeing the seeping wound. "There's a medpod in the back. Three cars down." She braced her shoulder under Byron's arm and helped him through the door, through the cars, all the way back. Despite his pain, Byron kept chuckling. As she pressed the red cross in the wall and watched the medpod emerge and lower itself, she met Byron's eyes. He was still grinning. "Now *that* was fun," he said. She grinned back.

* * * *

Later they all ate dinner together. Dirk had emerged from the sleeping car, startled awake by the Death Rider attack, and joined them for the meal. But after he picked halfheartedly at his food, he returned to bed. H124 knew how exhausted he was, how little sleep he'd gotten lately. He was a ghost of himself.

H124 brought a plate of food up to Grant, who looked drained. "Not used to making a continuous run," he told her. "But I don't dare stop now."

"We could take turns," she offered.

He regarded her with a shriveling look that clearly expressed his firm belief in her insanity. "No one drives her except me."

But in the end, they did all take turns, though Grant insisted on only taking very short naps propped up behind the temporary driver. During these shifts, he continually jerked awake, crying, "What was that?" even if it had been smooth sailing.

After dinner on the second day, she longed for some fresh air. She pushed the door release and stepped out onto the small platform between two cars. The hot, humid night air enveloped her. She climbed a ladder to the top of the neighboring car. Struggling to maintain her balance as the train rocketed down the tracks, she moved to the center of the roof. The wind ruffled her hair, a welcome breeze.

A sense of freedom washed over her, and a flurry of images hit her. She thought of laboring in New Atlantic, knowing only her small room and the tasks set before her each day, retrieving corpses and dragging them to the incinerator, then returning to her tiny room to do the same thing the next day.

She braced her feet, gazing out at the darkened landscape around her. She'd come so far. Her life felt so different now that she could barely grasp hold of it. The empty, aching feeling that had plagued her for as long as she could remember had now melted away. She'd found companionship, a sense of belonging, a greater purpose. For a moment her heart felt too big for her chest. She drew in a deep breath, smelling the tang of rain in the air. She was free. Her life could be anything she dreamed of. She could craft it exactly as she wanted to, her own choices guiding her. Her own conscience. Not someone else's orders, not the rules of a rigid society she'd been born into. Out here, she was free to build whatever kind of life she wanted.

She glanced skyward, the stars above brilliant in a sea of black. She had this one task ahead of her, and though stopping the asteroid was monumental, if they succeeded, the immense freedom of her life filled her with such longing and excitement that it was almost too big to process. Pure joy. Pure relief. What adventures awaited her out here? What grand experiences?

She sat down cross-legged on the roof of the train, the rhythmic clacking of the wheels echoing into the night. She heard the car door whoosh open, and a few moments later, Raven appeared at the top of the ladder.

"Mind if I join you?"

She smiled. "Not at all."

He worked his way deftly across the top of the train and sat down next to her. The landscape was flat, lit in silver and blues by a waning crescent moon.

When she'd lived in New Atlantic, artificial lights burned constantly, beating down on the city at all hours. To see the moon, you had to scan the sky, and even then it was mostly obscured by the ubiquitous amber glow of the atmospheric shield. The garish lights outshone the moon, and she'd never known the enchanting, silver light of the earth's natural satellite until she'd left the city behind her.

The arc of the Milky Way spanned the darkness, dense clusters of stars and dreamy nebulosity. They rode in silence for a time, and H124 couldn't help but think of the last time they'd sat together like this beneath the stars. She'd just lost Astoria. Her mind flashed on her friend racing toward the attacking soldiers, ripping the grenade belt off her chest, then the brilliant explosion as H124 had drifted helplessly toward the ground in her flight suit, unable to help her friend. She swallowed hard and looked over at Raven. His gaze was far away, his long black hair fluttering in the wind. He sat with his knees up, arms resting on them, staring up at the stars.

"What are you thinking about?" she asked.

He inhaled, leaning his head back. "My parents. They would have loved a night like this. They taught me all the names of the stars and the stories behind them." The crescent moon played silver over his face. "We'd play this stick game, *tsìdìł*, in the winter. I always loved that. I still have their set."

"We should play it," she said, then wondered if they'd see another winter. She glanced to the neighboring car holding the A14, the craft's sleek outlines cutting a dark shape against the stars.

"Yes, we should." He exhaled, staring off to the south.

She noticed a glow there. It had been dim at first, but now as they moved ever westward, it had grown brighter. It formed a dome of orange light to the south, no stars visible in that part of the sky. "What is that?" she asked.

"Delta City. We're passing to the north of it."

She thought about how far away they were from it, staggered the light was reaching them this far out.

"The light pollution there is terrible." He regarded her thoughtfully. "You must not have seen any stars growing up in New Atlantic."

Her mouth tightened. "Not a one. I can still remember the first time I saw them. I was so astounded I jumped out of my car and just had to stare up."

He smiled, shifting his weight toward her. "Did you know that birds migrate using the stars?"

She lifted her eyebrows. "They do?"

"Yep. They use the north star as a reference. The megacities are bad, truly, but in the past when people lived in conditions of urban sprawl, lights blanketed the entire continent from ocean to ocean. Migratory birds got lost, crashing into buildings and dying in urban centers. It decimated their populations." He sighed, craning his neck back to take in the expanse of the Milky Way. "If we're ever able to bring back enough birds, I'd sure like to see them on their migrations." He grinned, turning back to her. "One of them was this tiny little bird called a hummingbird. You can't imagine how tiny. Like this big!" He held up his thumb for reference. "Its wings beat seventy times a second. Can you imagine? It lived primarily on nectar from flowers. And this tiny bird would migrate hundreds of miles every year. I've seen photos of their brilliant feathers—sapphire, emerald, scarlet. They were like little flying jewels. They'd do incredible aerobatics, rising up and then diving more than a hundred feet straight down through the air. My ancestors said they did this to see what was above the blue of the sky."

"Have you brought any hummingbirds back?"

He pressed his hands together, pursing his lips. "No. So far we haven't located any of their DNA. But I have hope."

She smiled. "I know you do." Raven had enough hope for all of them. It was infectious. She breathed in the night air, her gaze moving from the amber light dome of Delta City up to the glorious dark to the north.

Her thoughts turned to James Willoughby.

Willoughby was a powerful figure in the Public Programming Corporation, but he believed in H124's cause and had considerable influence. He'd been helping them since her initial escape from New Atlantic, and he'd been close to getting caught.

And for H124 personally, the most surprising thing about Willoughby was that she'd just learned he was her father. She'd thought she'd never know her parents or even who they had been, so it was a welcome balm in a sea of loneliness to know that such a courageous, kind person was related to her.

But her family story had been an unhappy one. Willoughby had fallen in love with the daughter of a highly placed PPC exec, Olivia. Her daughter, Juliet, was an investigative reporter who had covered stories for one of the now-defunct PPC media streams. Juliet had stumbled upon a terrible story—that Olivia was dealing with Delta City's overpopulation problem by harvesting people who were living out on the streets for food. Before Juliet could have broken the story, Olivia had arranged for her to die in a transport explosion. Olivia had planned to raise infant H124 herself after Willoughby transferred to New Atlantic, a move that had been in the works. She'd wanted to raise H124 to take over her empire, to be a powerful player for the PPC, an existence that would have made H124's soul wither and die.

But Willoughby had learned of the plot and rushed to save Juliet. They'd staged an accident, faking the death of both H124 and her mother. Juliet had fled, agreeing to meet with Willoughby later at a designated place outside Delta City. But when he'd shown up there, smuggling H124 in secret, their contact had been murdered, the place burned down, and no sign of Juliet remained.

He'd never found her.

So the most anonymous way he had thought of to protect H124's real identity was by hiding her in the New Atlantic workforce and keeping an eye on her from a distance, playing the grieving father. That way she hadn't been fitted with a head jack and made part of the apathetic, opiated masses. And she hadn't been a target for Olivia, either.

Before New Atlantic was destroyed by the first asteroid fragment, Willoughby had escaped to Delta City, once again resuming an executive position there. Olivia had learned that H124 was still alive, and tried to have Willoughby fired on the grounds that he was a traitor to the PPC. But it had backfired. Because Willoughby had been so careful in covering his tracks, they hadn't found anything suspicious. It was close—he'd even packed up to flee Delta City before learning he'd been cleared. After that, the opinion of Olivia had lowered among the PPC execs, who felt that she had only put suspicion on Willoughby in order to get rid of him and gain more power.

Now H124 wondered how he was doing down there in Delta City. That glow there on the horizon marked his presence, and she felt a strange connection to him through the darkness.

"Raven?" she asked, unsure how to bring up the question she wanted to ask him. He'd been so close to his parents. Byron had, too. And they'd both lost them. She was having the opposite experience, thinking she'd never know her parents and finding out that one of them was still alive.

He turned to her, tucking his hair behind his ear. "Yes?"

"Can I ask you about your parents?"

He smiled. "Sure."

"What was it like? Having them, I mean?"

He shifted his arms on his knees and stared off into the distance. "Having parents is like...having a home wherever you are. The best ones, like mine, love you unconditionally. You feel like you always have somewhere to go. No matter how bad things get, you have people who love you no matter what." He looked down, shifting his feet on the metal of the train. "But when you lose them...it's the opposite feeling, like you'll never have a home again. There's no one left in the world who loves you unconditionally, or who's known you your whole life. No one to accept you in spite of mistakes or be there for you no matter what. It's the most desolate feeling I've ever felt." He hung his head, his hair falling forward.

She brought a hand up and placed it on his shoulder. "You've got us now," she said.

He lifted his head and smiled. "And you have us," he told her, "even if you do have a new dad and all."

She laughed. "I do, don't I?"

"And he doesn't seem half bad for a PPC guy."

She stared at the far-off glow. "Nope. Not half bad at all."

Raven shifted his weight and stood. "Well, I'm dead on my feet. I'll see you tomorrow."

He kept his balance, navigating the top of the train, and disappeared over the ladder.

H124 continued to sit outside in the night, the feeling of the train rushing across the darkened landscape, giving her such a thrilling taste of freedom she couldn't bear to leave. It was only when she started nodding off that she at last gave in to her exhaustion and stood, meandering down to her sleeping car and drifting off to thoughts of what lay ahead.

* * * *

On the third afternoon, she finished her driving shift and walked to the observation car, finding Byron alone there, playing the piano. She slipped quietly onto a sofa, delighting in the soft, musical tones, watching his hands move over the keys effortlessly, coaxing delicate melodies that enchanted her.

The light inside the car suddenly dimmed. She peered toward the vis-screens. "Why is it so dark? Did I lose track of time?"

She stood, staring outside. Dark clouds filled the sky. The light had a strange greenish quality to it. Overhead spanned a sky of green cottonball clouds. She recognized that kind of sky—she'd seen it when she and Gordon had first flown west to find the Rovers. Tornado weather. She turned to Byron. "We might be in for a rough ride."

He joined her at the vis-screen and for a few minutes they stared out as the sky grew darker. Winds buffeted the train. Then the rain started, lashing the roof with a drumming sound. Sheets of grey moved across the vast plains on either side of them, waving through the sparse grass and kicking up dust where land was too dry to maintain much plant life.

It grew so dark that Byron turned on a small stained-glass lamp on the piano. She took a red velvet seat by the vis-screen, watching the storm develop outside.

Part of the cloud off the right side of the train began to spiral downward in a thick funnel. A matching funnel rose up from the ground, and for a moment she thought they would meet. A crack of thunder shook the walls of the train. The cloud dissipated before the funnels touched. Then slightly to the left, another part of the cloud dipped down, churning. Lightning flashed overhead. A second funnel churned up to meet the one from the ground, brown dirt spiraling. The two funnels met, twisting and gaining velocity and diameter, grinding along the prairie.

"Tornado," she breathed, watching to see which direction it would move. It churned and tunneled toward them, and H124 stood, alarmed. Then a second funnel cloud touched down just to the right of the first. It spiraled and shifted, great clouds of dirt shooting up into its mass.

"Halo?" Byron said from the other window. "This doesn't look good." She went to him, kneeling on the seat in front of the other vis-screen, seeing three more funnel clouds touching down along the horizon. They spun and churned, sometimes moving toward each other, at other times parting and digging up paths in opposite directions.

As she watched, two of the funnel clouds dissipated, and a third dwindled to a narrow twister. Suddenly the two returned with renewed fury, churning due south, heading straight for them. She felt the train accelerate and imagined Grant in the engine compartment, pushing the Big Worm faster to try to outrun the storm.

But two funnel clouds closed in from the north, gaining speed, their bases growing wider and wider until they were massive black and grey funnels of charcoal. One grew so close she could see the debris cloud circling on the outside of the main funnel. Pieces of old wood, rusted metal sheets—the debris of a long-gone civilization picked up and hurled through the sky like a giant swinging a morning star. For a moment she thought the funnel might miss the train. Grant had picked up considerable speed, and the tornado shifted directions, moving parallel to the track for a solid fifteen seconds. But then it changed course again, its bottom twisting and bending, churning up earth on a direct collision course with them.

Outside, a loud reverberation thundered above the roar of the train's engine, like another train was barreling down on them.

The train shuddered, the metal groaning like a living thing. "It's going to hit us!" she cried, bracing herself against the back of a couch.

As it churned past their car, the debris cloud narrowly missing them, she heard impacts on the train's exterior. Metal pinging against metal. Dull *thunks* of wood striking the armor. On the vis-screen, the debris cloud wound closer and closer to them. Then it moved slightly off, giving them some breathing room. It had barely missed them. The real gravity of the situation hit H124. It had missed their car, but was heading straight back where the A14 stood exposed on the cargo platform.

"We have to move to the rear of the train!" she shouted to Byron above the roar of the storm. The engine thundered, pushed to its limits. "It could hit the A14!"

She raced to the rear of the dining car, pressing the door control there. It whooshed open, and she ran through the dining car, finding Raven at the far end, already pushing through to the next car with Dirk.

"If that thing hits the A14, this whole mission will have been for nothing!" Raven yelled, echoing her thoughts.

They reached the cargo car. Outside they could hear scraping and crashing as objects slammed into the side of the train. The car groaned, and H124 felt its weight shift. Suddenly the floor grew unsteady and lurched up at the far end. The tornado was going to pull them right off the tracks, A14 and all.

Chapter 6

H124 stepped into the space between the cargo car and its neighbor. At once her hair pulled upward, whipping around in the wind. Her ears popped. Raven emerged, his long hair instantly drenched, wet tendrils lashing out. She peered up at the ladder leading to the cargo platform. "What do we do?" she yelled over the roar of the tornadoes.

"We have to check on it," Raven called back.

Behind them Byron and Dirk stood in the doorway, rain soaking their faces. Raven gripped the ladder on the cargo car and climbed, his shirt buffeting his back as the wind tore at it. Once his boots cleared the ladder, H124 climbed up. As soon as her head crested the top of the car, she gasped. The debris cloud of the funnel was too close. She could see it churning just a few feet from the train, jagged pieces of metal whipping around at tremendous velocity, along with rocks and rusted debris. One of the securing chains had snapped off the A14 and now whipped around in the wind, lashing out. The A14 clattered on the platform, the strength of the tornado exerting tremendous force on it, trying to draw it near the edge of the train.

The funnel cloud angled away from them, but a second tornado had touched down, moving on a collision course with the train.

"If we could just get that chain refastened!" Raven called out in the wind. A brilliant flash of lightning lit up the dark afternoon, and a second later an ear-splitting crack of thunder rent the sky. Between the jarring motion of the train and the wind, H124 could barely stay standing. She went down on one knee to steady herself as Byron and Dirk climbed over the top of the ladder and joined them. She pointed out the broken securing chain just as a second one tore loose.

Now the A14 rattled on the platform, its wings tipping back and forth, and with a jarring rend of metal, it moved a foot toward the tornado, sliding on the platform.

Raven studied the flapping motion of the chain, and with a decisive strike lashed out his hand and grabbed it midair. He held onto it, pulling it taut. As he scanned the platform for the ring to attach it to, H124 saw that it had been snapped off at its base. Only the broken stem of the bolt remained.

"We'll have to replace it!" she yelled over the din.

"This one, too!" Byron shouted, pointing at another snapped off connector ring. He stood in front of a second whipping chain, waiting to seize it when he saw the opportunity. But it flapped around violently, and more than a few times it almost slashed him across the torso.

"I'll get more rings!" Dirk shouted, returning to the ladder and climbing down out of sight.

She knelt on the train, the wind hitting her back as Grant picked up even more speed. She dared a glance at the churning funnel cloud. It veered steadily toward them. She estimated it would hit the train again in maybe two minutes if it kept on its current trajectory—even sooner if it shifted to the south.

She fought off images of one of those jagged pieces of metal driving into her skull.

To her right, Byron traced the movement of the chaotic chain and darted his hand out, but the chain whipped erratically, cracking him on the arm instead. He cried out and brought his arm in to his chest.

"Are you okay?" she called to him.

"It was just a love bite," Byron called back, preparing to strike out again and catch it.

To her left, Raven held fast to his chain, but it yanked him around on the platform, and he struggled to maintain his footing. The A14 jolted slightly to one side again, and for a second Raven was lifted off his feet before his boots touched back down. He stumbled briefly, but caught himself before he went over the side of the train.

She stood, making her way unsteadily toward Byron. He lashed out again, and this time he caught the end of the chain and reeled it in. He braced himself on the platform. Behind her, Dirk appeared again, cresting the ladder. "Got 'em!" he called. He stumbled forward, the train jolting beneath him, and placed a ring in H124's hand. "You got your pocket pyro?" he shouted above the noise.

She nodded, then pulled hers from her pocket.

His dreadlocks lashing violently in the wind, Dirk staggered over to Raven, and H124 got down on her knees in front of the broken eye bolt near Byron. She placed the new bolt on top of the broken one and began to weld the two together. It melted quickly, and she had to keep wiping rain out of her face, though her sleeve was so soaked that it didn't do much good. At last the bolt was attached, and she tugged on it. It felt solid, but she knew her force of yanking on it was nothing compared to what it would have to withstand.

She glanced over her shoulder, seeing the tornado now mere feet away. Debris slammed into the side of the train, small objects pinging off metal as bigger ones *thunked* into the side.

"Try that!" she called to Byron, pointing to the replaced ring bolt. Gripping the chain, he maneuvered his way across the platform and bent down. With her help, they managed to steady the whipping chain enough to hook it into the eye. He let go. It held.

To their left, Dirk had just finished welding his eye bolt into place. He stood as Raven approached unsteadily. Dust, pebbles and ancient debris smashed against the train. Dirk and Raven were too close on that side.

"Hurry!" H124 shouted, staggering across the platform toward them. Dirk grabbed onto the chain with her, and they guided it to the ring bolt. It was much harder on this side, and a few times the wind-tossed chain dragged them toward the side of the train.

Something large from the debris cloud slammed into the side of the cargo car with such force that the whole thing shuddered.

They managed to clip the chain through the ring bolt. Byron reached the top of the ladder and called out to them. "It's about to hit!"

Dirk raced back to Byron, and they climbed down into the safety of the cars.

Just then a splintered piece of old wood struck Raven in the chest. Arms windmilling, he flew backward, slamming down hard on the platform. The force of the wind caught him, and he started sliding back toward the edge of the train. H124 leapt out, landing forcefully on her stomach and grabbing one of Raven's boots. His arms flailed for anything to grab onto, and as he and H124 slid more across the top of the train, they passed under the A14. Raven managed to grasp onto the A14's landing gear. H124 continued to hold onto his boot, but suddenly felt weightless. The tornado closed in, lifting her off the train's platform, her feet arcing toward the funnel cloud. She heard huge things slamming into the A14's wings above them, and squeezed her eyes shut, clinging to Raven's boot just as he clung to the landing gear.

The roar of the funnel cloud deafened her as she hung there, hair whipping wildly around her face for what felt like eternity. She held on to Raven and hoped they wouldn't go flying away with the A14.

The aircraft groaned and shuddered, metal rending, the roaring of the funnel cloud becoming one with the roaring of the train's engine. She felt something hit her leg and then slam onto the platform, sliding beneath the A14 with them. She opened one eye, seeing a rusted sign with a winged red horse sliding toward the edge of the train. It flew off over the other side.

Her body slammed back down onto the platform. Her ears popped. The roar diminished slightly. The cold of the metal platform against her wet face made her shiver. She opened her eyes to see they'd cleared the funnel cloud. It churned away, crossing the tracks and spiraling away to the south.

Raven let go of the landing gear and let his arms slump down to the platform. She released his boot and crawled to him, collapsing beside him.

Peeling his soaked hair away from his face, he stared upward at the underside of the A14. "It's still here."

Her heart thudded in her chest.

"Halo! Raven!" Byron shouted, emerging from the top of the ladder. He raced to them, ducking under the A14. "We thought you were right behind us!" He extended his hands down to them, but H124 couldn't budge. Her soaked clothes plastered her body, making movement difficult. He bent down, moving the hair out of her face.

"That was a hell of thing, wasn't it?" he said, a contagious smile on his face.

"I'm beginning to think you're an adrenaline junkie," Raven told him, managing to sit up.

Byron grasped one of H124's arms and hefted her up. "I just like a challenge."

Returning to the quiet of the train, they dried off and drank hot beverages in the dining car. Night fell, and H124 watched lightning jag across the darkened sky, the thunder booming later and later after each brilliant flash. The storm was moving in the opposite direction.

When day broke the next morning, Grant slowed the train, bringing it to a halt.

Moments later the door to the dining car hissed open. "We're at the pickup coordinates."

H124 smiled with relief.

Opening his comm channel, Raven called Rivet and Gordon.

In the meantime, they climbed up to the A14. A vast plain stretched out before them, with towering mountains in the distance. They detached the cargo chains, stowing them away inside the car. Soon dust appeared on the horizon, and four all-terrain vehicles came into view, moving in sync. As they got closer, H124 saw that a huge platform joined all four together. She spied Rivet and Gordon behind the wheels of the front two cars. They pulled up, and H124 saw that each all-terrain vehicle was far bigger than the one they'd taken to the radar facility. Cutting the engines, Gordon and Rivet piled out, followed by two Rovers H124 didn't recognize. They had driven the rear vehicles.

Gordon hugged H124. Rivet, her red hair blowing in the wind around her pink, freckled face, introduced the other two Rovers, Winslow and Rex. "Winslow is our aviation expert here at the satellite location," Rivet explained. "And Rex keeps the site running smoothly."

Winslow's blue eyes twinkled in a fawn-colored face under a short, spiky crop of black hair. She thrust out a hand.

H124 shook it, taking an instant liking to her. "H124."

Rex, his bronze face wrinkled and bearded, and his lanky brown hair hanging past his shoulders, gave hearty handshakes all around.

Back on top of the train again, they readied to shift the A14 from the cargo platform to the makeshift Rover carrier.

Using the recharged maglevs again, Raven managed to lift the A14 from the train and deposit it gently on top of the platform before the copters lost power and clunked on the top of the vehicles, bouncing off into the dirt. H124 picked them up.

Grant supervised, guarding his precious train against further damage. When they'd finished transferring the A14, they all stood out on the dusty plain, blinking in the bright sun, beginning to sweat. The day was going to be another scorcher.

Byron turned to Grant and extended a hand. "Can't tell you how much you've helped us."

"How much you've helped all of us," H124 added.

Grant scrutinized the Big Worm. "She got a scratch. She got more than one."

H124 winced as she looked back at the right side of the train. The whole side of it had been dented and scoured by the tornado. The A14 had also sustained damage, though thankfully most of it looked cosmetic.

"Going to take a hell of a paint job," Grant muttered, his bearded face looking grim.

He returned to the engine room and let out a giant puff of steam into the humid air. The engine churned and puffed, the wheels spun to life, and Grant was on his way, chugging down the tracks to the west.

"Interesting guy," Dirk remarked.

"Loves that train," Byron added.

They then piled into the vehicles and headed off toward the satellite location as the Big Worm wound away into the distance.

* * * *

At the satellite location, H124 climbed down the ramp of the all-terrain vehicle, taking in the place. They'd parked at a small airfield, with two hangars and a large warehouse at one end of the runway. The loading doors to the warehouse stood open, revealing workbenches, hydraulic lifts, tools, and a machine shop.

Rivet took over control of the maglevs, fitting them with freshly charged copters. She lifted the A14 from the makeshift platform and delivered it gently to the floor space inside the warehouse.

Long vines trailed off the warehouse and hangars, where verdant plants grew. She saw a lot of the same features she'd seen in Sanctuary City—glass that darkened and lightened to adjust the building's temperature. Gardens growing on roofs, wind turbines and catchers, and solar arrays set up in the distance. The place looked older than Sanctuary City, the buildings a little more worn. One large hangar stood off to one side by itself, no runway leading up to it, just a large grassy field.

To the west rose steep mountains, a couple peaks showing small snowfields. On the other side of them, she knew, lay the ocean. To the north and east, a small experimental forest grew.

At the base of one section of trees grew crops of vegetables. Agroforestry, she remembered Raven calling the practice. It helped keep in the moisture. She squinted up at the wind catchers, raising a hand to shield the sun. Rex noticed her interest and came over.

"This place has got everything you could need. Fresh water, food, solar and wind power." He pointed to a small, squat structure covered with pea vines. "We live under there. It can withstand a blast from an airship."

She regarded him, enjoying his twinkling blue eyes and friendly manner. "Could it withstand the effects of the impact?"

"We won't have to find out." He looked toward Rivet as she pulled over a rack of her tools. Gordon moved a step ladder on wheels over toward the engine. "We're going to stop this thing."

"We still need to find a nuclear payload."

"About that," Rex said. "Orion called down here earlier. He has a lead. He's in Sanctuary City with Onyx, waiting to talk to you."

After they'd settled in, they all gathered in Rivet's workshop and opened up a comm channel to Sanctuary City.

Orion's umber face shimmered on the floating display. H124 smiled at the sight of the astronomer. "I've been digging through the historical records with Onyx."

Onyx, the Rover's talented hacker, leaned into the frame and smiled, then saw her cousin Raven. *"Yá'át'ééh!"* she greeted him in Navajo.

"Aoo', yá'át'ééh," he responded.

Orion gave an ironic smile. "For once things aren't against us. Turns out it's not a question of where these nuclear payloads are, but where they *aren't.* Missiles are hidden all over the country in these underground silos. It's not going to be tough to find them. They're everywhere. There's a nest of them here," he said, sending coordinates to their PRDs. H124 brought up her floating display to see a cluster of red dots a few hundred miles to their southeast.

Orion continued. "Should be more than enough to get the payload we need."

"Do the Badlanders know about these missile silos?" H124 asked Dirk.

He shook his head, then thought a minute. "Although...a camp near where I grew up found a bunch of really deep holes in the ground. May have been empty silos. This camp wasn't the nicest group in the world. They used to...um..." He glanced around nervously.

"Yes?" Raven prompted.

"They used to throw people down there. Enemies mostly."

"Alive?"

He grimaced. "Kinda. Yeah."

"Enemies *'mostly'?*" she asked.

"Sometimes they'd throw people down there for fun."

She raised her brow.

"But the people had to be real jerks to deserve it. I mean, so I heard."

Not for the first time, H124 was grateful that it had been Byron's clan to find her on the road all those nights ago, though she'd nearly bought it that first night in the camp.

Onyx leaned in again. "There's been increased PPC drone activity up here," she told them. "They've flown over twice in the last few days."

Raven frowned.

"How often do they usually fly over?" H124 asked him.

"About twice a year. Onyx has a system to block them," Raven told her.

H124 looked back at the hacker. "When the drones fly over," Onyx explained, "I send up a jamming signal, so it doesn't pick up any of our communication or EM energy in the city. To the drone, Sanctuary City just looks like another stretch of uninhabited land. But the frequency of these fly-overs worries me."

"Do you think they know we're down there?"

She bit her lip. "It's more like they're searching for something. I don't know what."

"Keep me posted," Raven said.

"Will do."

Gordon spoke up. "I can fly us down to the missile silos."

Raven turned to him. "We've got a C-130 Hercules stored here that should be big enough to stow the warheads."

Gordon nodded. "Perfect."

Orion exhaled. "Good luck."

"Thanks," H124 responded.

"*Hágoónee',*" Onyx said to Raven.

"*Hágoónee'.*" He closed down the comm window, and they all looked at each other.

H124 stared back at the coordinates Orion had sent, the cluster of red dots showing all the missiles, then panned out to see the other silos, all along the coasts and the center of the country. "Why did they have so many of these things? Aren't they enough to destroy the world a thousand times over?"

Raven sighed. "Yep. But they kept building and stockpiling them. Apparently there was a time when world powers agreed to dismantle them, and partly did. But then for some reason, tensions returned and they started making new ones and stockpiling again."

As Gordon refueled and prepared the plane for the flight, H124 walked around the satellite location, taking in the vast mountains rising to west of her. Ancient burned-out forests lay between her and those summits. Most of the trees had toppled and now lay sun-bleached and white. Wind tore across the expanse, hot and dry.

Her PRD beeped, and she brought up her comm window to see Rowan's smiling face, his blue eyes squinting in bright sunlight. "How's it going out there?" he asked. His cropped blond hair looked sweaty and dirty, and he wiped a sleeve across his forehead.

"Pretty good. We're definitely on track."

He breathed out. "Here, too. Been doing pirate broadcasts, trying to warn people to leave Delta City. Relocating a lot of Badlanders to old bomb shelters. But a lot of them won't go. Don't seem to think there's a real threat." He shook his head. "Can't say I blame them. They've worked hard to claim territory in some of these places, and then some stranger comes along and tells them a rock is going to fall from the sky and kill them all?"

"I can see why they'd be doubtful."

"But I'm sure you guys are going to be successful, and moving all these people will all be for nothing. Then they'll really hate me." He gave a rueful smile.

"It's great of you to try, though."

They both went silent then, an awkward silence hovering. "You okay?" he said at last.

She bit her lip. She wanted to tell him about Byron, but wasn't sure how that sort of thing was done. She and Rowan had seen so little of each other lately. She didn't know how he felt about her.

A sudden shout on Rowan's side drew his attention. "Oh, man. Another fight is starting. It never ends. Where are you all off to next?"

She told him of the missile silo location they'd found.

He frowned. "That's right in the middle of Executioner territory."

"Who?"

"Some of the foulest Badlanders out there."

"Used to throw people down the empty silos?"

"So you've heard of them." He gazed around, and she could see two men fighting behind him. One staggered back under a brutal uppercut. "I think I'd better go with you all. I know them. Might be able to smooth some feathers before you head out there. Be there in case things go south."

She brightened. "We'd certainly love your help."

"Okay." He spun and shouted, "Will you knock it off? I can barely hear!" at the two fighting men, who completely ignored him. One bumped into him. "I can rendezvous with you at this location," Rowan told her, then entered some information into his PRD.

She opened her map screen when it beeped, seeing a glowing red circle about fifty miles from the missile silos. "I'll let Gordon know. And thanks, Rowan."

He smiled. "See you soon." His window shut down.

Outside she heard the sound of the C-130's engine firing up. Gordon's face appeared on her comm link. "Time to stock up on some weapons of mass destruction."

"I'm ready," she told him.

Chapter 7

H124 stood at the top of a silo, staring down the dark tube at the missile, its body stretching down into shadows. A vast plain extended to both sides of her, holding even more nuclear missiles. It made her nervous just to be around them.

They'd flown over some of the strangest terrain she'd ever seen. Vast flats of brown, waving grass gave way to abrupt cliffs and valleys filled with colorful geological formations—stark spires of dark brown, tan, and grey, like little canyons that appeared suddenly, sunk into the earth.

After picking up Rowan, they'd landed some distance away to stay clear of the cliffs. Wary of the Executioners, they'd deboarded with their equipment quickly: water, maglevs, pocket pyros. H124 still carried her small, brick-sized flight suit.

At the silo, Dirk had struggled with accessing the ancient doors that hid the missiles. But finally he'd succeeded, revealing the deadly projectile beneath their feet.

A metal ladder extended down the side of the tube. She and Byron climbed down, following Dirk and Raven. Rowan stayed topside with Gordon in case the Executioners showed up. They had to protect the plane.

H124 descended carefully, her clanking boots echoing in the chamber. Cobwebs caught in her face and hair. A platform opened up near the middle, with a walkway leading to a neighboring underground chamber. They moved toward it, finding a control booth and small storage area.

Returning to the tube, Byron stared up at the missile. "So we just need a tiny part of this thing?"

Raven nodded. "Just the payload, not the missile." He checked his PRD, pointing to the location of the payload inside the projectile.

Unfurling several maglev sleds, they powered them up. They went to work, using the maglevs to raise them up to the missile's side. With pocket pyros, they began cutting into the missile's exterior. At last they lifted out the warhead, placing it gently on a maglev. For now, they stowed it in the storage area, preparing to gather other payloads. They didn't dare bring it topside yet, when they could be spotted by Death Riders or other dangerous factions. They'd wait until they'd collected enough to deflect the asteroid. Then the warheads could be loaded onto the C-130 and flown to Sanctuary City to be hidden with the blast deflection craft.

Moving through the network of silos, they removed several more nuclear payloads. Raven had told her that this dry, inhospitable country had once all been farmland, people living in houses scattered across the landscape, the wind sighing in their corn and wheat crops. They'd been farmers, teachers, grocery store owners, all going about their lives. But even then, these missiles had waited under the ground, ready to arc across the earth and destroy similar communities in other countries.

She wondered how they'd felt, lying in their beds at night in the dark. Did they think of the dormant threat hiding under their fields, waiting for the push of a button or the mad whim of some leader either here or across an ocean?

When H124 and the others had gathered enough nuclear material, they started to load up the maglevs to deliver them to Gordon's plane. They moved a few payloads, then returned to the silos to transport the remaining warheads.

They had two more loads to go when H124 heard a deep thrumming. She froze in the middle of calibrating the current maglev sled. She met Raven's eyes in the gloom of the silo.

"Airship," he breathed.

Dirk creased his brow. "What are they doing this far out?"

Her heart started thudding. "Do you think a surveillance drone went overhead? Saw us?"

Raven's face had gone slack, his eyes glassy. He stood there unmoving.

H124's mind raced. Should they run out and try to cover the plane? Have Gordon take off before it got here? If it saw him, the airship pilot could easily outrun Gordon and bring down the C-130 Hercules.

She started to bring up her comm window, but Gordon beat her to it. "There's an airship out here! I don't see it yet, but I hear it." On her display, he searched the sky nervously.

"You have to get out of there," she urged him. "But don't do it in the air. Can you taxi somewhere with ground cover?"

On her display, she watched Gordon searching the area around him. "I see a cluster of buildings about a mile away. Might be something there." He pulled out a pair of diginocs and studied them more closely. "They're pretty beat up."

"Do it," she told him.

"What about you?"

"We'll stash these last two pieces somewhere and hide. Wait for the airship to pass."

"And if it doesn't?" asked Gordon.

"Then we get blown to kingdom come," Dirk said softly.

"Or burned alive," Raven added, his voice barely a whisper.

"They might already know we're down here," Byron put in. "If a drone did fly over earlier, they could have spotted our activity. We have to move these last two payloads to a different area."

Dirk ran to the missile silo control booth and shut the overhead doors. Darkness filled the underground chamber and they switched on their headlamps. To their right, across a metal catwalk, stood another door. They commanded the maglevs to follow them, and Dirk crossed the walkway, pausing at the door. He pulled out a multitool and pocket pyro and went to work disarming the lock.

Raven still hadn't moved; his breathing was shallow. H124 knew the horrors he'd seen, what an airship had done to his parents. She was halfway across the walkway when she realized he hadn't moved. She hurried back to him.

"Raven?" she asked.

His glassy eyes were a thousand miles away. Gently she touched his arm. "We have to go."

He blinked, looking down at her. "Of course."

She took his hand, and together they crossed the bridge, joining Dirk and Byron. The acrid stench of burning plastic filled the air. Dirk twisted a few wires together, and the door clicked. Pushing against it, he managed to slide it open, admitting them to a musty corridor with metal walls.

After the maglevs had passed through, she slid the door shut behind them. In this dark passage, with meters of solid earth between her and the surface, she couldn't hear the airship anymore. Her comm window beeped. She brought it up. Gordon sat in the cockpit of the plane. "I still don't see it. I'm almost at the buildings. Looks like one of them is big enough to cover the C-130. Holes in the roof, though. Some sheet metal is lying around. We might be able to drag some up on the roof. Cover the bigger holes."

A pit in her stomach turned, sour and unwelcome. She should have gone with him. Should have climbed the ladder out and ran to the plane. He and Rowan were out there alone now, two people who were supposed to heft huge sheets of rusted metal onto a roof.

She felt a strange flash of a new emotion. A contempt, almost a *despising* of herself. "I should have gone with them," she said aloud as he clicked off.

Raven turned to her, his shadowed face wary. "That thing would have spotted you and cut you down."

"We don't know that."

"Or it might have followed you right to the plane," Dirk pointed out.

It was all speculation, she knew, all of their points. Maybe it would have. Or maybe she could have helped. She thought of everything she and Gordon had been through together, and hated the thought of him exposed out there. Rowan was tough, sure. But Gordon was a pilot, not a fighter.

Dirk cracked a small smile. It was the first one she'd seen since he'd learned about Astoria. "I don't think you need to worry about Gordon. Dude's pretty resourceful, you know. He's made it this long, and he's not exactly a spring chicken."

She took a small breath. "Okay. True enough."

The gloomy corridor led to a second door, and they waited while Dirk rewired the lock. When it clicked, they pushed aside the door, finding another walkway. It went on for what felt like miles, lengths of underground tunnels with connecting doors, some leading to other launch tubes, some to control booths. She marveled at the sheer level of engineering, the expense and work that had gone into this entire network, all for the sole purpose of destroying someone on the other side of the planet. And at the same time, these people had cut funding to combat the biggest threat of all—the asteroid that right now barreled toward Earth.

She pulled up the map on her PRD and tracked their progress, showing how far she was now from the plane. She opened the comm window.

Gordon's face filled the screen, but there was very little light. Rowan brushed rust off his shirt behind him. "It worked. Got the holes covered," Gordon whispered. "But I don't know how hidden we'll be if they take a lot of time to search. I can still hear the airship, but haven't spotted it yet. It must be above the clouds." He paused. "Oh, no."

"What is it?"

She watched as he moved his body into a patch of light and peered up. "It's a PPC dropship."

Raven faced her display. "They're deploying ground troops?"

Gordon kept staring up, his mouth parting. "They're landing! They're right over your location!" He looked back at them. "Get the hell out of there!"

Chapter 8

They raced through the tunnels, trying to gain some distance from the dropship. Maybe they could cover enough ground and pop up somewhere far enough away that they could skirt around the PPC's troops and make it to the plane. But they'd been down in the dark for too long, the maglevs burdened with too heavy a weight. Without sunlight, their charges began to dwindle, the copters sputtering, just as they had when lifting the A14.

Dirk had gotten ahead of them. He slowed when he saw them pause. "What's happening?"

Raven glanced around. "The sleds are running out of power."

"Can we use the power cells from our PRDs?" H124 asked. As soon as she said it, she realized they couldn't. Their PRDs controlled and steered the maglevs.

"We have to get to the surface before they give out." Raven lowered the sleds to conserve energy.

H124 turned on her comm channel and called Gordon. His worried face came into view. He stood pressed against the inside wall of the weathered outbuilding, staring out. "What does it look like up there?" she asked.

His brow creased. "The dropship has landed. Two transports are now on the ground, loaded with troops." He squinted in a shaft of bright sunlight. "They're checking out the last place where you went underground. Trying to figure out how to get it open."

She looked down at the payloads. They had to get them to the plane. She regarded the others in the gloom of the walkway. "What if we split up? Two of us get these maglevs to Gordon's plane. The others create some kind of distraction so he can get out of here with them." She turned to

Byron. "Feel like stealing another transport?" she asked, recalling their attempt to rescue citizens in Delta City all too well.

He grinned. "You got it."

Rowan came into view on Gordon's comm link, holding up a hand. "Wait, wait. You think you can go topside and just steal one? They're all over the place up here. Those dropships can hold a hundred troops. There are only six of us. How are you even going to get to a transport? It could be filled with a dozen troopers."

Byron wore an expression of steel. "I'll play it by ear."

Rowan sighed. "You're so reckless. Remember the medical supply run on Murder City? You barely made it out. And almost got Astoria and Dirk killed." When he heard himself say her name, he grew quiet and swallowed.

"I've learned a thing or two since then," Byron said.

Rowan shook his head. "I don't like this."

"The most important thing is to get the payloads safely away," H124 reminded him. "If we stay down here, they'll find us."

"We don't know that. Gordon and I could wait until dark, continue to move farther away. You all keep moving through the tunnels. Eventually they'll give up and leave."

"And if they don't?" Byron asked him.

Rowan opened his mouth, but no words came.

"I like Halo's idea better," Byron insisted.

Dirk chimed in. "Me too. I don't relish the thought of hiding out down here, just waiting for them to stumble across us."

Rowan frowned. "You said yourself it's a labyrinth of tunnels down there."

Their PRDs had been tracking their path through the dark underground complex.

"You have to be our eyes topside. Send us coords of a good place to get out," H124 told him.

Gordon scanned the area with his diginocs. "They haven't moved into the following area," he told her, sending her the location.

She laid them over her map and nodded. "That's not too far from here."

Raven spoke up. "Let's move."

They ran now, rushing across catwalks and through old doors. Between gasps, they made a plan. Dirk and Raven would sprint toward the plane with the sleds. Once they were out in the bright sun, the copters would get a burst of energy. Byron and H124 would create a diversion to draw troopers away from them.

When they reached the coordinates, Gordon confirmed there were still no PPC troopers there. Dirk hacked another door, which led them to an emergency escape tube. There they climbed a ladder that ascended to the surface, leading to a locked hatch. Dirk grabbed the locking wheel and tried to twist it, but it was stuck fast. Byron joined him at the top, each hanging off one side of the ladder. Together they managed to unscrew the wheel, the old rusted metal screeching in protest.

"Everyone ready?" Byron asked.

Dirk climbed down, and H124 took his place on the ladder. Byron barely lifted the door to peer out. "I see them. About a quarter mile away."

H124 also peeked through the crack, eyes watering in the bright sunlight. She could see two transports parked by the tube where they'd gotten the last warhead. Ground troops patrolled the area on both sides. To the far right, a few hundred yards away, another transport was parked. Nearby two soldiers tried to open another emergency exit hatch there, while a dozen troopers had branched off on foot. "That transport looks like a good bet," Byron whispered.

Dirk looked up at them. "We'll go out another exit. Hope they don't spot us." He and Raven ran further along in the direction they'd been heading, disappearing through another door, the maglevs struggling along behind them.

H124 and Byron climbed out, opening their hatch as little as possible, and lay flat on their stomachs. Other than a few small bumps and rises, the barren landscape offered almost no cover, and H124 started to sweat in the heat, feeling exposed. This was a crazy idea. What had she been thinking?

Ahead, the two soldiers succeeded in swinging open the other hatch. They called out to the troopers who had moved away, beckoning them back. The soldiers filed into the hatch one at a time, vanishing down into the dark. It wouldn't be long before they found Dirk and Raven if they passed through the right doors.

When the last trooper had lowered out of sight, Byron and H124 took off at a run toward the abandoned transports. To her left, she saw troopers standing around a different hatch, and about half a mile away, the massive dropship waited on the ground, its gleaming silver sides glinting in the sun, its main hatch open, with two more sentries standing on the ramp.

When they reached the abandoned transport, Byron slid into the driver's seat. H124 climbed in beside him. These vehicles were different from the ones she'd seen in New Atlantic shuttling around soldiers. The inside had no seats except the two up front. In the back stood a side-loading door, a rack of energy rifles, sonic weapons, and flash bursters, and some kind of large cylindrical weapon mounted near a rear hatch.

Byron used his PRD to hack into the transport's navigation system. She turned in her seat, craning her neck to keep an eye on the troopers by the other hatch. So far they hadn't noticed them. She looked back by the dropship, staring beyond it. A squad of soldiers headed toward the collection of ancient buildings where Gordon was hiding. "We have to hurry!" she said. "They're about to find the plane."

At that, the transport's engines hummed to life, and she felt it lift gently off the ground. Byron grinned at her. "We're airborne."

He veered the transport around, speeding toward the squad of soldiers nearing Gordon. H124 scrambled back to the weapon rack. She handed up an energy rifle and sonic weapon to Byron, then took the same for herself.

She cranked her rifle up to the lethal setting and moved to the side-loading door. Waving her hand over the control she opened it. A blast of hot air hit her as she kneeled, ready to fire.

Byron moved alongside the squad, who took no notice of the transport, which to them could have just been dropping off more soldiers. As he passed by them, H124 let out a stream of fire, catching them unawares, taking out half the squad. They turned, horrorstruck, and loosed their firepower on the transport. Byron hit a handful of them with his energy rifle, then swung the transport around, heading for the troopers at the hatch where they'd first entered.

The remaining soldiers from the injured squad gave pursuit.

Byron slammed into the group at the hatch, taking out at least a dozen. H124 fired her rifle out of the open door, hitting even more. She could hear their commanding officer shouting orders over their panicked cries. The troopers who had entered the underground system came pouring back out of the hatch. Byron veered toward them. Again H124 fired, the snaking, bright energy knocking them all down. Byron sped away, drawing their fire. A few survivors climbed into transports and took off after them. She pulled out her diginocs and looked back to where Dirk and Raven had been heading. She saw them emerge from a hatch, sprinting toward the buildings where the plane hid.

But all eyes were on her and Byron, the troopers pulling out and streaming toward them. She counted two transports in pursuit.

Other troopers, farther away on foot, ran back toward the dropship. The guards on the ramp stood aside as they poured in. She heard its engines kick on.

"Dropship's about to take off."

Byron wheeled violently to one side as a transport came up behind them. She almost fell over, grabbing onto a stabilizer bar to keep her balance.

Struggling to stay upright, she stumbled to the back, grabbing onto the cylinder that was mounted on a stand. She studied the controls, spotting a fire button and several control switches for intensity and range.

"What is this thing?" she asked Byron.

He craned his neck back to see as he veered wildly to the left, forcing her to grab the walls of the transport. "It's an EMP gun."

"A what?"

"Electromagnetic pulse weapon. Fire that sucker at these bastards behind us!"

She waved her hand in front of the rear hatch window. It slid down. One of the transports was right behind them, so close that it would soon ram them. A soldier leaned out of the passenger window, leveling an energy rifle at her. She cranked up the controls on the EMP gun and aimed it at their transport. She pressed the fire switch, and the enemy transport's engine cut out. The trooper tried to fire her rifle, but it wouldn't work. The transport crashed to the ground, the inertia driving it along the dirt, sending up a huge dusty cloud.

"Way to go, Halo!" Byron shouted, punching the air.

The gun's charge went down to seventy-five percent. It had to recharge before it could fire again. The second transport in pursuit veered away, trying to move up alongside them. She tried to swivel the gun, but the stand wouldn't allow it to move to a ninety-degree angle.

"Can you get that other one?"

"The mount won't let me!"

She knelt beside it, hands moving over its connection to the stand. Her fingers found a latch there. She snapped it open. But when she tried to lift the gun, it was too heavy. She'd wouldn't be able to hold it. She had to prop it up. The charge display read eighty-five percent.

She lowered it down off the stand, then moved to one of the side windows. Waving the pane open, she returned to the EMP and dragged it across the floor. The transport was close now but wary, changing its course, weaving, clearly concerned about another EMP blast.

She leaned the gun against the wall, then hefted it up onto the windowsill. The enemy transport was only a few feet away. The pilot saw her and sped off to the side, trying to pull ahead of them. In the back, she saw a solider at their own EMP weapon, struggling with the stand's limitations just as she had. She checked the charge on the gun. One hundred percent. She fired. The enemy's engine cut out. The transport slammed into the ground, hitting a small rise and vaulting up onto its side, then tumbling, rolling, the troopers inside tossing about. It slid to a stop in the dust. Dirt clouds obscured the wreck.

"Nice!" Byron called back. He whipped the transport around.

She stuck her head out and looked up. The dropship was in pursuit. She pulled out her diginocs, looking toward the buildings where Gordon hid. It was too far away to make out much detail. Then she spotted it. A tiny speck of movement. The plane. Taking off in the distance, moving in the opposite direction.

"They made it! They've taken off!"

Byron's voice went grim. "And our problems are just beginning."

H124 looked behind them. The dropship was lowering, keeping pace with them. The main ramp opened, and a stream of transports poured out. Troopers stood on their roofs, strapped into racks, all holding energy and sonic weapons.

She hefted the gun back to the rear window, and looked at the charge. Eighty-seven percent. "It's not ready to go again!"

Transports continued to stream out. She counted more than a dozen, and a few moments later, twice that amount. The EMP read ninety-eight percent.

Byron weaved as the troopers started shooting at them, the energy blasts hitting their transport. On top of a bigger transport in the middle of the enemy group, she watched two troopers readying a massive sonic weapon, the same kind she'd seen decimate Black Canyon Camp. They swiveled it around, aiming at her. Her EMP beeped, indicating it was fully charged. She fired without hesitation, targeting the sonic weapon transport. Its engine cut out, and it smashed into the dirt, crashing end over end, crushing the troopers on top.

Caught in the collateral blast, two adjacent transports also plummeted, sending up huge billows of dust as they rolled to a stop.

But there were still dozens more, and the EMP took too long to recharge. It was back down at seventy percent. The other transports fanned out, making it so that she couldn't hit more than one target with a single EMP blast.

Suddenly the dropship, in the middle of spewing out two more transports, flew up and to the side erratically. The deploying transports fell out of the hatch, too high up. They crashed nose-first into the ground, one of them falling over upside down. The dropship careened off to one side, then blasted away into the distance, completely out of sight.

She heard another engine replace the dropship's deep thrumming in the sky. She looked up, where Gordon's plane shot by. Raven's face shimmered on her comm screen. "Took me a while to hack into the dropship. Controls are a little different than the airships Onyx designed the hack for."

"Uh...Halo?" Byron said, as she turned to him. "We kind of have a problem. Or as I like to think of it, an opportunity."

She rushed to the front of the transport, and looked out to where he pointed. They'd reached the end of the flat grassland. Stretching out before them now was the endless landscape of canyons and cliffs they'd seen from the air. In just a few minutes, they were going to drive right off a cliff. "You still got that flight suit?"

"I've only got the one, and it can't hold two people!" Her heart hammered as she flashed back to that rooftop in Delta City when Astoria's flight suit malfunctioned. She hadn't been able to help her. She couldn't go through that again.

Next to them, the enemy transports gained ground. If they got within reach of their EMP guns...

Rowan's face flashed on her vid screen. "You're going to go off the cliff!" he shouted.

"Byron knows."

"Goddamn it!" Rowan shouted.

They had two choices: Try the flight suit, or be blasted into oblivion by the enemy transports.

She grabbed the flight suit out of her pack. "You take it," she told Byron, heading forward through the transport.

He shook his head. "Strap it on. I've got an idea."

"It can't support both of us."

Byron glanced back at her, his eyes gleaming with adrenaline. "Maybe it can just slow our descent, and we'll only *sort of* plummet to our deaths."

"Sounds like another one of our usually well-thought-out plans."

She could hear Dirk over the comm link. "Get lower!" he was shouting to someone. "Reel it out!"

They raced toward the cliff. Three hundred yards. Two hundred. H124 strapped on the flight suit. Byron put the transport on autopilot and climbed into the back with her. She grabbed some straps from the weapons rack and strapped Byron to her body, then fired up the flight suit controls on her PRD. As soon as the transport went over the edge, they'd have to jump out of the door.

"Reel it out more! We need more!" she heard Dirk yelling.

The ground sped by beneath them. A transport had pulled up beside them, and she could see two troopers struggling to aim the EMP while another scrambled furiously to detach it from its mount.

The ground began to blur. Her heart raced as they went over the edge, the yawning expanse of canyon opening up beneath them. She felt herself go weightless as Byron grabbed the edges of the side door, propelling them out into the air.

She deployed the chute, watching the empty transport plummet. Two enemy transports, caught up in the thrill of the chase, also went over. The others pulled up short.

She angled away from the cliff, but it felt nothing like diving into Delta City. They were too heavy, and the suit couldn't compensate. Over the air surging past her ears, she heard a droning engine. She glanced up to see Gordon's plane. The rear cargo bay door yawned open. Dirk and Rowan stood out on the amp, held in by straps.

Gleaming metal flashed in the sun, and she saw a thin winch cable lowering out of the open hatch. She angled the suit for it. But they were coming down too fast, too chaotically. She managed to straighten them out. Gordon slowed the plane, and Byron stretched out his hands. The cable lashed in the wind, whipping around them. It caught her painfully on the shoulder, and for a moment she worried it would tangle in the chute. Then Byron's hands closed around it. He made a loop in the bottom of it, using the hook to secure it. Then he stepped into the loop, and she felt a crazy, powerful jerk.

The ground rushed up to meet them. She could see spires of mud and sandstone, the grey and white and red bands of strange rock, just before Gordon lifted the plane. They narrowly missed a spire. She felt another violent tug as they surged upward. She hung tightly onto Byron's chest, pressing her face against his back as they jolted up, her stomach plunging down.

Above, Dirk and Rowan reversed the winch, reeling them toward the plane.

The wind caught them, whipping them out of control. She adjusted the chute with her PRD, trying to steady them. She gazed back to see the tiny white dots of the transports at the cliff's edge, and the colorful aggregate of spires deep down in the canyon below.

Alarmed shouts sounded closer. She looked up to see they were only a few feet from the plane's ramp. Dirk and Rowan reached out, grabbing Byron's hands. They hefted them up into the plane. Dirk ran over and slammed the button to close the hatch.

The wind shrieked and howled. She stood on the ramp with shaky legs, still holding on to Byron with everything in her.

Then the ramp sealed, cutting out the wind, leaving her deafened by the quiet. Byron whipped off the straps binding them, and turned and hugged her fiercely. She pressed her face into his warm neck, her heart still thudding.

"That," he said, "was amazing!"

"Don't ever do some crazy thing like that again!" Rowan yelled.
Byron burst out laughing.

"I thought it was pretty damn cool," Dirk added, managing a smile.

"You all okay back there?" Gordon called.

She rushed to the cockpit and gripped her friend's shoulders. "That was some amazing flying."

He reached up and squeezed her hand. "You had me pretty scared."

"*I* had me pretty scared."

Chapter 9

British Entertainment Corporation City
Across the Atlantic

Tony had just wrapped up a rather successful media pitch and retired to his seventy-first floor office to drink a twenty-year-old Scotch and unwind. The pitch had been stressful, with a producer who had the reputation of getting rid of people before they'd even had the chance to prove themselves. But he'd had two successful AI reality shows in the last four months, and his new one, *Weight Loss Death Match,* was even better. The BEC City execs had flipped when they realized the potential impact the show would have. Already they'd been cutting into New Atlantic and Delta City feeds across the ocean.

They'd had a population plunge due to drinking water shortages, and the infrastructure of BEC City was falling into disrepair and neglect. They'd finally decided to build a stronger transmitter to start poaching the workforce of other megacities, and it had paid off. They'd been able to keep BEC City up and running with half the population of twenty years ago.

At first the execs had been reluctant to upgrade the transmitter. The tech was old, and no one was too sure anymore how it all worked. But Tony had found a team of engineers who were able to reverse-engineer existing transmitters and figure out how to make them even more powerful. And with the kinds of programming they were putting out, like *Footwear of Famous Chefs* and *Toupee Factory Understudy,* it was easy to poach viewers from other cities who still relied on entertainment like *Measuring Cup Wars.*

Tony poured two fingers of Scotch and stood looking out over the city, the strange shimmering of the atmospheric shield slightly obscuring his view of a grey, cloud-laden sky. Below him the city stretched out as far as he could see, a cement paradise bristling with buildings and antennae, none as tall as the BEC tower, but some almost as high.

He'd been born in this tower, raised on the twenty-second floor, his parents ensuring he received promotion after promotion, moving higher and higher in the building as his career prospered. He was now a full dozen floors higher than they were, his career far more lucrative than their own, a couple of low-end producers who picked up throwaway shows like *The Laundry Room Sock Matching Game* and *Cupcake Smash*. They were nobodies now, and he was on the rise. This new show would probably get him another ten floors up, and then he'd be able to see even more of the city.

Not that he ever went out in it. The streets below looked tidy enough, but he didn't relish the thought of going out in all that heat below, breathing in the refuse of all those residential buildings, or seeing the laborers going about their duties of cleaning living pods or doing laundry. All those things should be invisible to someone like him.

He sipped his Scotch slowly, swirling the amber liquid in the glass, watching it cling to the clear sides. He stared up at the roiling grey clouds, briefly wondering what it would be like up there, exposed to the elements, and gave a small shudder. It wasn't worth thinking about.

A bright light seared across the sky, something that lit up the clouds and made him squint. Then a flash erupted that was so impossibly bright, he threw his arm up to shield his eyes, dropping his Scotch with a curse. The glass fell to the floor, landing with a thud on the thick carpet and leaving a half-circle of liquor as it rolled to a stop.

He staggered back, shocked that he could see the bone inside his arm. He brought his hand up, staring in horror at his fingers. He could see every blood vessel, every bone, right through his skin.

He fell back against his desk as a sudden heat wave blasted over his body. It was so intensely hot that for a moment he thought he'd caught on fire. It felt like a flaming specter had embraced him. Then the heat passed and he gasped. He stepped closer to the window, wondering what was going on.

A shockwave blasted toward him. It thundered for a fraction of a second against the glass, then shattered the window, driving him back. It bowled him over, flattening him against the floor. The wind gusted over him, rippling his skin. When it passed, he sat up, realizing he'd landed on the fallen drinking glass. Blood seeped down his arm.

Another bright light drew his eyes to the sky. A strange cloud grew on the horizon. It billowed upward, its zenith spreading out. The bottom remained tall and thin. It reminded him of an old drawing his grandmother had of an ancient oak tree, with a tall, thin trunk and myriad branches thrusting out above.

The cloud swirled and bloomed, the grey billowing with hints of orange and gold.

He saw another fiery streak in the air, then another. These were far closer, a string of them arcing straight for BEC City. He gasped at the next burst of light, and had only the briefest impression of all of BEC City erupting in sudden flame, burning upward instantaneously, exposing him to an unbearable, searing heat.

In seconds, BEC City was gone.

Chapter 10

The flight back from the missile site was uneventful. They dropped Rowan off among a group of Badlander camps that had yet to be informed of the asteroid. Then they continued on to Sanctuary City.

Once there, H124 settled in. They awaited news from Rivet's team that the A14 was ready. They were still converting it.

She met Raven and Gordon for lunch the next day, thrilled as usual by the delicious food in the commissary. Raven was strangely preoccupied. Several times he opened his mouth to say something, then seemed to think the better of it.

Her PRD beeped. She opened the comm window, watching the now familiar series of numbers scroll across her screen. "The Phantom Code is coming through again." The strange sequence of numbers had been streaming into Sanctuary City from an unknown source for a while now.

"Let me see that," Gordon said, watching beside her. "Huh." He scratched his chin. "Back in the day, I was something of a treasure hunter. Used to crack codes for fun."

"Want to give this one a whirl?" Raven asked. "It's been coming in for months now."

Gordon brought up his own PRD and saved the numbers. "I'll take a crack at it."

Raven looked at them all in turn, his face growing stern. "I need to say something. An opinion that's not going to be very popular."

"What is it?" H124 asked, taking the last bite of her dessert—something called orange sherbet.

But before he could go on, Nimbus, the Rover meteorologist, rushed into the commissary. She spotted Raven and hurried over. "You've got to have a look at this."

They got up at once, following her to her lab.

"This is crazy," Nimbus said, tucking her long, wavy black hair behind an ear. She brought up a series of readings on her display. "Something massive just exploded over BEC City." She'd explained to H124 earlier that she used ancient satellites to monitor different parts of the globe. The tech was old, but they were self-course-correcting and powered by solar energy, so some of them were still functional. She'd been able to receive sporadic images from them. Now Nimbus's bronze hands flew over her button display as she brought up an aerial image of a megacity on an island. Its orange glowing atmospheric shield covered most of the southern portion of the landmass. It was a daylight image, with the blue ocean surrounding the brown island and a few high, scattered clouds.

"This is BEC City about a month ago, looking much as it has for years." She waved through the display, bringing up a second image, this one taken at night. "Same with this one, taken about two weeks ago." In this one, the atmospheric shield glowed, and beneath it H124 could make out millions of gleaming lights from the city.

"Now look at this. I thought it was a mistake at first, that the coordinates were off. This came in a while ago." It was another night image, but this one was almost completely black. No shield, no artificial lights, just a few bright, irregular patches of red and orange. "I double-checked the coordinates, and this is where BEC City should be. So I waited a bit for the satellite to pass again when it was light. And check this out."

She brought up another daylight image, this time showing the blue ocean, but where BEC City had been lay a smoldering pile of grey rubble. Fires burned in a number of places.

"Then I tried to tune into BEC City's feed. Nothing." She swiveled in her seat and faced them. "They've just been wiped off the planet."

H124 kept staring at the image of the destroyed city, disbelieving.

"What was it?" Raven asked. "An asteroid fragment we didn't know about?"

"That's what I thought at first. But look at these atmospheric readings." She brought up a series of numbers and graphs. "Whatever it was, it was more than one hit, each with an intensity of 1200 kilotons of TNT, and the radiation readings are off the charts, higher than anything I've ever seen."

"Nuclear radiation?" Dirk asked.

Nimbus nodded.

He and Raven exchanged glances with H124. The missile silos. The PPC showing up there, learning of the location. H124's mouth came open. "You mean the PPC launched nuclear missiles at BEC City and destroyed it?" Nimbus cringed. "I think so."

"My god..." Raven breathed. "They have no idea. They just have no fucking idea!" He paced furiously around the room. "The blast, the radiation poisoning alone!" He brought a fist down on the table before him, causing H124 to jump. "They are un-fucking-believable!" he roared, and stormed out of the room. She'd never seen him like that.

She hurried out after him, finding him halfway down the hall, leaning against the wall. "You okay?" she asked.

He shook his head. "I don't see how we can proceed with the PPC here. Not only do they destroy our experimental forests, but they kill their own kind without flinching. All they care about is power. They don't care about the planet, or other living things. They'd destroy countless species just to get a hit show, and these megacities are completely unsustainable. Do you know what the latest thoughts are on Delta City? They won't last the decade. Their water sources are contaminated, and their air quality index fluctuates between 250 and 350. People are already starving there. Yet they go on as if they're going to last forever, as if humanity hasn't already destroyed this planet and every other living thing on it, and as if none of those things even matters as long as they have their powerful positions and luxury housing. Goddamn it!" He pushed off angrily from the wall. "Do you know what that radiation is going to do to the atmosphere? The ocean? To any organisms who managed to survive there until now?"

She placed a hand on his arm. What could she say? He was right.

Onyx came running down the hall, out of breath. "Guys? We have a problem." She stopped, gasping.

Raven looked up, instantly alarmed. "What is it?"

"You know those PPC drones that have picked up in frequency? Well, my cloak didn't work this time. It saw us. The PPC knows where Sanctuary City is now."

The color drained out of Raven's face. "They'll destroy us." His eyes went wide. "My god. They could even nuke us." They ran back to Nimbus's office. "We need to evacuate now!" Raven called out.

The others looked at him in shock.

"The PPC knows where we are."

Onyx followed them in. Raven turned to her. "How much time do you estimate it would take for airships to arrive?"

"I'd say less than two hours."

Raven looked back at the others, all still too stunned to move. "We need to move personnel, equipment. Get the blast deflection craft out of here." He reached over to a panel in the wall and waved his hand in front of it. It slid open, revealing a red lever with large white letters above it: "Emergency." He took a deep breath. "From the day we installed this thing, I hoped I'd never have to do this." He pulled the lever.

Out in the hall, a bright red light began flashing, followed by a klaxon blaring in their room. She could hear other alarms ringing in labs all the way down the corridor. "I need to secure the DNA samples in the lab, move the creatures that are in the incubators and newborn pods. We need to get to the blast deflection craft. Rivet's team are all with her at the satellite location, so that thing has no one looking after it right now." He started out of the room at a sprint.

"I'll help you," H124 told him, following close on his heels. She glanced back as the others all piled out of Nimbus's lab. "I'm going to the armory," Byron called out.

"Me, too!" Dirk yelled, turning in the same direction as Byron.

She and Raven sprinted down the corridor, running through the large double doors that led to the de-extinction lab. Already a few Rover techs were packing up samples and had secured the baby muskox that she'd first watched Raven remove from its amniotic sac. It looked up at them in surprise, its large brown, watery eyes startled as they moved it into a comfortable transport enclosure.

An automatic sorting arm was pulling out samples and placing them inside metal cases with handles. She grabbed the cases as it finished and loaded them onto maglev sleds.

Raven checked all the nursing pods, making sure all the young creatures had been moved to transportation enclosures. "I think we're good."

She loaded the last few cases onto a maglev. His team took them out of the room, running down the hall.

"What now?" she asked.

"The blast deflection craft."

She stared out into the hall, watching fleeing Rovers carrying books and equipment, the blaring klaxon and flashing red light making her heart pound. "Where will everyone go?"

"We've prepared for something like this. People will evacuate to the satellite site where Rivet is. We can all rendezvous there and come up with a plan."

They took off down the hall. A tech in front of her tripped, a box full of ancient maps spilling out onto the floor. Some, held in tubes, rolled across the hall. H124 stopped to help the woman, picking up the tubes as they rolled away into a neighboring lab.

"Thank you," the Rover told her, stacking them back inside the box.

"Raven! H!" She heard Orion's voice calling through the chaos. He stopped in front of them, catching his breath. "I've got bad news. We don't have nearly the time we thought we would. I was just up in Cal's radar lab. There's an airship less than thirty minutes out, heading this way. It must have been in the area for some other reason. Why it would be all the way up here, I don't know."

H124 thought about Dirk and the deadly sphere that had been inside his head, transmitting. Had it given away their location to Olivia? If so, why had she waited so long to attack?

Raven gaped at Orion with wide eyes. "Less than thirty minutes?" He pivoted, staring at the Rovers rushing past him. "Send the new timeline to everyone's PRD. Get as many people to the hyperloop as possible."

Orion sped off and Raven took off at a sprint, H124 beside him. "Do you have any defenses?" she asked him. "Anything that can fend off an airship?"

"You've seen our armory," he said, jogging around two Rovers with a maglev loaded with antique books. "We don't have anything big. Just small arms, really. Our defense was our invisibility."

"You said when I first came here that you could survive in tunnels beneath the surface."

"That's true, but only if the PPC didn't know we were here. We always thought we'd have more time than this. From the air, it's hard to make out the living buildings unless you know to look for them. We could have hidden down here. But they know the location now. They know exactly where to look."

When Raven and H124 reached Rivet's lab, they found the doors closed and all the lights off. Raven waved his hand in front of the door and it slid open, lights blinking on. The blast deflection craft stood in the center of the room, completely assembled and covered with a clean skin. A special maglev sled had been built to accommodate the craft's size and weight, and it stood curled up against one wall.

Raven unfurled it while H124 started up the copters with her PRD. They aligned themselves to each other as Raven spread the cover over them. They levered beneath the craft and lifted it, arms whirring and gently maneuvering it onto the sled base. When it was secure, H124 programmed the maglev to follow them.

As big as the doors to Rivet's lab were, the craft barely made it out. H124 didn't think it would fit, but the maglev slowed to an agonizing pace as it turned and lowered and readjusted itself to pass through the opening without damaging its cargo.

Then they there were in the hall, Rovers dodging out of their way as they dashed down the corridor, the massive craft in tow. There was no way it was going to fit onto a lift, so they had to take the long way through the facility, using one of the large ramp exits that led up to the surface.

When they got close, the loading doors slid open, and the sunlight poured in. She squinted, watching chaos unfold before her eyes. Everywhere Rovers ran with equipment, all streaming toward the hyperloop entrance. She knew its large doors had to be firmly shut before the PPC's arrival. They could never know about the hyperloop. She knew from experience that the doors were so well hidden you wouldn't know they were there even if you *did* know to look for them. Even trees grew on their surfaces.

A Rover transport waited outside by the de-extinction lab building, hovering as techs ran back and forth, piling crate after refrigerated crate of DNA samples into it. Then the scientists piled into the transport and took off for the hyperloop doors. They vanished inside. A few moments later the transport emerged again, empty save for the driver, who made a trip out to the farthest outbuildings to pick up Rovers and supplies. She watched it disappear into the hyperloop entrance again.

She and Raven fell in with a bigger crowd, the maglev whirring along behind them, the rotors sounding like they struggled to keep up with the weight of the craft. A few times they sputtered and the sled tilted before correcting itself. They were halfway to the hyperloop doors when she heard the unmistakable sound of a descending PPC airship.

The hyperloop doors clanged shut just as a gleaming silver airship, its familiar, triangular shape striking a chord of panic within her, descended through the clouds into view.

The Rovers left exposed on the surface, unable to make it to the hyperloop door on time, shouted and scattered as H124 heard the terrifying thrum of the airship's main weapon warming up.

Chapter 11

H124 braced herself for the brilliant blast that would destroy her and a chunk of the land around her, but it didn't come. She glanced over at Raven, who was transfixed on the airship with a defiant jaw.

A gravelly voice boomed out from the airship. "We've come for the A14 and the blast deflection craft. Hand them over and no one gets hurt."

"What the hell?" H124 breathed. "How did they even know about them?"

Raven shook his head, his mouth a grey slit. "They are listening in somehow."

"How do they expect to use them? They don't know anything about how they work."

"They're probably paranoid. Think we're going to let the asteroid drop on Delta City like how they tried to destroy BEC City with the fragment."

She frowned. The PPC may have failed in that, but they'd found another way to destroy their competition.

A troop dropship came over the horizon, its low engine thrumming, its sides glinting in the sunlight. It dropped low to the ground, disgorging hundreds of troops. Then a second dropship glided into view, stopping near the airfield. Transports of soldiers emptied out, moving to flank Sanctuary City on all sides.

H124 was frozen, watching as more and more soldiers came forth. Raven appeared panicked.

"We've got to hide the deflection craft!" she told him.

Coming to, he blinked. "Follow me!" He took off at a sprint, maglev in tow. She followed, feeling as if they were a huge target with the massive blast deflection craft hovering along behind them.

Spotting them, five soldiers driving a transport sped in their direction. Why hadn't she gone to the armory with Byron? There hadn't been time. She and Raven kept running, glancing back to see the troopers gaining on them. They couldn't run faster than the transport or leave the blast deflection craft unattended.

The soldiers quickly caught up with them. One was punching furiously on his PRD, and suddenly the maglev stopped. The blast deflection craft teetered slightly, and H124 stared up at its gigantic bulk, expecting it to come crashing down on her. But it stabilized.

Raven waved through his PRD screens, commanding the maglev to follow. But instead it started to move slowly toward the transport. Raven tried again, the blood draining from his face, then looked to H124. She brought up her display, trying to command the maglev to return to them, but it wouldn't respond. It picked up speed, moving into position beside the transport. The soldiers turned, heading back toward the closest dropship, the maglev and blast deflection craft following.

Frantically, Raven searched the area around him. "Onyx!" he shouted. "Onyx!"

The hacker was nowhere in sight. He brought up his comm link, but she didn't answer.

Though they couldn't catch up, she and Raven ran after the maglev as it sped away, and watched in disbelief as it powered up the ramp into a dropship and disappeared. Immediately the ship rose up and shot off into the distance.

H124 stopped running, a stitch in her side, blinking at the spot in the sky where it had vanished.

"Where is the A14?" the voice boomed from the airship.

All around them, troopers stormed into Sanctuary City buildings, shooting and killing any Rovers they encountered. They shot out windows and placed detonator charges that brought down walls. The commissary collapsed in a cloud of dust and debris.

She saw enemy transports speed along the airstrip, checking all of the hangars and demolishing the buildings after they were searched. She spotted Gordon on the far end of a hangar building. He dashed to another structure, keeping out of sight.

One Rover, a young man with long blond hair, ran from the seed storage vault with a crate. The soldiers didn't spot him right away, so he made it to a grove of trees and hunkered down. A wave of troopers passed him obliviously, fire and smoke billowing around him and masking his location.

He took off after they were gone, heading for a group of undamaged buildings near the airstrip. He'd only taken a few steps when another squad of soldiers appeared from the opposite direction, spotting him at once. He tried run back, to find more cover, but the trooper in front raised his energy rifle and fired. H124's breath caught in her chest when she saw it hit the man. The weapon must have been turned up to lethal, because as the energy snaked around his body, the young man's face blackened. His hair went up in flames as he fell, screaming, then convulsing and burning on the ground. The squad never slowed, but ran right over his prone body, trampling him. The last trooper turned and smashed a boot into the man's face, stomping him again and again until his head was a caved-in mess. Then the soldier turned and caught up with his platoon, not once glancing back.

H124's heart pounded. Everything slowed. She watched as Rovers were shot in the back, falling, Sanctuary City on fire, flames shooting up into the trees and consuming the branches.

"Raven..." she breathed.

He grasped her hand.

A trooper spotted them and leveled his energy rifle at them. H124 sucked in a breath and dove to the side. Raven did the same. She hit the ground hard, glancing up to see the trooper's chest burst. Someone yanked her up by the arm. The barrel of Byron's Henry repeating rifle was still smoking.

"Why are you two standing out in the open?"

"They got the blast deflection craft," she told him as they all sprinted for the nearest cover, the only remaining wall of the radar building.

Smoke billowed out from the doorways of the buildings, the underground tunnels now on fire.

A loud boom resounded in the distance. Raven ran out around the side of the building to look east.

"What are you doing?" Byron shouted at him.

A trooper spotted Raven, firing his rifle. It hit a metal girder next to him, white hot energy coursing through it, melting it. Byron pulled him back to cover.

"They're bombing the outer city...the forests, the crops. It's all on fire! I...I saw a herd of caribou out there..." His whole body shook. "I don't know what to do!" He looked at them in desperation. "What do we do?"

Byron gripped his arm. "We get out of here alive." He slung two energy rifles off his back. "They're at the lethal setting. Don't even think about arguing with me, Raven."

H124 took one, the cold metal reassuring. She focused on the smoldering buildings, the dozens of soldiers pouring in and out of them, the troopers shooting Rovers as they tried to escape.

She took aim at one trooper as he emerged from the mechanical engineering building, bringing his rifle to bear on a fleeing Rover. H124 fired, the electricity streaming out, hitting him full in the chest. He jittered and collapsed, a corpse by the time he hit the ground.

"What's the plan?" she asked.

Byron reloaded his rifle. "They still don't know about the hyperloop. We take out as many as we can, then hold off here until they go."

Raven gripped his energy rifle. "There are some old maintenance tunnels running on the southern side of the city. We haven't used them for years, and access from the living areas was sealed up from the inside. There's no water or food down there, nothing like the survival tunnels under the city. But at least the troopers won't know they're there." He pointed to the south. "There's an old maintenance hatch in the forest where we can access them. Let's get as many survivors as we can and hold out there until the troopers leave."

"Sounds like a plan," Byron said, a slight smile coming to his face.

With the security leak, they didn't dare send out a message over the Rover network to rendezvous at the hatch, so instead they had to search for survivors one by one.

H124 surveyed the chaos, the burning buildings, the troopers looting and destroying, then looked toward where the hatch lay. Already that part of the forest had caught fire. She could see a herd of elk fleeing the flames, their golden coats flashing in the sun. She stifled a cough as smoke drifted in their direction.

"This isn't going to be easy," Byron said, mirroring her thoughts. "Brace yourselves."

Chapter 12

As they snuck through Sanctuary City, a group of soldiers spotted them and reeled around, their squad leader barking orders. As the troopers brought up their rifles, she barely had a chance to dive and roll. She stayed down, belly in the grass, and fired at them, hitting two troopers in front with an electric shock. They went down, bodies shuddering on the ground. She started crawling away toward a patch of taller grass, but fire from the rest of the squad kept her pinned down. She raised the barrel of the energy rifle above the tall, verdant vegetation. A jolt from an enemy gun blasted her weapon. The rifle sizzled in her hand, heating up fast, and she slung it off. The metal barrel melted, the cylinder drooping and hissing in the grass.

Glancing around, she couldn't find Raven or Byron. She crawled on her elbows into a grouping of trees, then got to her feet and ran, zigging and zagging away from the enemy squad, heading for the shelter of a nearby horticulture lab. Just as she almost reached the door, it banged open and another squad of soldiers poured out. In the confusion and smoke, they didn't spot her, and she veered away quickly, whipping around the corner and pressing her body flat against the wall. She heard them sprinting in the opposite direction, the sizzling and whining of their energy rifles fading away.

She dared to peer out, knowing she'd completely lost track of her friends. She tried to spot them through the chaos of marching phalanxes, fleeing Rovers, and explosions wracking building after building.

To her left, another retinue of troopers approached, moving as a solid mass, their boots marching in double-time through the smoke.

She withdrew from the safety of the building, spotting a cluster of bamboo nearby. At a crouch, she ran toward it, staying low, and entered the dense growth of tall, green plants. They swayed in the breeze, knocking against one another in a musical serenade. The quiet of the bamboo grove struck a harsh contrast to the destruction raining down beyond.

Still moving at a crouch, she peered out, hoping to spot Byron or Raven. She hoped Gordon and Dirk had made it to the hyperloop doors. She hadn't seen Dirk since they'd gotten the news of the probe spotting Sanctuary City.

As she moved along, not watching her feet, she tripped over something sticking out of the ground. Grabbing onto a solid stalk of bamboo, she caught herself. Turning, she spotted a bamboo cutter hastily dropped in the dirt, its handle sticking up. Next to it leaned a bamboo stalk that had been partially cut through, but remained upright.

Her head snapped up as she heard voices. On the far end of the bamboo patch, Dirk came into view, two PPC soldiers closing in on him. He was unarmed.

"Would you look at all those scars and tattoos?" one of the troopers sneered. "You're Badlander scum, aren't you? What do the Rovers want with you?"

Dirk backed away, trying to keep the soldiers from flanking him.

H124 cursed the loss of her rifle. She had no weapon, and the two soldiers were certainly armed. One raised his energy rifle. "Your kind are a waste of space. Scavengers scrambling in the muck. A quick death is too good for you." He gritted his teeth, advancing on Dirk.

H124 bent down and grabbed the bamboo cutter. She went to work on the existing cut in the bamboo, sawing quickly through the rest of the stalk. She caught the pole as it started to fall, then used the cutter to trim off the end.

It made a handy staff, long and tough, yet light enough to wield.

As soon as the two soldiers were facing away from her, exposing their backs, H124 burst out of the bamboo grove, slamming the pole horizontally into their backs. They went down hard. Dirk raced forward and kicked one so savagely in the head that she heard the man's neck snap. The second one struggled to get to his gun, so H124 turned the bamboo pole end-first and ran toward him, driving it into the back of the man's neck. He cried out, the blow catching him partially on the helmet. An angry cut opened in his skin. H124 swung the pole swiftly, catching him in the ribs. He fell and rolled into a fetal position.

Dashing forward, Dirk ripped the rifle off the man's body and fired it point blank into his face. His skin bubbled and melted as he screamed in agony. Dirk fired again and again until the man's features turned into a viscous soup.

Then Dirk stopped, chest heaving, rifle gripped so tightly that his hands shook.

Finally he looked at her. "Thanks."

A cry of help brought their attention to a group of soldiers advancing on three Rovers carrying boxes of books. Dirk ran toward them, H124 trailing closely behind. A sudden blast hit the ground between them, sending up a plume of dirt. She checked over her shoulder, horrified to see three soldiers carrying a fifty-caliber weapon. She careened to one side, crouching and running with the pole. The three Rovers fled. She lost Dirk in the madness.

Stepping into a plume of smoke, she came upon a lone solider standing over a Rover, grinning down as he trained his gun on her. H124 surged forward, swinging the pole up to sweep the soldier's feet out from under him. He crashed down on his hip, and H124 drove the pole into his stomach. He groaned and rolled into a ball. She lent her hand down to the Rover. The woman took it and swung upright, then ran off, trying to skirt around the fighting.

H124 looked back at the soldier just as he was drawing a flash burster from the holster at his hip. She had started to swing the pole around, intending to hit his hand, when suddenly his lower arm disappeared in a spray of blood and bone. The flash burster went flying. The soldier screamed in pain, grabbing the stump of his arm, and seconds later another round tore through his neck.

H124 spun, pinpointing the direction of the shots. She saw Byron standing twenty feet away, the barrel of his Henry repeater smoking. She ran to him, spotting Raven crouched down a few feet behind him, talking to a woman with a head wound.

"Let's keep moving," Byron said.

Stealthily they crept from one outbuilding to the next, avoiding the troopers as the soldiers blasted off doors, wielding flamethrowers as they exited the searched buildings.

Acrid smoke spiraled around H124 and the others, and they used it for cover. On the far side of a residential building, they came across four Rovers huddled behind the smoking wreckage of a west-facing wall. Raven waved them over. At a crouch, they joined groups.

Slowly they made their way toward the forest, pausing at each section of cover—a building not yet burned, a dense cluster of trees. They picked up fifteen more Rovers along the way. Finally they entered the treeline.

Dense black smoke spiraled through the shadowed trunks. The hatch lay a mile away, and H124 was relieved to see it had been so long since anyone had used it that any footpath leading out this way was now overgrown. The soldiers wouldn't know to look for them out here.

They picked up twelve more Rovers who had taken sanctuary in the shadows of the forest, some pressed up against fallen, mossy logs.

Raven paused over a piece of ground covered in vibrant green moss, grey lichen and fallen pine needles. "This should be it." He knelt and started feeling around in the soil. "It's a round hatch," he added, putting both of his hands to work.

H124 knelt and helped him, feeling for the rough edge of metal beneath the soft moss. The tips of her fingers scraped against something hard as she probed the ground. "This might be it."

Raven moved to her position, and together they explored beneath the soil, finding a round edge. Her fingers stopped at what felt like a handle. She excavated it, revealing a rusted latch. Other Rovers quickly bent down, removing the rest of the dirt off the hatch, and Raven threw it open.

A ladder descended into darkness. Raven went down first, using the light from the floating display of his PRD to illuminate the shadowed space.

H124 stayed topside, helping people down. Many had armfuls of equipment and old books, and one person held a delicate, curling fern in a pot. A musty scent issued up from the hole, one of mold and stagnant water. She stifled a cough as a sudden gust of wind kicked up, mixing the smell of mold with smoke.

She and Byron were the last to go below, lowering the hatch after themselves and sealing them all in the dark. Someone switched on a headlamp, infusing the place with a feeble glow.

She thought of the people trapped in the hyperloop area, hoping they had left and weren't waiting for the rest of them. Someone had to get out of here and continue this work. She felt sour bile rise up within her. Now that they'd lost the blast deflection craft, she didn't know how that work could proceed. At least the A14 was safe, she hoped.

Her eyes found Raven's in the dark. "What about Rivet?"

"With this leak, we can't risk contacting her. If they're listening in, the last thing we want to do is reveal her location. We'll just have to wait and hyperloop down there. Rex has a drone watch system in place there, too, so they'll have a heads-up if the PPC locates them."

H124 hated this, biding time, wishing there were more she could be doing. She hoped Gordon and Dirk had found safety. She gazed around at the distraught faces, and Byron met her eyes. For now, they just had to wait. Above them airship blasts shook the earth, raining down a thunderous dirge.

* * * *

When everything grew quiet above, Raven lifted the hatch and peered out. She heard him gasp. When he vanished over the lip, she climbed after him, instantly choking and coughing from the smoke. At first she couldn't see anything but billows of black ash. Then a breeze parted the smoke and she saw that the forest had been incinerated in every direction. It wasn't even on fire anymore. Nothing was left to burn. Charred, broken tree trunks dotted the desolate landscape. In the distance, blackened lumps littered the ground. At first she thought they were rocks, but then she saw a branch sticking up from one of them. No, she realized, not a branch. An antler. The lumps were the burned remains of the elk and caribou, littering the grassland to the east.

A gigantic smoking crater stood where the airstrip and hangars had been. The living buildings that she'd marveled at when she first arrived were completely gone; blackened holes smoldered in the soil where they had once stood, the rooftop gardens destroyed.

As Byron and the others climbed out of the hatch, Raven stood dumbfounded, staring in disbelief. His chin trembled. H124 came up beside him. His mouth parted, and his brow was distorted in sorrow and confusion.

"Good god," Byron breathed when he saw the destruction. "They didn't leave anything." Then he spotted the charred lumps out in the burned grassland, and sucked in a breath.

H124 scanned the sky, where smoke streamed ever upward, searching for any hint of an airship. It looked clear.

Byron moved ahead of the others, checked his rifle, and started skirting the area, searching for soldiers.

Raven still hadn't moved.

H124 took his arm and led him gently away, toward the closed hyperloop doors. A few other Rovers joined Byron in searching the smoldering remains of the city. No soldiers had been left behind. H124 walked past the Rover corpses, feeling a powerful new emotion rage through her body. She'd heard Byron and Astoria talk about it. *Hate.* It flared up inside her, and as she passed the dead body of a trooper, she resisted the urge to kick the body and stomp on the soldier's slack face, much as she had seen one of them do to the Rover earlier.

Raven walked beside her, an automaton, chin trembling, eyes dull and lifeless. She led him around rubble and guttering flames toward the hyperloop doors.

"H!" She spun as she heard her name. From behind a plume of smoke, a figure in overalls limped forward, leaning on someone else. As the smoke cleared, her heart soared when she saw Gordon and Dirk. She raced toward them, hugging both.

"You're alive!" Gordon said, pulling away.

She grinned before looking down at his leg. Blood soaked the cloth over his left thigh.

"It's nothing," he said, waving a hand in the air. "Cut it on some metal." He winked. "I'll be right as rain."

Sweat streamed down Dirk's filthy face. His shirt was ripped, but other than that, he looked okay. An energy rifle hung across his chest. "Can't believe this," he said quietly, taking in the destruction.

With Raven and a few others, they picked through the wreckage of Sanctuary City, coming away with a few damaged pieces of equipment that could be repaired, as well as a handful of singed books. But everything else was gone. The agroforestry areas had been burned; the forest, the grassland.

When they were sure no PPC presence remained in the city, H124 brought up her display and commanded the hyperloop doors to open. The massive doors lifted upward. The trees on their surfaces were likewise blackened and smoking.

Light streamed into the tunnel below, where the Rovers waited anxiously. Onyx was the first to run out. Instantly H124 saw that the hacker had been shot in the arm, her PRD destroyed. It must have been why she hadn't answered when the troopers had taken the blast deflection craft.

Onyx dashed toward her cousin. She was halfway there when the surrounding destruction hit her. She stopped abruptly, staring incredulously at the charred remains of the city. Finally she turned to Raven. "The blast deflection craft?"

Raven merely stared back in silence, so H124 shook her head. "They got it."

Onyx went slackjawed. "What?"

"We need to get to the rendezvous point where Rivet is. Take stock of who survived," H124 told her.

Onyx blinked. "Right. Okay." She looked as frozen as Raven.

"C'mon everyone," Byron called out. "Get into the hyperloop. We're moving out." He gestured for everyone to move inside the tunnel. Then Raven spoke for the first time. "We...we have to check for survivors." He pointed east. "Out there. The animals." H124 nodded. "We'll go together."

Three hours later, they'd skirted the grasslands in the only remaining transport they had—one that two Rovers had taken with them down into the hyperloop tunnel. As they sped over the terrain, stopping repeatedly, their spirits sank lower and lower. Caribou, elk, bison, muskoxen, saiga antelope. Nothing had survived. In some cases, the grassland around the bodies hadn't been touched. It was clear the airship had purposely targeted individual animals simply for the sheer joy of killing them. The wind turbines had toppled, the wind catchers were scorched and fallen. The once-amazing paradise of Sanctuary City was gone.

Chapter 13

H124 stood beside Raven at the hyperloop doors. He took a long, last look at the destruction, then turned silently and descended the stairs to the hyperloop. She followed.

The transportation pod rustled with somber activity as equipment was stowed and secured and Rovers settled into their seats for the journey. She and Raven took a couple of empty seats next to Byron.

H124 had noticed that Rovers kept their distance from Byron. One look at him and you could tell what a rough life he'd had. He was hard around the edges, a cactus in their garden of roses, and it was easy to see why people who had led peaceful lives might be instinctively wary of his combative presence.

She collapsed into the seat next to him, momentarily laying her head on his shoulder. He brought an arm around her, and for a moment they settled into a comforting embrace. Gordon sat down on the far side of Byron, wincing as he bent his leg. As soon as they got to the satellite location, they could get him into a medpod.

Raven helped secure the last of the cargo, then slumped into the seat next to H124, still mute.

A Rover at the back asked if everyone was ready, and a murmur of assent spread through the pod. H124 felt the gentle tug of the pod's securing mechanism releasing, followed by a gentle acceleration.

She lifted her head and scanned the survivors. Many stared off into the distance with eyes like glass. Tears streaked down their dirty faces. The woman with the fern cradled it in her lap, her eyes fixed on its greenery.

H124 had no idea what they would do now.

* * * *

When the hyperloop dropped them off at the satellite location, she escorted Gordon to a medpod. All around her, Rovers helped their wounded comrades. She spotted the Rover doctor, Felix, applying pressure to a head wound while the person waited for an available medpod. She helped where she could, comforting people and attending to minor wounds.

Raven found H124, an injured woman leaning on his shoulder. "Can you go talk to Rivet? I just learned she was out scrounging for parts. She just got back. But in all this chaos, no one's been out there to talk to her. She still doesn't know." Rivet's workshop lay on the far edge of the satellite location, and all this commotion wouldn't have reached her there.

"Sure."

"Tell her...tell her to keep working on the A14. We can get the blast deflection craft back." But his words fell like dead stones, and his eyes showed no trace of hope.

H124 found Rivet in the hangar, working on the A14. She stood at the top of a ladder, arms covered in grease up to her elbows, happily digging around in the fuel system. She was midway through converting it to run on their specialized methane fuel.

When she saw H124's face, the soiled and ripped state of her clothes, she descended from the ladder and strode over to her, wiping her hands off on her coveralls.

"What happened?" she breathed.

H124 described the attack, the Rovers who had been killed, the seizure of the blast deflection craft. Rivet rocked back on her heels in disbelief. "They got the craft?" She shook her head and added, "I'm sorry. Are *you* okay?"

"I'm fine," H124 mumbled, a painful knot scratching at her throat. "But a lot of the others didn't make it." She briefly ran down a list of the survivors, at least the ones she knew.

A long, slow breath left Rivet's chest. She turned and looked at the A14 over her shoulder. "Without the blast deflection craft..."

"Raven wants you to keep working on it. We'll get the craft back."

Rivet nodded, the uncertainty plain on her pale face.

When H124 returned to the main compound, she spotted Nimbus. The meteorologist hurried over to Raven, and they talked gravely before rushing off together. Nimbus had been lucky to be in the first evacuation wave out, safely away in the hyperloop as the attack had raged on in Sanctuary City. H124 flashed back to an image of the Rover shot with the energy weapon, his hair bursting into flames, his body trampled by indifferent soldiers. She returned to the main building to see if she could help unload the hyperloop car.

Raven appeared and intercepted her. "Can you come join us in the engineering lab?"

"Yes." She followed him outside, weaving through a number of Rovers carrying rescued equipment.

When she entered the building, she found Nimbus, Dirk, Orion, and Byron sitting at a table, waiting for them.

"Have a seat," Raven said, taking one next to her. She assumed they were going to come up with a plan to locate the blast deflection craft, so Raven's unrelated first sentence surprised her.

"Something bothered me about the labs we found in Basin City," Raven started.

H124 swallowed. She'd never forget the rows of operating tables with shackles, the hideous videos of torture and genetic manipulation. Ground zero for the night stalkers.

"And not just the horror of it all," Raven went on. "I mean the tech. I've never heard of the PPC doing that kind of genetic manipulation. Sure, they physically alter people's brains, but that's after they're born. The kind of genetic engineering we saw in Basin City was entirely different."

"What are you thinking?" she asked.

"That the tech wasn't theirs to begin with. I think they found it and tried to adapt it to their own ends."

"Found it where?" Dirk asked.

"That's what I wondered." Raven leaned forward, resting his arms on the table. "While we were waiting for Marlowe to pick us up there, I powered up an old terminal using our PRD power cells and hacked into the mainframe. I downloaded everything I could find, but only recently had the time to look over it."

"And what did you find?" Dirk asked.

"It's both exciting and terrifying." He met their gazes in turn. "Apparently, on one of their routine scouting missions, looking for new transmitter sites, the Basin City PPC came across an ancient genebank."

"A genebank?" H124 asked. "You mean like what you have in the de-extinction lab?"

"Kind of, but not as sophisticated. It sounds like it was an old storehouse of some kind, a vault where a number of plant and animal DNA samples were kept as a sort of safeguard against extinction. But that wasn't all that was there."

"Why am I worried now?" Dirk asked.

"There was a device that used something called CRISPR, a tool for manipulating genomes. The Basin City PPC took DNA samples back, along with the CRISPR setup. They modified it and began to create their new workforce that would be able to work in volatile, near-pitch black conditions."

H124 sucked in a breath. "The night stalkers."

Raven nodded. "Exactly."

"Well, that turned out great for them," Dirk said. H124 thought of the swarms of night stalkers infesting the abandoned city. Even if the earth weren't on fire beneath the place, no one could live there among the sheer multitude of night stalkers. The PPC had completely destroyed their own home.

Raven raised a brow, looking hopeful. "But while it ultimately led to their downfall, it could be an absolute boon to us."

Dirk crossed his arms. "In what way?"

"That vault, if it's still there, could supplement the DNA samples we have in the de-extinction lab. And the Basin City records show that it was only one of a handful of other genebanks. They were planning to visit the others, but by then night stalkers had overrun the city, and the coal seam fires had spread to the point of making the city uninhabitable. When the execs there assimilated into other cities, the plan to visit the other genebanks evaporated. So the vaults might still be out there."

Byron brought a hand up. "Why do I have a feeling this is all leading to some crazy, foolhardy mission to travel to these places and secure the vaults?"

Raven cracked a smile. "Because that's exactly what I want to do."

"Shouldn't we be concentrating on getting the blast deflection craft back?" Dirk asked.

Raven bit his lip, looking gravely at each of them. His smile dissolved, and he didn't continue.

Beside him, Nimbus, who'd been quiet, stood up. She shifted her weight from one foot to the other, looking away to the floor.

"Okay, what is going on?" Byron demanded.

"The asteroid impact," Raven began to say, then went quiet.

"The main show, you mean? The big one?" Byron prompted him. There was still another fragment that would hit the Pacific Ocean before the main asteroid fell.

"Yes. The big one."

When it was clear no response was forthcoming, Dirk prodded. "What about it?"

"It's what I wanted to talk to you about back in Sanctuary City. A natural disaster like that can lead to great diversity. When the dinosaurs went extinct, it led to the rise of mammals. Before that, mammals were tiny creatures, barely eking out an existence. Think of all the diversity of creatures that happened when they had room to grow and evolve."

H124 had read, enraptured, about dinosaurs and other animals that went extinct millions of years before humans evolved. She'd found an old, tattered book in the Rover library at Sanctuary City and scanned it into her PRD. She swallowed, realizing that that library was now destroyed.

Raven continued. "Though the dinosaurs had already been experiencing a decline in population and a number of other factors were leading to their extinction, an asteroid strike dealt a powerful blow to their chances."

H124 thought of all the animals that had existed, even just hundreds of years ago. But it hadn't been disease or an asteroid or massive volcanism that had led to the recent extinctions—it had been humans. Other animals hadn't had the chance to expand into new territories, to evolve into new creatures. They had died off at a terrible rate, over hundreds or even tens of years instead of millions. Humanity had stolen their chance to live on this amazing planet.

Raven set his jaw. "I'm just going to say it." He stood up, resting his fists on the table. "If we let this thing hit, if we secured all the DNA vaults we have and take shelter to wait out the worst of it, we might have a chance to make some of humanity's destruction right."

Nimbus grimaced and spoke up. "I admit I've been thinking along similar lines. I didn't want to say this before, but the Apollo Project..." Her voice trailed off.

H124 had learned of the Apollo Project in one of Raven's lectures she'd found in her first weather shelter. Instead of using preventative measures to curb anthropogenic climate change, people had attempted geoengineering, sending up millions of particles into the atmosphere that would reflect back sunlight and stay suspended. The first attempt had led to the particles crashing down in one tumultuous event that created a devastating heat wave. The second attempt, designed to make the particles stay up longer and come down gradually, had backfired. The particles had remained in the atmosphere, forever falling and rising, but never coming down completely.

The particles had been designed to flip as the composition of the two different sides warmed or cooled at differing rates. While originally they'd been spread uniformly, the particles had eventually migrated, growing erratic, clustered too densely in some places and completely absent in others, drifting chaotically around the globe and causing the already unusually violent and damaging storms brought on by anthropogenic climate change to reach a cataclysmic level. The atmosphere's relationship with the ocean, the continents, and the fresh water cycle was much more complex than anyone had understood at the time. Predicted catastrophic scenarios of such a geoengineering project had fallen short of what the fatal reality turned out to be. Lethal heat waves and unprecedented blizzards befell the planet, killing millions. Drought, which had already taken countless lives, became devastating in some regions, while calamitous flooding claimed lives in others.

No one knew what government or private corporation had launched the particles, but they were still up there, altering the sun's natural incoming solar radiation with disastrous results.

"What about the Apollo Project?" Dirk prompted her.

Nimbus took a deep breath. "Because the first Apollo Project came down so suddenly, they wanted to avoid that problem with the second. It's not just that each particle has differing material on its sides, which heat up and cool with the sun's radiation. If a particle began to lose its loft, it would emit a negative charge, which would attract a healthy, positively charged particle. The two would glom onto each other, with the failing particle leeching what it needed from the healthy one. Then when its charge went positive again, they would separate, and the failing particle could remain aloft."

"You mean they fix each other, like the agrobugs?" Byron asked, referring to the deadly engineered swarms they'd encountered at the radar astronomy facility.

Raven stepped in. "Exactly. It's not going to come down. Not any time soon, not before this planet has become uninhabitable for the life that evolved on it during humanity's time here. Coupled that with the current methane and CO_2 output from the PPC, and we have even less time than we thought. The PPC is everything bad about humanity boiled down to a refined brew, laser-focused on selfish gain at the expense of all other life. They are dangerously short-sighted, and have a stranglehold on the planet."

Nimbus continued hesitantly. "While no one now knows the exact composition of the Apollo Project particles, from what I've been able to determine sending up weather balloons, they seem to be in a layer lower than where dirt and sulfate aerosol particles become suspended, say, after a volcanic eruption."

"Or an impact?" Dirk asked.

"Exactly."

"So when all that dirt and dust gets kicked up into the atmosphere and blocks out the sun, it will also block off the source of light to the Apollo Project particles," Nimbus concluded.

Dirk stared at her in amazement. "You're saying they'd come down?" She couldn't help but smile a little. "That's exactly what I'm saying."

"For good?" Byron asked. "No more intolerable heat and cold swings? No more constant violent storms?"

She nodded. "The earth's systems can start to return to what they were before the project was launched."

"Wouldn't it cause another massive heat wave?" Orion asked, speaking up for the first time.

H124 listened, riveted.

Nimbus nodded. "Initially. But we're looking at a probable global firestorm when the asteroid hits anyway, so things will be a little hot regardless."

Byron rubbed his stubble thoughtfully. "Firestorm? That's interesting."

H124 looked at him, puzzled. "Interesting?"

"Yeah. Agrobugs."

She frowned. "Agrobugs?" The tiny engineered robots had been built in antiquity to replace extinct pollinators, but they had ended up destroying far more than the pests they were intended to control. They'd begun killing any living thing where they'd been released, from plants to grazing animals. And they'd killed the Rover radar expert, Cal.

Byron glanced around at them all. "After the disaster at the radar astronomy facility, I asked around the Badlander camps to see if anyone's tried to expand into that territory in the west, and what they did about those things. They used fire. Flamethrowers. Said it was pretty effective, but they just couldn't cover a large enough area. But a global firestorm?"

H124 lifted her eyebrows. "You're right. Interesting."

"So this natural disaster could undo a lot of fucked up things humanity has done," Dirk added.

"But to let it hit…" H124 said in a pained expression.

Raven spoke up. "I've been reading a lot of the research we've found over the years about natural disaster mitigation. Did you know that long ago, they used to try to stop forest fires? They worried about the forests and private property being destroyed, so for decades they actively fought any fire that sprang up. But something strange happened. The forests became monocultures, with very little biodiversity. And then when there *was* a forest fire, it would sweep though these overgrown forests with wild abandon, entering cities, ending up being far more devastating than they would have been if the smaller forest fires had been allowed to burn naturally over the years. So they started *setting* fires, fires they could control, to burn out the underbrush. And it even turned out that some pine trees *required* fire for their cones to open and propagate, so it not only prevented massive, devastating fires, but the forest would come back afterward, refreshed, with new plant growth, new diversity, aspens among the pines, and open spaces where grazers like deer and elk could forage."

Dirk cleared his throat. "It would also deal a blow to the PPC. New Atlantic was the cream of the crop for them, and it's gone. Basin City is gone. BEC City has been nuked, and it was the second most powerful city. That leaves only two bastions for the PPC—Delta City and Melbourne City. With the Delta City PPC wiped off the map after this asteroid strike, that gives this plan a hell of a better chance at success. All the shit they've been doing—destroying these experimental forests, setting off nukes for god's sake—all that would be over."

H124 hadn't heard of Melbourne City. "Where's that last city?"

"On a continent in the southern hemisphere," Raven explained.

"Is the PPC big there?"

Raven shook his head. "From what we know, they're not as big as they once were. They put out a minimum of programming that we've picked up over the years. Nothing on the scale of Delta or BEC City. So we think they have a pretty small population."

Orion held up his hand. "So let me get this straight—you want to let this sucker hit so that the earth can come back naturally on its own?"

"Think about it," Raven went on. "We've caused 98.5 percent of species to go extinct. Just us. Humans. Not volcanism. Not disease. Us. We let this thing hit, and when the initial disaster is over, we go topside and de-extinct as many animals as we can. Give them a fighting chance. Right now they don't have any. And what you're saying about the Apollo Project and the agrobugs...things will start to return a little bit to normal. Eventually those places where the agrobugs are could become natural grazing lands again. New species would evolve. It would be a whole new amazing world."

Seeing that everyone remained silent, Raven went on. "The question we have to ask ourselves is do we preserve the earth now, like it is, destroyed by geo-engineering, with almost no biodiversity and a devastating regime in power, or do we give it a chance to reset, put some of all the wrong we've done back to right, and once more give wildlife and humans the chance to live and thrive?"

Everyone glanced around the table, the tension palpable.

Orion spoke up. "If we do this, we'd need to up the game to urge people to get out of Delta City and seek shelter. The shield there can protect against a lot of things, but not a direct hit from the asteroid."

Byron nodded. "Rowan's pirate broadcasts just aren't enough. The PPC gets them offline in a matter of minutes."

Raven agreed. "We need a bigger plan. A sweeping broadcast that people are forced to pay attention to. One that repeats, over and over, and isn't immediately replaced by the usual mind-numbing programming."

All eyes turned to H124, who was suddenly on the spot. Then she realized. "Willoughby. I'll contact him now." She stepped outside so they could continue their meeting.

She brought up the comm window, using the Badlander coding that would cloak their communication, and called him. He answered right away, his alabaster face beaming. His perfectly coiffed black hair, longer than usual, hung to the back to his collar. He wore an immaculate black suit, white shirt, and purple tie. "H! I was going to call you later today." He noticed her downcast expression. "What's wrong?"

She struggled to find the words. "The PPC destroyed Sanctuary City."

He gasped. "What?"

"You hadn't heard?"

His mouth fell open. "No, I hadn't." He looked toward the door to his office, his mouth an angry slit. "Olivia?"

"We don't know. But probably. They knew about the blast deflection craft and the A14."

"Did they get them?"

"They got the blast deflection craft. The A14 wasn't there." She hesitated. "And then they burned Sanctuary City to the ground."

"Good god." His face went pale. "Want me to figure out where they've stashed the blast deflection craft?"

She grimaced. "Actually, we have a different plan now."

"Your expression is worth a million words. Why do I get the feeling I'm not going to like it?"

"We are going to let it hit."

His eyes went wide, and he cocked his head. "Excuse me?"

"This is what we're thinking." She went on to explain how the Apollo Project would finally come down, the agrobugs would be destroyed, and how decimating the stronghold of the PPC would be a strike that would allow the Rovers' restoration work to finally succeed, to return the planet back to a healthy state.

He spoke the obvious reaction. "But what about all the people in Delta City?"

"That's where you come in."

"Go on."

"Rowan's been doing pirate broadcasts, urging people to flee the city and find shelter."

"I know. Olivia's been in a fit about them."

"But they just aren't having a big enough difference. We need a message that will take over all feeds for a lengthy period of time. Even the floating population control signs in the streets so people not jacked into the network can see the warning."

Willoughby stroked his jaw thoughtfully. "I've actually been thinking about this. About a way to do this very thing. Where is Rowan now?"

"He's at a Badlander camp west of Delta City."

"Tell him to contact me. I'll arrange a way in for him. I'm going to need his help to pull this off." He met her gaze. "And what are you going to do?"

"We're still figuring that out." She worried about saying anything about the genebanks before they figured out the source of the leak.

"Be careful," he told her. He hesitated, as if he wanted to say something more, but didn't.

"You, too. Let me know when your plan is underway."

"I will."

Reluctantly, she closed the comm window. She wasn't sure how she was supposed to act around Willoughby, knowing he was her father. She wanted to say more, but didn't know how to express the conflicted emotions within her. Being around people, people she cared about, was so new to her. She didn't know how to talk to Rowan about her feelings for Byron, or the other way around. She felt awkward and out of place when someone near her cried, because she wasn't sure how she should respond. Hug them? Put a hand on their shoulder? The Rovers and Badlanders had been around others their whole lives, fighting, loving, expressing their feelings. It all came so naturally to them. Often she felt like an outsider, all elbows and knees with her tongue tied.

When she returned to the engineering lab, Gordon had joined them.

"So what's the next step?" Dirk asked.

"Some of us should travel to these DNA vaults and secure them," Raven said.

"Where are they?" Gordon asked.

"Farther than we've traveled before. The first two I think we should check out are to the extreme northeast of this continent. They're both on large islands. One's called Newfoundland, and the other was named Greenland to attract settlers, but apparently it was covered mostly in ice." He paused, then grinned at Gordon. "You might be interested in a new method of transport recently discovered by one of our scouting teams."

He lifted his brow. "Do tell."

"It's an airship. But unlike anything we've found before. Apparently, it was designed to stay aloft for weeks at a time, and carry more than 30,000 pounds of cargo. It can cruise at altitudes of 30,000 feet and reach speeds of 210 mph. We call it the *Argo*. And it's roomy enough to transport any DNA samples we may need to move."

Gordon cracked a grin. "And you have it here?"

Raven smiled. "Yep. Brought it here just two months ago. One of our aeronautic engineers, Winslow, has been undertaking restoration and repairs." He looked at the others. "It's just what we need for an expedition like this to the genebanks."

* * * *

When Raven had mentioned an airship, H124 immediately thought of the sleek, metallic triangular ones used by the PPC, with a tiny cabin underneath that could hold only a pilot, a weapons officer, and a handful of other crew members and PPC officials.

So when they walked out onto the airstrip and saw it, her jaw hung open.

It was massive. Not metallic or silver, but blue-black and reflective, with three tremendous air sacs above a capacious structure beneath. Four fins jutted out from its hull, like airplane tail fins. On the rear and sides of the craft, four engines fitted with propellers stood out. For landing, two long pneumatic tubes ran along the length of the ship on either side, so it could even land on water. Even the landing rails stood a good foot taller than her, and the entire airship itself towered at more than ninety feet.

On the *Argo's* sides stood two self-defense pods. Gunners could climb into them and use weapons that swiveled on mounts to defend the airship. H124 hoped they'd never have to use them. The *Argo* didn't look like the most maneuverable of ships, and she imagined that in an aerial battle, everything would ride on the successful operation of those guns.

"We've modified the airship a bit," Raven continued. "It was originally designed as a luxury craft. There are about six sleeping rooms, a main dining room, a recreation room, and enough cargo space for pretty much whatever comes up."

Gordon gave a long, low whistle as he circled the airship. The entire surface of the air sacs was coated with dark, reflective material. When H124 drew near, she saw that they were all tiny solar cells, the smallest she'd ever seen.

Raven followed her gaze. "These are the most powerful solar cells we've built to date. Originally this ship was filled with helium, making it lighter than air. But helium is hard to come by, and difficult to extract. So we made some modifications. All of these solar cells power a super heater that fires up the air inside it, giving it lift."

The thing towered over them, and when they'd walked up to the cabin entrance, the shadow beneath the ship extended far out on every side.

She walked into the cool just as Gordon completed his circuit. "This is amazing. I flew a zeppelin once, but that was years ago."

"The controls probably aren't much different. You want to take a look?" Raven offered.

Gordon grinned. "Hell yes, I do."

Raven opened the main cabin door, and they filed in. She had expected a utilitarian inner cabin, but what she saw surprised her. It was even more posh than the Big Worm, though the furnishings were decidedly more contemporary. A large lounging area opened off to the right, while the control booth lay to the left. Floor-to-ceiling windows took up all the walls.

Two Rovers bent over the flight controls, checking off items on their PRDs. Gordon joined them. H124 walked through the lounge into another big room. Here a collection of tables and chairs sat neatly arranged, and a pair of swinging doors on the far side of the room led to a small kitchen. She returned to the dining room and walked down a hall, finding small, individual rooms opening up on both sides of the narrow corridor.

She opened one of the doors, finding a small bed and desk. She ran her hand along the bedframe, finding that it was made of what felt like lightweight aluminum, but it had been handcrafted and shaped beautifully into the pattern of a swan, its neck arcing gracefully to form the crown of the headboard.

She was so used to the stark, pragmatic designs of the megacities that craftsmanship like this completely surprised and pleased her. She left the room and opened several other doors, finding that each had different bird sculptures for their beds. She recognized some of them from the field guides she'd been reading: great blue heron, bald eagle, albatross, flamingo, sandhill crane.

She returned to the control room, where Gordon was still talking with the Rover techs. Winslow stood with them. She noticed H124 and smiled.

"I'm going to be piloting this baby," Winslow told her. "The ship should be ready for flight in a few minutes if you want to tell the others."

A rush of excitement pulsed through H124. She grinned. This was going to be completely different from traveling in a plane—sitting in this luxurious lounge, gazing out of the large picture windows at the terrain below. And they were going to a completely different landmass, out over the sea to an entirely new place where none of them had ever stepped foot. She wondered how long it had been since a human had visited the place, and what they'd find. But she also felt nervous. The thought of letting the asteroid strike still hadn't truly set in.

She walked down the small ramp to where Raven stood talking with Gordon.

"Shame to miss this magnificent beast in flight," Gordon was saying.

"You're not coming?" H124 asked.

Gordon hooked a thumb back in the direction of Rivet's outbuilding. "Kind of want to see the A14 in action. See if we can fix it. Thing like that could prove useful."

"You'll be missed," she told him.

Raven turned to her. "Ready to get our gear and push off?"

She nodded, ready to see what lay ahead.

* * * *

Once they were aloft, H124 couldn't believe how quiet the engine was. They rose magically above the trees, and she could see the expanse of grassland beyond the satellite site.

Byron had elected to take over Rowan's task of moving Badlanders into bomb shelters, now more important than ever. They dropped him off west of Delta City and continued on.

They drifted speedily over the landscape, moving at a much higher elevation than they had with Gordon's planes. Beneath her, ancient ruined structures and streets passed by. She brought up her PRD display. She'd captured images from a collection of old paper atlases and entered them into her PRD's basemap as an extra layer. They sailed over a dead forest that stretched to one side of a series of circular streets. The trees ended abruptly as dilapidated houses came into view, crumbling along the avenues. The sun-bleached forest continued on the other side of the development, most of the trees having fallen long ago. She looked at her map. The place was called "Forest Acres," but not a single tree stood inside the housing development—not even a dead one.

They sailed on, passing through more of these outlying communities that sprawled along the edges of bigger cities, pressing into what would have been undeveloped land back then before it was covered with houses. They passed over an ancient community built along a river that had dried up long ago. A series of crumbling dams had been installed, with fallen bridges spanning the river bed. The old map described this community as "Homes at the River Walk."

They flew on, traversing a large expanse of land where all the trees had been removed. Artificial hills, now brown with dead vegetation, had been stacked up around strange sand placements. "Golf Meadows," read her old map.

Next they sailed over "Deer Brook," which sported a crumbling array of houses so close together that she didn't see how a deer could possibly survive in the community. A long-dried up creek sported many human-made dams and diversions, rerouting the path of the stream around the development.

"I don't get this," she finally said to Raven. "So they named these places after whatever they destroyed to build them?"

He peered down. "It seems they did."

When they weren't passing over the endless sprawl of abandoned housing developments, the land was broken and fragmented. Old fences, now tangled messes of wire and rotten wood, lined every open piece of land. Old scars pitted and excoriated the ground, like a giant hand had reached down from the skies with a rake and placed furrows in the dirt.

Strange, rusted metal skeletons spanned some of these raked fields. Other metal skeletons were circular in shape, with the spikes branching out from the center.

Wind gusted across the soil's surface below, kicking up a funnel of dust. It twisted across the land, churning along like a solitary ghost in this desolate place, before losing momentum and dying in a puff of dirt.

Raven noticed her gaze. "Old farms," he said. "Those metal structures delivered water to them. But then the megadrought came and water become more and more scarce. Crops died, people lost their livelihoods. Food became more and more scant. Most farms were abandoned as people were forced to leave for the megacities."

They continued over the desolate land, heading northeast. They passed over a narrow strip of ocean. Winslow announced that they'd reached the coordinates of the genebank. H124 saw a narrow spire reaching up into the sky, marking the entrance. The rest of the building was underground.

As they hovered above it, looking for a good place to land, Raven stood against one of the windows, looking down. He sucked in a sharp breath.

Even from this height, she could see the source of his dismay. Dark shapes littered the ground, and the door to the vault stood open, partially blasted off its hinges. Its contents lay scattered for a quarter mile around the entrance.

The genebank had been raided and damaged.

Chapter 14

Raven waited anxiously for the landing tubes to fill with air, then Winslow gently set the *Argo* down a couple hundred feet from the vault doors. Raven raced out as soon as the craft touched down. H124 descended the ramp, keeping close. Raven hurried to the littered contents, picking up half-buried vials and trying to read worn-off labels, making his way quickly to the door. "Maybe there are still some viable samples inside," he called back to her.

She paused on the soggy ground, looking around. A huge solar array, thankfully still intact, towered over the vault's entrance. The genebank had been placed here in antiquity because the area was cold and snow-covered year-round. Her boots sank in the spongy soil, water seeping around her soles. A strange, vaguely rotting smell drifted on the breeze. Not a single snow patch remained up here, and the ground was far from frozen. A few scraggly bushes struggled to survive in the boggy soil, comprising plant communities that should have been growing much farther south. It was just like the area around Sanctuary City, where trees that had normally grown in more southern latitudes had crept north as the earth warmed.

Raven disappeared through the vault door. As H124 approached the entrance, she saw how weathered and dirty the discarded samples were. This damage had not occurred recently. It looked decades old. Maybe longer.

Dirk caught up with her, and they followed him into the darkness. Beyond the door was an entryway with a power panel on one wall. A shadowed set of stairs led steeply downward. Years of windblown dirt covered the steps. Next to the staircase, an old elevator stood open, one of its doors broken and leaning outward. The car inside was littered with broken glass from shattered vials.

Raven stood at the power conduit along the wall, attempting to turn it on. "Something's wrong with the power."

He returned to the daylight and stared up at the solar array. "This should be working." He bent over its control panel, pulling out his multitool and checking all the connections, adjusting a few things and stripping some old wires to make new connections. He returned to the vault and tried to restart the power. They heard a dull thump from a deep part of the structure, followed by a rhythmic hum. Lights flickered on above them.

As she squinted from the sudden brightness, H124 peered down the stairs.

"Let's go," Raven said, already jogging down the steps. They followed, descending deep into the ground. Raven talked as he took the stairs. "Originally, this facility probably relied on the cool of the permafrost to naturally refrigerate this place. But now that it's melted..."

When they reached the bottom of the stairs, a set of steel doors waited. The metal leaned precariously, blackened by soot, as if someone had blown the doors off their hinges.

She stepped into the room beyond, taking in the scene of chaos around her. Shelves that she imagined had once been orderly, holding DNA samples of plants and animals, now lay mostly bare, spilled and broken vials littering the floor. A few of the shelves had been tipped over. Tall vats labeled "Caution—Liquid Nitrogen" had been toppled, their contents spilled and rotting. Doors leading to other sections of the genebank stood open, broken glass scattered on the floor in their entryways. The rotten smell was almost unbearable.

"No! No!" Raven said aloud, approaching the shelves. He jogged down their considerable lengths, moving faster with each pass of a destroyed shelf.

H124 and Dirk searched the floor for intact samples, their boots crunching the broken glass. The containers that had spilled out of the liquid nitrogen tanks still held their labels, though the samples were smashed at her feet. She read a few of them:

Q234984 - Vaquita porpoise *Phocoena sinus*
JCP32094 - White rhinoceros *Ceratotherium simum*
NJS02935 - Green sea turtle *Chelonia mydas*
GPH4059 - Blue jay *Cyanocitta cristata*
AWH201 - American pika *Ochotona princeps*
RAF2423 - Sea otter *Enhydra lutris*
SPP64202 - Snow leopard *Panthera uncia*
SGO2304 - Wolverine *Gulo gulo*
WPG6920 - Greater bonneted bat *Eumops perotis*

XOI29405 - Panamanian golden frog *Atelopus zeteki*
OWD0528 - Giant ground pangolin *Smutsia gigantea*
RNS10456 - Lord Howe Island stick insect *Dryococelus australis*

"Weren't some of these species' DNA also in the Sanctuary City lab? Did they make it out with the evacuation?" she asked Raven.

Despair crept over his face. "Yes, but it's always good to get genetic samples from a variety of individuals to make viable populations."

She moved to one of the doors and felt for the light switch along the wall. As light flooded into the cavernous space before her, a similar scene revealed itself. In this room, the labels were different. There were no liquid nitrogen tanks here, just empty shelves. She read a few of the labels:

Artifact 201234 - Mountain gorilla paw ashtray *Gorilla beringei*
Artifact 234092 - African elephant foot umbrella stand *Loxodonta africana*
Artifact 482590 - Plains zebra rug *Equus quagga*
Artifact 340592 - American alligator suitcase *Alligator mississippiensis*
Artifact 723631 - Diamondback rattlesnake belt *Crotalus atrox*
Artifact 925061 - Bengal tiger rug *Panthera tigris*
Artifact 525321 - Guitar made from hawksbill turtle shell *Eretmochelys imbricata*

The shelves above the labels were empty. She noticed that Raven stood in the doorway, dismayed. "I can't believe it's all gone."

"What are these?" she asked him, pointing at the labels.

He came closer, reading them, his expression pained. "These vaults were constructed before de-extinction had been attempted. Back when this was built, they stored all kinds of samples from extinct animals."

She pointed to one of the labels. "Elephant foot umbrella stand?"

"Yeah. In a lot of cases, samples of DNA left from extinct animals were in the form of decorations that had been made from their body parts."

"That's horrible."

"They were enormously popular. And not just when they were made, but well into the future. In fact, one of the only Sumatran rhino DNA samples we knew about was a wall decoration made from a rhino hide that a PPC exec had in Basin City. I remember my parents talking about how years before, back when Basin City was still up and running, a group of Rovers had infiltrated it to steal that hide." His expression clouded suddenly, his gaze growing distant. "The PPC..." He gazed around. "At first I thought this destruction was the work of Badlanders or Death Riders, but…excuse me." He left the room, turning on the display to his PRD.

Dirk's voice sounded from another room. "You guys should take a look at this." He sounded spooked.

H124 left the room, seeing Dirk gripping the doorframe of a neighboring room, his back to her. She moved to his side and peered in, instantly assaulted by the powerful smell of decay.

Tall glass cylindrical enclosures filled the room, some still intact, others shattered, thick ooze caked and dried on the floor. But the most startling thing was the contents of those cylinders. Dozens of human skeletons leaned against the glass walls. Thick, gelatinous soup pooled around the calves and thighs of the bodies in the intact tubes. The stench of decay was overwhelming.

She stifled her gag reflex and pulled the collar of her black shirt over her nose. "What are these?"

Raven's voice behind her made her jump. "Cryogenic chambers. But without the power on, the bodies broke down and decayed."

She turned to him, her eyes watering from the stench. "Why would they be here?"

"They aren't meant for DNA samples. They were probably kept here for resurrection."

Dirk's eyes went wide as he took a step back.

"Back when this was built," Raven went on, "if you were rich, you could pay to have your body stored here, to be awakened when the technology to do so was developed. People who had incurable diseases or had grown old and infirm but didn't want to die yet, paid to have their bodies kept here."

"Poor souls," Dirk breathed. He turned, gazing out over the wreckage. "Who did this? Death Riders?"

"That's what I thought at first, some kind of raider who was here looking for tech. I didn't see why the PPC would destroy everything like this. But I just hacked into the last security recordings before the power was cut." His face looked grim. "It *was* the PPC." He brought up the video window on his PRD and played the footage.

H124 watched as a huge PPC cargo ship landed outside the vault, followed by an executive airship. Four smartly dressed execs emerged, their suits and hair impeccable. Soldiers escorted them, looking officious and anonymous in their black body armor and helmets with the face shields down. The execs entered the vault with maglev sleds, picking every endangered species collectible off the shelves. When they'd gathered them all, she watched as one of the execs gestured to the soldiers, who then stormed through the facility, overturning shelves and smashing samples. Then they cut the power, and the video went black. They'd left the door open, and with no power, it had ruined the place for anyone who could find future use for it.

When the video ended, H124 stared in disbelief, then met Raven's gaze. His eyes had narrowed, flashing with anger. "I guess they didn't want anyone else discovering this site," he said quietly.

"This is unbelievable," Dirk breathed.

In the end, H124 and the others found nothing left to salvage. They walked quietly back to the *Argo*, boarding it in silence. Winslow started up the engines, and they took off.

H124 stared down at the ruined vault as they flew away.

"Let's hope Greenland will be better," Raven said.

They motored on, covering vast, empty stretches of dry terrain. Hungry, she grabbed some food and sat down next to Dirk, who had made some earlier. But when she looked at his plate, the food had gone cold. He hadn't touched it, though he held a fork poised over the meal. He stared blankly ahead, the utensil in his hand forgotten.

"Are you...are you thinking about Astoria?" H124 asked tentatively.

Dirk blinked, then lowered the fork. He stared down at the food, his face slack, like all the life had drained out of him. At first H124 didn't think he was going to answer. Then, in a quiet voice, he said, "I feel half empty without her. We balanced each other out. I was the peace to her vengeance." He paused, looking out the window. "Now I can almost feel that white hot rage she carried with her, like somehow it's moving into me. She treated it like it was her best friend. Sometimes I think that rage was closer to her than I was, that it had been born out of some kind of primordial pit inside of her."

"Where did that rage come from?"

Dirk sighed as he tucked an errant purple-and-black dreadlock behind his ear. "She wasn't always like that. She was one of the happiest kids at our Badlander camp. Our parents had been trying to have kids for a long time, so when we came along they really lavished attention on us. Astoria laughed a lot. She'd make up these creative games and all the other kids would play along. Treasure hunts, stuff like that.

"We were nine when a contingent of PPC soldiers rolled into our camp. We'd had no warning. They burned the place to the ground. Smashed or took everything we had. Astoria and I managed to hide, but our mother..." Dirk's chin trembled, and his eyes fell away. "Our mother was trying to help these other kids hide. The PPC grabbed her. My dad tried to stop them.

They'd picked up a harpoon gun from our stockpile and shot him with it. Pinned him to the wooden side of a building like it was a game. Then they laughed as he screamed at them. They drove away with our mother.

"We got our dad down, and the camp's sawbones started patching him up. Astoria ran after the PPC troopers, tracking them. I followed her. We ran after their tracks for two days. Astoria was relentless. And then…on the third day, we were getting close. The tracks were fresher. We came over this rise, saw this dusty lump on the ground up ahead." He swallowed, staring out of the window. "I thought it was an old bundle of clothes or something. Astoria ran forward, crying out. It was our mother. They'd dragged her to death behind one of the transports. Her body was all torn up. We could hear their engines roaring away into the distance. Astoria stood there staring after them. I'd never seen her like that before. We carried our mother's body back to camp.

"It took weeks for our dad to recover from the harpoon wound, but eventually he did. Everyone moved to a new camp. But as it turned out, this one was no safer. Between Death Rider raids and a neighboring group of Badlanders who constantly robbed us and savagely beat anyone caught near their camp, we were always on guard.

"When we were twelve, we moved to a different area. The place seemed peaceful. Astoria still made up games for us to play, though she didn't smile or laugh as much as she used to. That summer Death Riders found us. They tore into camp, stealing everything we had, smashing up our living quarters, setting the camp on fire. My dad tried to fight them, and they chained him to a pole. They locked us in these metal cages, and we watched while…"

Dirk swallowed, his voice caught in his throat. When he spoke again, he rasped out the words. "While they carved off pieces of his body and ate them. He was still alive."

"Oh, god," H124 said, closing her eyes.

"A neighboring group of Badlanders happened to be passing by and saw what was going on. They drove the Death Riders out of camp. But not before our dad had died from blood loss."

"This is terrible, Dirk."

He picked absently at his food with the fork, moving it around without eating it. "After that we didn't have much left. Hardly any belongings, no food. One of the kids we grew up with, Dooley, started going on these scavenger runs, finding things to trade or sell. We went with him sometimes. He was brash and fearless. As we got older, Astoria really fell for him. Hard. And he loved her, too. Or so I thought. Some of the levity she'd had as a kid returned. She smiled more. Dooley started disappearing for longer and longer stints of time. Astoria was always so happy when he returned to camp. By this time she'd been training as a fighter—the best in our camp. The best on the Badlander circuit, as a matter of fact, and she was only fourteen.

"Dooley heard about this massive score of PPC weapons that had been stashed at a satellite site. He wanted to break into it. Astoria thought it was too dangerous. She didn't want me to go. So they stole away together in the middle of the night.

"But they didn't come back the next day, or the day after that. Me and some others checked out the weapons stash. It hadn't been touched, and was there no sign that someone had been there recently. It was old, probably forgotten about ages before.

"Astoria didn't come home. I searched for her for months, asking questions, traveling from camp to camp. No one had seen her. Then a few months later, I was coming back from a neighboring camp, and I happened to see Dooley, bouncing along in an old jeep. He didn't see me. I followed his tracks way out to this camp on the plains. He'd amassed a fair amount of wealth in stolen goods. I thought maybe I'd find Astoria there, though I couldn't understand why she would have been out of touch for so long. I entered the camp and asked him where she was.

"He...he actually laughed at me for looking for her for so long. He told me she was probably long dead. I didn't understand. He said how naïve she was, falling for his every line. He'd sold her, H," Dirk said, meeting H124's gaze. "He'd sold her to this traveling Death Rider fighting show, all for that beat-up old jeep he drove." Dirk looked back out the window. "He had no remorse. I asked where this show was now. I remember he said, 'How the hell would I know?' and I could see then he had no conscience, no feeling." Dirk swallowed with a downward gaze. "I don't know how I had missed that. How I'd let her go with him.

"I kept looking, asking questions about the Death Rider show, where it went. But by the time I caught up to it, Astoria wasn't in it. I couldn't just go up and ask them, so I spied at night, eavesdropping. Then one of them mentioned her, that they'd lost a fortune when she'd killed her handler and fled a month before.

"They laughed that the area had been so inhospitable, that she was surely dead.

"But I knew that wouldn't have stopped her. I remembered her determination when we'd searched for our mother. She wouldn't give up, even when we were dying of thirst. I put the word out in every Badlander camp I came to. That's how I met Rowan and Byron. I walked into their camp one day, barely alive myself. I'd had no food or water for days. And there she was, wounded and half starved, but alive. They'd found her and helped her. But she was so different, H. All that joy? That laughter? It was gone. She'd been beaten, starved, betrayed. We'd lost our family. When she healed and was strong enough to move, she vanished one afternoon. A few days later, she returned, her eyes like cold steel. I'll never forget that look. It was a few days later when we learned the Death Rider fighting camp had burned to the ground, fleeing stragglers picked off as they tried to escape, their bodies viciously beaten. No one said anything, but we all knew it had been her.

"Word got around that Dooley had been found, his skull smashed so brutally that all that was left were bone splinters and brain matter. She never trusted anyone again."

"Except you," H124 said quietly.

Dirk clasped his hands. "Except me. I don't know what she endured in that fighting camp, but anything left of the sweet kid was gone. They'd robbed her of it."

"I'm so sorry," H124 said, feeling the sheer uselessness of the phrase; her sympathy was nothing in the face of such loss. They ate in silence, but it seemed to have done Dirk a little bit of good to talk about his sister. He perked up just a tiny bit, and managed to eat a few mouthfuls of food.

Afterward, H124 resumed her place by the window. She marveled as the coast drifted away and the blue of the sea opened beneath them. She'd already been astounded by the ocean when they'd visited the sunken facility, but now, flying over a wide expanse of it, was a completely new experience. Wind tore across the surface, kicking up the whitecaps and creating hypnotic rippling patterns in the undulating water.

"How soon until we see the ice?" she asked Raven. She'd seen pictures of it in Rover books, a vast white sheet.

He peered down. "You might be disappointed. I'm not sure how much of the ice cap still exists. But it shouldn't be long until we find out. Greenland is fairly close to the coast of North America."

She stared down, her view momentarily obstructed as they passed through a bank of thin clouds, the vapor parting around them, its white tendrils curling around the ship.

"You might want to catch some Z's," he suggested.

She nodded, exhausted. She took his advice, plopping down on one of the luxurious couches and stretching out. She covered herself with the coat the Rovers had given her, the soft black one with the red sections on the back. The low thrumming of the *Argo's* engines lulled her to sleep.

* * * *

She awoke to Raven gently touching her shoulder. "We're almost there." She sat up groggily, wiping her eyes and stretching. She couldn't wait to see the vast expanse of ice. Other than the blizzard she and Gordon had encountered on her way to find the Rovers, she'd never seen a lot of snow, certainly not a vast sheet of ice.

She couldn't imagine it. She tried to picture an ice sheet 10,000 feet thick covering an entire landmass.

Moving to a window seat, she gazed down. The sapphire sea sparkled below, and a coastline was coming into view. But it wasn't icy. In fact, as far as she could see, there was no ice at all, just brown and green mountains forming steep fjords dipping down to the sea.

"What happened to it all?" she asked him as they began to descend. "The ice."

He too looked out the window, squinting in the brightness of the afternoon. "It's been disappearing. As the planet got hotter, more and more surface ice began to melt, creating these large lakes on the ice cap. The water, warmed by the sun, would sink through these cracks and fissures to the bottom of the ice sheet. This caused even more warming, and more fissures to open, draining lakes in the neighboring areas, bringing more water down. It made the ice cap unstable, and melting occurred more rapidly. When it started to collapse, the flooding was catastrophic."

H124 thought of the buildings far out in the sea, the ones off the coast of New Atlantic. All that had once been above water.

"There might be a little left, right where it was once thickest, but it's nowhere near as massive as it once was."

H124 leaned her head against the glass, staring down as they readied to land. The quiet hum of the *Argo's* engines vibrated through the glass where her forehead met the cool surface. She couldn't believe how different the planet had once been, and so recently too.

"The melting all happened much quicker than they'd anticipated; the positive feedback loop surprised them with its speed," Raven added.

"So this genebank," she asked, pulling away from the window, "was originally placed here because of permafrost too?"

He nodded. "It looks that way."

She thought of the rotten smell and disaster of the one they'd just come from. "Will everything be ruined here too?"

"I think we need to brace ourselves for that possibility. If there was no backup refrigeration system, and if the PPC has cut the power to the liquid nitrogen tanks again…" His voice trailed off as they felt the *Argo* set down gently in front of a tall structure that rose out of the side of a mountain. In the center of it stood a pair of thick double doors. They were still closed.

"That's a good sign," she said hopefully, standing.

In a nearby couch, Dirk stretched and rose with a yawn. He ran a hand through his long dreads. "Fingers crossed," he said, and approached the exit.

They filed out the descending ramp, toward the genebank doors. They were locked. "Even more promising," Raven said. "Dirk?"

Dirk cracked his fingers, then moved to an ancient keypad behind a protective Plexiglas box. He opened the case and studied the keypad, then pulled out his multitool. In a moment he'd jimmied off the cover, exposing the wires beneath. He rewired them, twisting some together, and before long they heard a dull clunk as the lock disengaged. "We're in." He folded his multitool and put it back in his pocket.

He pushed open the door, revealing a similar setup to the one they'd just come from. A dark stairwell led steeply down, and an elevator waited to transport visitors. H124 sniffed the air. It smelled a little musty, but no hint of decay hung about. Raven moved to the power panel and switched on the lights. They powered up instantly, flickering on in the stairwell. "Shall we?" he asked.

They started down, the musty smell growing stronger. Mold and mildew grew along the walls, growing thicker as they went deeper inside the mountain. When they neared the bottom, she saw a dark black stain forming an even line all the way along the wall. "What is that?" she asked, pointing.

Raven paused to consider it. "It looks like a high-water mark."

The musty smell suddenly made sense. All the water streaming off the ice cap had caused the facility to flood.

They descended lower, finding another high-water mark below that one, and yet another as they reached the bottom.

"Looks like the water receded in stages."

The lights had burned out at the bottom of the stairs. H124 stepped into darkness. As she crossed the stairwell landing to another door, she stumbled on something. Shining her headlamp down, she found a huge crack in the foundation that had been patched up. The floor was uneven where water had made the ground swell.

Raven opened the door at the bottom, admitting them into a large series of rooms. All along the floor and bottoms of the walls, other gaping cracks had admitted water. But all the cracks had been repaired, and the floor was dry in here. The liquid nitrogen tanks were all still functioning, and the shelves containing seeds and animal artifacts still held all their supplies. Raven walked along the rows, grinning and turning, taking it all in. "This is amazing!"

Dirk knelt down by one of the cracks, feeling it. "This work is recent," he told them, standing back up. "Someone's been here."

Raven inspected one of the liquid nitrogen tanks. "All these fittings look new, too," he said, walking around it.

She surveyed the area carefully. "So who's been maintaining this place?"

Raven met her gaze. "I don't know." He turned in place. "But this is incredible. This is a wealth of DNA material. And so far deep underground, it should be shielded from the effects of the impact." He moved to a nearby terminal. It wasn't as old as the ones she'd found in the university beneath New Atlantic. But it wasn't as new as their PRDs, either. It had a floating display. Raven powered it on and paired it with his PRD, then downloaded the contents of the genebank. He scrolled through countless DNA samples. "H! There is hummingbird DNA in here!"

She smiled, already imagining the little jeweled birds he'd described on top of the train.

Raven was still midway through the download when her own PRD beeped. She brought up the comm window, expecting to hear from Byron or Gordon. Instead a familiar string of numbers played out in her message window.

It was the Phantom Code.

"Look at this," she said, moving closer to Dirk and Raven.

They watched the numbers scroll by. "Isn't this the strange message we were getting in Sanctuary City?"

Raven nodded, approaching her display. "Yes, but...wait...there!" he said, highlighting some of the numbers. "I've seen that code so many times I know most of it by heart. But these numbers are different. Most of it's the same, but..." He studied it a while longer. "Yes, some of these numbers are definitely different."

She brought up her saved version of the Phantom Code from Sanctuary City, and they compared them side by side.

Dirk came closer, scanning it. "Yes. Here," he said, pointing out one sequence of numbers, "and here, too. It *is* different."

"But what is it?" she asked.

"I wish I knew," Raven said. "And why receive it here?"

"Have you ever picked it up anywhere but Sanctuary City?"

He frowned. "No. Never."

They puzzled over the code a few minutes more, and H124 forwarded the new message to Gordon and Onyx, who'd been taking a stab at deciphering the string of numbers from Sanctuary City.

"Well," Raven said as the contents of the genebank finished downloading into his PRD. "Let's seal this place back up and move on to the next genebank."

They checked over the other rooms, ensuring no more flooding was seeping into the foundation. Whoever had repaired it had done an amazing job. She wondered if it was the PPC. Maybe they had realized what a mistake they'd made by destroying the other facility, and wanted to keep this one around for future use.

Raven hacked into the security footage, but it had been wiped recently, and the mystery of who had been maintaining the vault remained.

They climbed the stairs and locked up the vault again. As they walked back to the *Argo,* Dirk's PRD beeped. He brought up his display, watching for a minute, then waved them over eagerly. "Hey, come take a look at this!"

H124 hurried to him, and peered over his shoulder.

"This is the live feed from Delta City," he said, looking at them poignantly. "The *only* live feed."

Willoughby's face filled the display. He spoke with gravity. "For months now you've been seeing pirate broadcasts warning of an imminent danger to you all. These broadcasts should be taken very seriously. An asteroid, a giant rock that orbits the sun just as our planet does, is on a collision course with the earth. It's going to fall on Delta City like a bomb, and it will obliterate this place. This is not a hoax. Check your feed source. You can see this is an official PPC transmission. I'm a high-level producer, and I'm here to tell you that this is a very real threat."

It flashed on images of New Atlantic, the city a smoking crater with no sign of life. "This is what happened when just a fragment of the asteroid hit New Atlantic. The one coming here is far bigger." He stared intently into the camera. "Each of you, *every single one of you,* must seek shelter. There are refugee camps located in bomb shelters to the east and west of the city, as well as a vast network of tunnels located deep beneath the city that can offer shelter. You must leave your living pods and seek safety. There is very little time now. We have arranged for water and food cubes to be available at these locations. But you must get there yourself." He paused, glancing at someone off camera, then returned his intense gaze to the screen. "Again, I cannot stress this enough, the broadcasts you've been seeing are *not* a hoax. You must seek shelter, and you must do so now." The screen briefly went blank. Then Willoughby appeared again, his message looping from the beginning.

She stared up at Dirk. "They did it! They got the broadcast out. How long has this been looping?"

Dirk checked the source feed. "About six hours now."

She grinned. "Amazing! And the PPC hasn't figured out how to shut it down yet?" She thought of Willoughby, and a knot formed in her gut. "I hope Willoughby got the hell out of there."

Chapter 15

They flew on to the next genebank, in a place once called Siberia. The old maps she'd scanned and overlaid onto her PRD map called the area the Yamal Peninsula. The brown terrain rolled beneath them, with snow dusting certain parts. The area had once been freezing cold for much of the year, and permafrost had been locked up in the soil. Vast grasslands had spanned the entire region, home to grazers such as mammoths, woolly rhinos, saiga antelopes, reindeer, and muskoxen.

She could imagine these creatures moving in mixed herds across the landscape, eating leisurely in the sunshine. Now, no animal caught her eye as they rumbled over the landscape. Strange, nearly perfectly circular holes dotted the ground here and there. Even from their altitude, the depressions appeared large. In other places, odd little hills appeared, like a giant had pressed up on the earth from beneath, splitting the soil.

"We're nearing the coordinates," Winslow called from the cockpit.

H124 peered out of the window, trying to spot the genebank entrance. A tall spire flashed in the sun, catching her eye. It rose from a hillock, a towering metal structure similar in design to the first one they'd visited. As before, the spire was only the entrance, the vault itself deep underground so as to take advantage of the natural cold there.

About a quarter mile off, she spotted another of the strange round holes. She pointed it out to Raven. "What's that?"

He wrinkled his brow. "Not sure. Sinkhole, maybe? The ground here is likely unstable with all the melting permafrost."

As the *Argo* set down on its inflated landing rails, H124 studied the entrance. Relieved to see nothing scattered on the ground around it, she hoped the PCC hadn't found this one. The exterior of the spire had oxidized, and some kind of green mold or moss grew in some areas.

Winslow opened the doors, and H124 grabbed her toolbag. Eager to explore a new place, she was the first one off the airship.

Blinking in the sunlight, she breathed in the air. Something vaguely rotten met her nostrils, and she wrinkled her nose. As Dirk emerged beside her, he covered his nose with his arm. "What is that? Decay?"

"Something's gone off," said Raven, stepping out beside them. "But it's not the same smell as the first vault we visited."

Raven cupped his nose. "No, this is something else. Maybe decaying plant matter."

They crossed to the entrance, the ground soggy, giving way with every step of her boot. Nearby stood another of the hillocks, the soil on its perimeter broken and fractured.

They were almost halfway to the entrance when a loud boom wracked the quiet afternoon and the ground shook. H124 went down on her hands and knees. Dirt rained down on her head, rocks peppering her back.

"What the hell?" she heard Dirk cry, whipping her head to see him lying on his side, shielding his face as pebbles and soil cascaded over him.

The ground settled, and the last of the dirt fell. H124 rose, confused, looking around. Behind her, Raven struggled to his feet.

She looked up, expecting to see a PPC airship that had fired on them, but only clouds dotted the searing blue sky. She looked back at the ground. The little hill was gone. In its place stood a gigantic hole, identical to the ones she'd spotted from the air.

"Look at that!" she shouted, pointing.

Raven followed her gaze. He glanced around nervously. "Methane. It's so warm that all that buried organic matter is decomposing and building up gas."

Dirk stared at the ground at his feet. "You mean the ground itself could explode at any moment?"

"In a nutshell."

Alarm swept over his face. "I don't like that nutshell."

"Do we stay or get out of here?" she asked.

Raven inclined his head. "We hightail it into the genebank."

"And if the whole thing gets blown skyward while we're in there?" Dirk asked.

"That would be unfortunate," Raven responded.

They all jogged to the entrance. Dirk worked more quickly than usual, removing the door lock panel and twisting wires together. The door slid open, and they piled inside.

As Raven worked to the get the lights on, H124's PRD beeped. She lifted it, opening the comm channel. A stream of numbers flashed across it. She recognized the familiar pattern now—the Phantom Code.

"Check this out," she said. "It's coming in again."

Raven lifted his own PRD, watching the scrolling numbers, and recorded the whole sequence as it repeated. "Curious. It's different again."

H124 sent these numbers on to Gordon and Onyx while Raven messed with the power grid. The lights flickered on with a hum. A staircase led off to their right, and so they descended deeper underground. The temperature grew noticeably colder. H124 zipped up her jacket.

Inside, they found the genebank wonderfully intact. Signs of updates and recent repairs were evident once again. Someone was looking after these sites. Raven downloaded the DNA database and tried to check the security footage, but it too had been recently wiped.

They returned to the *Argo* in higher spirits.

H124 looked to the sky as she boarded it. Part of her was terrified they were just going to let this thing hit. She felt a bit of panic, a scared voice inside her telling her they should be getting back the blast deflection craft. But if they could undo some of this damage…

They took their seats as the *Argo* rose into the air. Raven was smiling to himself, looking over the Siberian genebank's contents on his PRD.

As the quiet hum of the *Argo's* engines threatened to lull H124 to sleep, she sat up straighter in her seat. Dirk sat across from her, frowning at his PRD's display.

"This isn't good," he mumbled.

H124 moved beside him.

"This is the only thing streaming in Delta City now." It was still an image of Willoughby, but this time it was an animated version of his face. It was so realistic that if you didn't know him in person, you could definitely be fooled into thinking it was the real thing. In big red letters across the top and bottom the screen read: "Fake news. Do not be alarmed. Go about your duties."

The fake Willoughby smiled, and he said in a nearly identical simulated voice, "I created this scare as a hoax. There is no real threat."

Then it cut to Olivia's face, her real face, and at the sight of her grandmother, H124 felt a mixture of revulsion and fear for Willoughby. "Earlier, this man made a broadcast claiming that a giant rock from space, of all preposterous things, was going to fall on Delta City and destroy it. I assure you, no such threat exists. Some of you may have seen images of New Atlantic, but I assure you that an asteroid will not fall anywhere near Delta City. Check the source feed, and you'll see this is not only an official PPC transmission, but is coming from the highest office here at the media tower. This so-called 'producer' was fired earlier this week and took it upon himself to try to cause chaos here in our fine city. So rest assured, no such disaster will befall us, and you can resume enjoying your entertainment. We're even rolling out some new media streams we've dreamed up just for you."

It then cut to a "reality" show called *Living Authentically with Throw Pillows,* where two people sat around a table discussing their latest finds. H124 knew that unbeknownst to the citizens who viewed these shows, they didn't feature real actors. Instead the shows used realistically animated people who often acted out scripts randomly generated by AI.

"Mine has little feet and a crown," one woman bragged to her friend. She cradled a throw pillow with a crooked sewn-on face, along with pink velvet arms and legs.

Her friend looked at her and snarked, "But look at the footwear for the feet! They aren't even sandals. They're like pumps. And they're so plain." She rolled her eyes. A laugh track giggled away.

A couple minutes into the show, the feed cut back to Willoughby's face. A mocking, high-pitched voice had been dubbed over his own. "It's an ASS-teroid!" the voice said, tittering. Then a cartoonish rock fell into view. Willoughby's eyes grew wider, and his nasally voice said, "Uh-oh!" When the rock hit him, he exploded in a comical animation.

The feed cut back to the reality show.

Dirk bounced around between media streams. "There are number of feeds up now. Delta City is streaming as usual." He flipped to the different stations, all of them showing some inane program, but this time inundating the viewer with cuts of the space rock blowing up the goofy Willoughby.

"She's made a meme out of it," Dirk breathed. "This will totally discredit him."

H124 stood stunned. "She's…she's completely diabolical. I don't get it. She knows that one already destroyed New Atlantic. Do the citizens really believe they're safe?"

Dirk shook his head. "It's entirely possible they believe her. She's made it all seem like a hoax."

H124 blinked. "So…so she can what? Just keep working there till the last minute? Then bail somehow while the city perishes?"

"They still hope to get the A14."

"That's a huge gamble."

"One she's obviously willing to take."

Just then H124's PRD beeped, the comm system signaling her. She saw it was from Rowan and opened the comm window, worried to hear how things were going. They'd taken over the feeds successfully, but it wasn't looking good now.

On her display, chaos reigned behind Rowan. He stood outside the atmospheric shield wall, people streaming down from the wall behind him on ladders and ropes, leaping onto the ground and fleeing. The shield was down. With fewer people manning their consoles, the shield had collapsed, allowing people to escape en masse.

Though Olivia had restored the streams, it wasn't yet business as usual. Delta City was in a state of panic.

Rowan helped up a person who had fallen, and the man limped out of sight. "It's amazing, H. People listened. They've been evacuating for hours. We've been trying to get them to safety, to the bomb shelters. But it's been a nightmare. People are trampling each other. One PPC exec even killed someone to jockey for position. Everyone fell on him like lunatics."

"That's terrible."

He glanced over his shoulder. "But already the flow is ebbing. Now that Olivia has the feeds back up, people are being reassured and returning to their consoles."

"Can you try the broadcast again later?" Dirk asked.

Rowan's face fell. "There's a problem with that." He hesitated.

"Yes?" H124 prompted.

"Willoughby was supposed to meet me at a rendezvous point. He never showed."

H124 felt her stomach clench. "How long ago?"

"More than five hours. He closed down all the other feeds and replaced them with his transmission. He was out of his office by then, transmitting from a sub-tower that doesn't get used anymore. It should have been an easy escape. We'd already stashed a transport for him to take to the shield wall. But he never showed." People pushed against Rowan as he fought to stay upright. "I can't stay here much longer. I've got to oversee their escape."

"But where is he?" she asked him.

Rowan grimaced. "I'm sorry. I just don't know."

Desperate people streamed around him. She saw an exec in a suit, a cluster of dirty, ragged people who likely lived on the street, then a handful of clean, comfortably dressed individuals who must have been citizens. Their eyes bulged at the scene around them, mouths open in vacant confusion. It was probably the first time they'd been unplugged from the network in years.

All the same, the variety of classes showed that the signal had reached everyone—citizens, workers, execs, even the homeless. A woman in rags bumped into Rowan, grabbing onto him. "Which way do I go?" she pleaded, the panic clear in her eyes. "How long till it hits?"

"I have to go," Rowan told them. "I'm sorry." He signed off.

H124 stood there in awe. Her mind raced over the possibilities. What had become of Willoughby? Had he been captured? Killed? Merely delayed somehow? Maybe his transport had broken down.

They continued back to the Rover satellite location, this time flying over the top of the world. She'd read from old books that a great pack of sea ice once covered the ocean there, but now there was nothing of it left.

As they sailed over the vast blue, H124 tried to call Willoughby a number of times, but couldn't get through.

At the satellite location, Rowan and Byron rendezvoused with them. They'd done all they could for now. The bomb shelters were full. They needed the Rovers' vast database of historical knowledge to search for additional shelters where people could hide.

H124 was happy to see them and Gordon, but couldn't fight the terrible feeling in her gut. Something bad had happened to Willoughby.

Everyone converged on Orion's lab to come up with the next stage. They planned to pick up a larger crew and head to the biggest genebank of all, located in a place called Antarctica, at the very bottom of the world. Some adjustments had to be made to the *Argo* to keep rime from building up on the exterior.

As they collected around a table, H124's comm window beeped on her PRD. She looked down, stunned at the name blinking on her display. She looked to Raven in horror. "It's Olivia."

"Why would she reach out to you?" he asked.

"She wants the A14," H124 gasped.

"Don't answer it!" Dirk said, his eyes flashing with rage. "She can go to hell!"

H124 was ready to ignore the incoming call, but a thought came to mind. "She might know something about Willoughby."

"Or she might be trying to get a handle on your location," Rowan said warily.

"I can mask your location," Onyx offered, already typing in commands in her virtual keyboard. She looked up. "Okay. It's safe to answer if you want to."

Hesitantly, H124 moved to face a blank wall, where all Olivia would be able to discern was a featureless grey surface.

She opened the comm window, and the woman's perfectly coiffed silver hair and conceited appearance turned H124's stomach. She wore a red business suit, her matching red lips smiling smugly in her ivory face.

"I have a little present for you, my dear," Olivia oozed. She stood on some kind of white surface, with a staircase rising in the background. In the distance, H124 could make out a blue expanse of seawater. The camera bobbed up and down somewhat with the motion of the waves. Then it panned down and revealed Willoughby, on his knees and badly beaten. Deep purple-and-black bruises masked his face, and his lip was busted. One eye was swollen shut. He hung his head, his usually impeccable suit torn and bloodied. Behind him stood a man clad entirely in black, the brim of his hat shading his cruel, black eyes and glistening pale skin.

A Repurposer.

He held a gleaming tool to Willoughby's skull, ready to dig in through the bone. His slit of a mouth was drawn up in a tight little smile.

"Deliver the A14 to the following location," Olivia went on, "and I'll spare him." Coordinates streamed into H124's PRD, her map bringing up a location near the outskirts of Delta City. "If you don't, well…" She smirked, her eyes cold and calculating. "I'll do worse than kill him." She gazed down at him, grasping his chin. "I've always believed he would best serve the PPC as a Menial. Just sitting there, with vacant eyes, pressing a button now and then. He deserves a break after all the hard work he's done." She sneered into the camera. "You have twenty-four hours."

The transmission ended.

H124's mind exploded. "We can't let her do this! Where is she?" It had been a strange location, one she didn't recognize. In the wider shots, she could see more of the sea stretching out. With the bobbing motion of the camera, it must have been on a boat of some kind.

Onyx's hand flew over her virtual keyboard. "Let me see." The hacker continued to work, eyes narrowed on her display. "She shielded her location. I'm having trouble getting coordinates."

"We can't let them get the A14," Raven said firmly, stepping toward her. "If they divert the asteroid, everything we've been hoping for will be for nothing."

"And we can't just let her destroy Willoughby!" H124 cried, her voice rising. Her temperature shot up as she began to simmer.

"He knew what he was doing," Rowan told her. "Knew it was a huge risk. And it paid off. A lot of people got out. And if we get a stream back up, even more will get out."

H124's eyes had gone wide. She fought back a well of emotion surging up inside her. She blinked back stinging tears, the image of Willoughby kneeling before Olivia seared into her mind.

"He knew the risks," Rowan went on. "The needs of the many outweigh the needs of the few." Rowan seemed so calm about it, so certain that they should turn their backs on Willoughby, as if the decision were so simple.

She opened her mouth, but Byron beat her to it. He jabbed a finger at Rowan's chest. "How can you be so cavalier about it? It's her father, for god's sake."

Rowan looked back at her, somewhat apologetically. "I know. I'm sorry. But you know I'm right."

H124 started pacing. "No, I don't know that. We owe him. Let's not forget he saved our lives. More than once." She glanced up at Raven. "I agree we can't let them have the A14. But I can't let her do this to Willoughby." She clenched her jaw. "I'm going after him." She turned to Onyx. "Any luck with the coordinates?"

The hacker's face was screwed up in concentration as she tapped a final key. Her face lit up. *"Aoo',"* she said in Navajo. "Got 'em!" She brought up a map, zeroing in on a location in the Pacific Ocean, off the western coast of North America. "They must be on *The Morning Star.*"

"What's that?" H124 asked.

"A PPC luxury ship," the hacker answered. "It's gigantic." She pulled up an image saved on her PRD. "Here." The photo revealed an enormous ship with so many decks it towered over the water. Onyx leaned forward in her chair. "They have conferences on it and summits. Meetings. The thing's a floating city."

H124 set her jaw. "I'm going there. I'm not going to let her repurpose Willoughby." She started pacing again. "I'm going to tell her we're delivering the A14. By the time they realize we're not showing, hopefully I'll have gotten to Willoughby." She raised her hand to her PRD, but Byron stopped her. "Wait. Don't do that."

"Why not?"

"If Olivia is as evil as we think she is, the minute you accede to her demands, she's going to kill Willoughby anyway. Or worse."

H124's hand halted before she opened the comm window. He was right. "Then I don't have much time." She looked to Gordon. "I need something fast. Something long-range that can land on water."

The pilot scratched his head, his white hair rumpling. "I'd say we could take the A14, but we're still converting over the fuel system. And besides, we couldn't land it on the water."

"What about Marlowe's helicopter?" H124 asked.

Gordon shook his head. "It doesn't have the kind of range or speed we'd need." He cocked a brow. "But I might have just the thing." He pulled up a map on his PRD and moved it to a location southeast from where they were presently. "There was a long-range helicopter stashed at this location. It's old military, armed to the teeth. And boy, is she fast."

"Do you think it's still there?" Raven asked him.

"Got to hope it is. We could take the Vega down there, pick it up, and be out on the ocean in no time."

H124 lit up with gratitude. "Would that work?"

"If it's still there," Gordon added, "and the Death Riders haven't found it." He looked at Byron and Dirk. "Or your lot."

"I haven't heard of us picking up something like that," Dirk told him.

"Then it's a plan," Byron said to H124. "We go for the helicopter."

H124 felt a surge of affection for him having her back without question.

Just then Raven gave a haunted frown. "I just realized something."

She turned to him. "What is it?"

"Olivia's location…" He brought up his map. "Orion, where is that third fragment due to hit?"

Orion leaned over his display, bringing up a map. A red circle marked the location in the Pacific Ocean. "Somewhere inside this circle."

"Overlay the ship's coordinates on that."

Onyx sent the coordinates to Orion's display. The ship was right on the edge of the red ring.

"What the hell?" Orion breathed.

H124 gulped. "What is it?" She hurried to peer over Orion's shoulder. She looked anxiously to Onyx. "When they hacked the blast deflection craft last time, didn't you say they could see everything? The orbits of the fragments, all the data you'd put together?"

Onyx nodded. "They got everything."

H124 stared back at the red dot, the ship, floating just outside the impact zone. "So they know they've sailed out to the spot where the fragment will hit."

Onyx looked perplexed. "They'd have to know."

"So they're out there to what, see it fall?"

"I can't begin to guess," Raven said.

H124 leaned over Orion. "When is the fragment due to hit?"

He checked his PRD. "Fifteen hours and four minutes."

"I have to get out there."

Rowan gripped her arm. "This is crazy. It's *suicide*. Even if you manage to save him from Olivia, there's still the impact, the air blast, the tsunamis. You'll be killed."

"I'm going," H124 resolved. "I have to." She turned away and headed out the door to the makeshift armory where they'd all piled their weapons after evacuating Sanctuary City.

Bootsteps followed her down the hall. She braced herself for further argument with Rowan. Instead Byron's voice called out, "So what's the plan?"

She smiled over her shoulder. "Get in. Get out."

"I like the complexity."

They jogged down to the weapons room.

She grabbed an energy rifle and a handheld sonic weapon, along with a grenade belt. She slung it over her shoulder, the second time she'd worn such explosives. The first had been when she and Astoria had parachuted into Delta City. "I sure would have liked to have Astoria with us on this." She thought of her friend, running toward the PPC soldiers, the brilliant explosion lighting up the night.

"Well, you've got me instead," he said, grabbing his Henry repeater, a Glock 9mm with a laser sighting, and a flash burster.

She cinched the grenade belt over her torso. "Thank you, Byron."

"Besides," he added, buckling on a holster. "This sounds like fun."

She shook her head with a smile. "You're crazy." She threw the energy rifle over her shoulder, draping her body with all the weapons she could carry. "Let's go."

As they left the armory, Raven appeared in the hallway. "Be careful. She may be anticipating a rescue."

H124 nodded. "Thanks, Raven."

Behind him, Rowan peered out from the room, but he didn't say anything.

She and Byron sprinted outside, where Gordon readied the Lockheed Vega. The rescue mission was under way.

Chapter 16

"Let's hope no one raided this place," Gordon said from the cockpit of the Vega.

H124 gazed down. A series of immense sandstone spires rose out of the desert floor. Sands blew in tan dunes around their bases. Long-dried-out river channels meandered across the barren land. As they descended, she marveled at the spires, her imagination transforming them into whimsical shapes. They looked like sentinels standing guard over this magical landscape.

The Vega touched down on a stretch of flat desert. Nearby, in the shadowed side of a red sandstone butte, a great cave mouth yawned.

"It's in there," Gordon said. "At least it was last year."

They piled out, Gordon taking the lead. H124 squinted in the glare of the bright desert sun, the heat punching her the moment she stepped out. The air hung heavy and dry, and she instantly grew parched. Reaching into her toolbag, she donned her goggles, then took a swig of water.

Gordon marched up a steep incline to the mouth of the cave, his boots leaving swirls of dust in his wake. She and Byron followed him up the precipitous rise. They were all panting by the time they reached the top, and had to stop twice along the way to drink water and catch their breath.

As they stepped into the cave, she welcomed the cool dark that enveloped her. Positioning her goggles on top of her head, she stopped, waiting for her eyes to adjust to the shadows. Gordon pulled out his multitool, turning on its small but powerful light. The focused beam penetrated the darkness. Eroded holes in the cave's ceiling let in shafts of light, and she marveled at the interior colors—deep reds, chocolate browns, and caramel curves, all weathered smooth in antiquity by water.

Gordon moved to the rear of the first large chamber and entered a side tunnel. H124 followed, having to bend over to navigate the narrow channel.

"This place is stunning," Byron said behind her, his voice echoing off the walls. Sunlight filtered up ahead. They emerged from the tunnel into a great sandstone cavern. A large hole in the roof allowed in another shaft of sunlight. In the middle of the chamber's floor stood a sleek black-and-red helicopter, far more streamlined than what Marlowe flew. A layer of dust coated it. Gordon hurried over, yanking out the red cloth that perpetually hung out of his back pocket and running it gently over the chopper's frame.

"It's still here," he breathed with relief.

"This thing's a beaut!" Byron told him, his voice resounding once more. H124 had to agree.

"How fast you say this baby can go?" Byron asked him.

"Almost 300 mph," Gordon told him proudly.

Byron looked up, beaming. "Wow."

On the far side of the cavern, in the gloom, H124 could make out a series of methane fuel holding tanks.

"Let's fill 'er up and go!" Gordon shouted, rubbing his hands together.

As Gordon climbed into the cockpit, H124 and Byron hefted the hoses over and fueled the helicopter. Gordon started it up, checking over the controls and engine status readout. Then he calculated the flight plan.

H124 and Byron boarded the helicopter. She stood in awe as she stepped through the door. It was very different from the other one she'd been in.

Where Marlowe's helicopter had room for at least six people to ride in the back, as well as open space to store cargo, this one was jammed with so many different glowing instruments, H124 was relieved she wasn't the one who had to fly it. Gordon sat nestled in the front in a cushioned black seat with straps, his fingers gliding over a plethora of controls, dials, and switches. She didn't know how he kept them all straight.

In the middle of the chopper was a similar seat, positioned in front of a control console. She leaned over it, reading the various switches. Buttons for missiles, forward, rear, and side guns, and a number of other weapon options glowed in the darkness. In the very rear were two jump seats that didn't look very comfortable.

"Does it still have all these armaments?" she asked Gordon.

"You bet it does," he replied eagerly.

The rotors beat overhead as they moved to their seats. H124 took the seat behind Gordon, as Byron piled their weapons onto one of the jump seats and strapped himself into the other.

They were airborne in moments, lifting deftly through the hole in the ceiling.

"Hold onto your hats and secure your valuables," Gordon said, and as soon as they cleared the aperture they shot forward, the engines roaring with startling fury. H124 fell back in her seat, held there by G-forces as they rocketed forward. They maneuvered around the sandstone spires, shooting across the desert like they'd been fired out of a cannon. She clenched her teeth.

"Woooo-hoooo!" Gordon whooped, and H124 grinned uncontrollably. "Hot damn!" he roared, and punched them even faster.

H124 managed a look back, where Byron was sinking into his seat, gripping the harness, and gritting his teeth. He caught her grin, and burnished one of his own.

Finally the acceleration evened out to a constant speed, and she peeled herself away from the seat. Looking out the windows, she watched the sandstone terrain speed by.

As they passed over a wide desert, H124 wondered how close they were to the radar facility they'd visited to image the incoming asteroid and its fragments. The land rose abruptly as they raced over a valley between foothills and the coastal mountains. Dead urban sprawl, swallowed by drought and sand, spread out as far as she could see: old roads, dead power plants, highways littered with rusted cars. They raced over the coastal mountains, and the seashore came into view, black and stained from oil spills, flotsam and jetsam piled up along the dirty beaches. They screamed past it. In seconds they were out over the open ocean, the deep blue churning below them, whitecaps dancing on its surface.

For a long time she observed the vast ocean blue, staggered by its sheer immensity. Soon it was all that occupied her sight. She tried not to imagine the helicopter going down, leaving them to scramble among pieces of sinking debris as those depths claimed them.

After some time, the ocean took on a strange appearance in the distance. No longer deep blue, it appeared mottled grey and white. She withdrew her diginocs, zeroing in on the surface. Instead of flowing waves, her eyes fell on trillions of floating pieces of trash.

She saw undulating rafts of plastic bottles, crates, floating fishing nets, pieces of broken-down garbage she couldn't distinguish. "What is all that?"

Gordon peered down. "That, my dear, is the Great Pacific Garbage Patch."

She wrinkled her brow. "Garbage? In the middle of the ocean?"

"Yep. It's home to trillions of pieces of plastic, big and small. Because of converging currents, it all collects here in the Pacific, just one huge gyre of floating garbage."

"That's insane!"

"And it's huge. More than a million square miles, and it's estimated to weigh a hundred and sixty million pounds."

H124's jaw fell open. "What?"

"It's been collecting here for who knows how long. People throw stuff away, it ends up in the water, and floats out here."

She studied it with the diginocs, spotting tangled fishing nets, industrial trash, and pieces of plastic boat hulls. "You have got to check this out," she said to Byron.

He unbuckled and came forward, taking the nocs and gazing out. "Holy hell."

"I heard a long time ago there were plans to clean it up, but they had too little funding to make much of a dent," Gordon told them.

"There's something else out there," Byron said as they drew closer to the PPC ship coordinates. "Floating on the plastic."

"Like what?"

He handed her back the nocs and pointed. "What do you make of that?"

She followed his finger and trained the nocs there. He was right. Something *was* floating on top of all the garbage. She zoomed in, the image resolving into a series of rusted hoverboats, all tied together against a floating structure with makeshift walls. Fires burned in barrels placed regularly around the mass of trash. Whatever this place was, it wasn't abandoned debris. It looked occupied. She scanned the area, discerning more boats and other structures. Tall spikes adorned the corners of the buildings, objects with streamers mounted at the top. The streamers glistened in the sun, white and red. She zoomed in further still, and a lump caught in her throat.

They weren't streamers. They weren't pendants. They were human heads, mounted on spikes, bone exposed and long, bloody hair flailing out behind them on the ocean breeze.

Just then a hulking man strolled out of one of the floating buildings. He wore a jacket with twin epaulettes on his shoulder. She zoomed in to see that the epaulettes were made of human skull caps, with strings of dried meat hanging down from the jaws. The teeth cupped his shoulders, while above, empty black eye sockets stared out.

She lowered the diginocs. "It's a floating Death Rider city."

Gordon's hand trembled on the flight stick. "What?" He pulled out his own diginocs, studying the throng of rafts and rusty boats tied together in the garbage. "Do you think…" He blinked in the brightness. "Do you think they have ranged weapons? As soon as they hear this engine…"

Through the diginocs, she watched as the man with the skull epaulettes spoke to a group of Death Riders, who scurried off after he pointed out to sea and barked orders. She didn't think he'd spotted them yet.

She followed in the direction he was pointing, and at first she couldn't make out where his attention was focused. Then she zoomed in on another part of the garbage gyre out in the distance. A massive ship cut through the dense layer of trash, plowing through the decaying carcasses of a past civilization. Before its bow churned a mass of old tangled fishing nets and chunks of unrecognizable sun-bleached plastic debris. She zoomed in and sucked in a breath. The luxury ship came into sharp focus, towering twenty stories over the water, multiple decks with sparkling swimming pools and an outside dance floor of coveted rare wood. Lettering on the side read, *"The Morning Star."*

"I see the ship. It's humongous," she told the others.

"Do you see Willoughby?" Gordon asked.

She scanned the people on board, but they were too far away to make out details. "I'm not sure. We need to get closer."

Gordon slowed the helicopter and hovered. "If we get any closer, those Death Riders will hear the engine. And if they *do* have ranged weapons…"

She pointed the diginocs to the water directly beneath them, wondering if they could walk on the garbage. The Death Riders had built an entire floating city on it. The layer was thick, a mass of gyrating trash.

"Do you think we could—" Her words were cut short as a deafening boom sliced through the air. She stared down to see a massive gun mounted on one of the floating platforms. It swiveled in their direction. Its huge barrel jutted out over the waves, a large white cylinder mounted above it.

"Is that a CIWS?" Gordon cried, banking violently. He pronounced it like "sea-whiz." H124 to cling to the armrest as they dipped sickeningly to the right.

She saw the barrel spin, plumes of smoke and ammo blasting from the gun. But the shots went wide. "I think it's safe to say they noticed us!" Gordon shouted.

As he banked away, she trained the diginocs on the man with the epaulettes again. He pointed at the helicopter, shouting orders at one set of Death Riders while commanding another contingent toward the PPC ship. Five Death Riders ran to one of the moored hoverboats and leapt in, casting off.

Water plowed up behind them as they roared toward the PPC ship.

She scanned back to the commander, diginocs falling on the CIWS, which was pivoting and aiming, readying to fire again. She swept over the floating mess of trash, spotting another group of hoverboats to the far right, on the outer edge of the floating city. She pointed them out to Gordon. "Do you think you can drop us off over there?"

He gazed down. "It'll be close."

"We'll take it."

Dipping the helicopter's nose down, he raced for the hoverboats, which bobbed abandoned on the waves. All the attention was in another part of the city, with Death Riders either rushing toward the PPC ship or feeding more ammo into the CIWS. The barrel swung in their direction.

H124 took off her headset and unbuckled her safety belt, stepping around her seat to the back of the helicopter. Byron unlatched his safety belt as well, handing weapons to her and slinging his own over his chest. She grabbed her toolbag and slid the door open.

As Gordon dipped low, she saw that a group of Death Riders were already racing across the trash, trying to head them off before they reached the boats.

Gordon screamed down, pulling up just a few feet above the water. She leapt down, landing hard in one of the boats. It sloshed chaotically in the water. Byron jumped next, landing beside her. The boat threatened to tip as they tried to steady themselves, but it remained upright. Byron whipped out a tangle of wires from the ignition as another pounding clatter erupted from the spinning barrel of the CIWS. Gordon banked away, the rounds narrowly missing the helicopter. He sped away, engines roaring.

Byron twisted the wires together. "Damn, this is old tech. Wish Dirk were here." The wires sparked in his hands as she heard the lift fan whir to life.

The Death Riders closed in, only a hundred feet away now, drawing their guns. Her heart thudded at the sight of an AK-47 aimed at her head. She reflexively gripped Byron's shoulders as he moved to the controls. "We're off!" he cried, opening up the throttle. They shot forward, bouncing off the waves. She almost flew off the boat. She wrapped her arms tighter around Byron, looking back over her shoulder. The Death Riders piled into boats and took off, but the ocean's undulation kept them from aiming properly. A round whizzed past, hissing into the water.

Gordon shot into the distance, well out of range of the CIWS.

Swinging the hoverboat around the edge of the floating city, Byron raced for the PPC ship. Another round clanged into the fan behind them. H124 flinched. Byron careened the boat to the left, zigzagging to throw off their pursuers' aim. Still the Death Riders closed in, and a round struck the deck only a foot from H124. Waves sprayed up behind them, hailing down tiny pieces of microplastic. She gripped Byron's shoulders as he sped around a mesh of tangled junk. She didn't see how they were going to lose them.

She startled as the pursuing boat erupted in flames. The Death Riders screamed as fire consumed them. One managed to dive over the side. His lifeless body bobbed back up to the surface, facedown. The thudding of a helicopter rotor brought her eyes up as Gordon raced by overhead, the port missile bay smoking.

Byron punched the air as Gordon banked away. He steered the hoverboat for a direct intercept course with the PPC ship. Already the Death Rider hoverboats had reached the luxury ship, throwing grappling hooks up over the rails to board it.

PPC troopers emerged from the bowels of the ship, wheeling out a sonic gun. More soldiers loosed their energy rifles upon the attacking Death Riders, who fell over the sides and back into the ocean, struggling in the soup of garbage.

The sonic gun fired at an oncoming Death Rider hoverboat, and the attackers dropped instantly, some slumping down into the waves, others collapsing onto the deck. She and Byron had to steer clear of the sonic gun.

He wheeled the hoverboat around to the back of the ship, skirting past two Death Rider boats. In the chaos, the marauders didn't notice that H124 and Byron weren't of their ilk, so they sped by undetected.

Byron slowed the craft at the bow, next to an emergency ladder leading down the side of the ship. "We can climb up there!"

He pulled up next to it and cut the engine. Grabbing a tattered rope from the back of the craft, he tethered the boat to the ladder. Then H124 grabbed the rusted metal and started to climb, the rungs cold and slippery in her hands. Her boots slipped, but she regained her footing and continued upward. Beneath her, Byron stepped out of the boat and followed.

The sides of the ship flared out near the top, making the climb more difficult, and in the last stretch, her feet swung free as she pulled herself up with just her arms. At last she reached the bottom deck of the ship and grasped a railing. As she pulled herself up, a sudden pain flared in her fingers: a PPC trooper had slammed his boot down on her hand. She reached behind her, slinging the rifle off her back, and shot him at close range. He flew back, jittering from the electric jolt. Two more soldiers closed in, and she shot them too, then crested the railing.

Chaos reigned on deck. PPC troopers dressed in black held their positions behind pillars as Death Riders streamed over the railings. Smoke drifted over the deck, the biting smell of cordite from the Death Riders' guns palpable in the wind. PPC execs escaped to the upper decks, while some were gunned down on the stairwells. A Death Rider with a bone breastplate reached an elevator just as five execs tried to pile into it. He mowed them all down, their blood spraying the walls of the lift. H124 scanned the maelstrom for any sign of Willoughby, but the noise and smoke overwhelmed her senses as dozens of PPC execs fled the area and Death Riders swarmed the blood-soaked deck.

Byron appeared over the railing. "How the hell are we going to find Willoughby in this?"

And then she saw him, two decks up, kneeling before the railing, hands bound behind his back. Two Repurposers stood over him. "There!"

Chapter 17

"I see him," Byron told H124.

The nearest stairwell stood twenty feet away, across a deck slick with blood. She rose and raced toward it, unslinging the rifle from her back. She tore up the stairs, whipped around the landing, and started to climb the next set to the third level. She crouched, ascending quietly, peeking her head above the staircase. Between her and Willoughby lay the dead bodies of three PPC soldiers and a Death Rider, his face melted, distorted by a lethal blast from an energy rifle.

The two Repurposers didn't see her. They simply stared at a fixed location to her left and out of sight, their black eyes beady and cruel.

"Bring him in here!" cried a familiar voice. "We still need him as a bargaining chip."

H124 froze. Olivia. She must be just inside one of the cabin doors.

The two Repurposers grabbed Willoughby roughly under the arms and dragged him toward Olivia's voice. H124 inhaled at the sight of Willoughby's face. He'd been beaten so severely that both eyes were swollen shut, his handsome face a mass of bruises, his cheekbones crushed. Hands and feet bound in chains, he dripped blood and sweat onto the deck as they heaved him along.

She was about to leap forward when Byron gripped her arm. She gave him a backwards glance. He motioned a ring with his hand. "We don't know if she has troopers with her," he whispered. "I'll circle around. Let's meet in the middle." She nodded, and Byron skirted back down the stairs. She watched him round the corner, springing for the stairs on the other side.

She heard a door close above her and had crept back out of sight when a Death Rider bounded up the stairs to her rear. She turned and fired the rifle at his chest, sending him sprawling back onto the deck. From her perch, she had only a limited view of the bottom of the stairs. Another Death Rider came into sight, glancing down at his fallen companion before aiming the barrel of an AK-47 up the staircase. She sent another lethal blast coursing through his body. The man collapsed, jittering on the floor. Above, she heard boots slapping the deck. She dared a glance out of the stairwell to see twenty PPC troopers marching toward her. At the bottom, two more Death Riders appeared. Soon she'd be trapped between them.

Grabbing the railing, she swung herself up the rest of the stairs and darted around the bannister, fleeing from the advancing soldiers. The lead trooper spotted her, raising his weapon. She flung herself flat on the ground, bringing her rifle around, but before she could fire, the trooper's chest exploded like a volcano. A Death Rider crested the stairs, holding a smoking sawed-off shotgun. Painted in blood, with black teeth filed to a point, he screamed in delight as he unloaded another round into the next trooper's face. The PPC phalanx fell out of formation, its troopers scattering as a stream of Death Riders emerged from the staircase, blasting away.

H124's ears rang. She ran along the deck. To her right stood the interior of the ship, posh etched glass and wooden walls. Inside she spied a fancy dining area and a large ballroom with entertainment monitors lining the walls.

Holding a position within, at least a dozen advancing troopers headed toward the stern of the ship. She spotted Olivia standing in the middle of them, using them as a protective barrier. At the rear, dragged by the two Repurposers, Willoughby scraped across the floor.

H124 sped along the exterior wall, taking cover when she passed by windows. Rounding the corner at the stern, she nearly collided with Byron. She grabbed his arm, glad to see he'd made it around without more than a fresh cut on his forehead. "Looks clear on that side," he said. "Did you see all the troopers in there?"

She nodded.

Together they advanced to the nearest door, an ingress of swinging wood and glass that admitted them into the interior of the ship, just a few rooms away from Olivia's troops.

H124 glanced down at her PRD. Just sixty-six minutes until the asteroid fragment would hit.

She and Byron passed through a small food preparation area, then to another room that sported an extravagant bar made entirely of intricately etched mirrors. Bottles with amber and silver liquid sparkled beneath the recessed lighting.

At the next door they paused. Byron opened the door a crack and peered in. "This is it," he whispered. "I count twenty-four troopers guarding her, plus the two Repurposers." He gasped and quickly shut the door. "Oh, no."

"What is it?"

"Company."

Rifle and shotgun blasts erupted on the other side of the door.

H124 stood up and looked through the window. Death Riders from the stairwell poured in through the door. Muzzle flashes blinded her. The PPC troopers fired their energy weapons, felling a handful of Death Riders, but the PPC were greatly outnumbered.

Olivia vanished through a door on the far side of the room with a contingent of soldiers. She gestured for the Repurposers to follow, hauling Willoughby in tow.

This was H124's chance. Olivia and the troopers were distracted. H124 kicked the door in and stayed low, moving against the wall to stay out of sight. Amid the roar of gunfire, the Repurposers carrying Willoughby didn't hear her approach. She brought her rifle around to shoot them, but a trooper checked their six, spotting her. She dove as he fired. The Repurposers spun. One wheeled around and kicked the rifle from her hands, but not before she managed to squeeze off a shot. It hit him in the leg, and his electrified body keeled over. Her rifle skittered across the floor, toward the struggle in the center of the room.

Olivia's guards surged forward. Byron rolled and fired, reaching a table. Flipping it up, he made a shield, popping up and firing, holding them at bay.

The second Repurposer strode toward H124, removing a flash burster from his long black coat. A shotgun blast splintered the chair and table next to her, hurling shards of metal and wood in every direction. She backed up, scrambling for a weapon. Her hand fell on the metal leg of the destroyed chair. She clenched it firmly, this singular object that stood between life and death. Just as the Repurposer got a bead on her with his flash burster, she thrust the chair leg into his stomach, driving it upward. A foul stench blossomed. She let go of the metal as a thick, black ooze seeped out of the Repurposer's body, creeping down his leg and onto the floor. He slumped down, his black eyes somehow even emptier.

The Death Rider with the sawed-off shotgun appeared nearby, a look of unbridled glee on his face, his mouth filled with blood. Then his grinning, painted face melted like wax as a PPC trooper hit him with a lethal blast from an energy rifle. She could hear Olivia barking orders in the next room. "Get up to the security floor! What are you doing! Bring Willoughby!"

The gored Repurposer groaned on the floor, breathing his last. The Death Riders rushed the retinue of soldiers, pressing H124 into the throng. An elbow slammed into her shoulder, driving her to her knees. She pushed through the tangle of legs, spotting Willoughby just feet away. He lay on the floor in a fetal position, trampled underfoot in the clamor. Despite the odds she reached him, closing her hands around his shoulders. She shoved her foes out of the way, helpless as boots stomped them indiscriminately. Pulling him backward, she slid across the slippery floor, blood soaking her clothes. The chains binding Willoughby's hands and feet made it an impossible chore.

Then Byron was beside her, shoving away the crowd. A shotgun went off inches from her face, deafening her world. Byron grabbed the chain between Willoughby's feet as she cinched the links between his hands, and together they scrambled to their feet, lifting him between them. With her free hand she aimed her rifle on three Death Riders who burst through the rear door. She released a stream of electric fire, sending them skittering to the floor.

Willoughby soon proved too heavy to carry with one hand. She slung the rifle around her back and grabbed the chain with both hands, hauling him through the bar, then the small kitchen, where they burst outside into a world of smoke and fire. The deck below had ignited, spitting red and orange embers into the smoldering sky. As the auto-fire suppression systems rained a foul-smelling, puffy white substance over the deck, she slipped, struggling to keep hold of her father. He lagged in his chains, drifting in and out of consciousness. Bound as he was, there was no way he was going to walk on his own. And they couldn't carry him any longer.

She directed Byron to a recessed doorway. They dragged Willoughby inside.

Troopers clashed with Death Riders just beyond the entryway. She saw the man with the human skull epaulettes, thrusting his finger into the air, directing his fighters toward the upper floors. "Seize the helm!" he shouted. She spotted a small craft on the top deck, glistening in the sunlight, resembling a tiny PPC airship that probably couldn't hold more than a few passengers.

To her right, a group of troopers attempted to set up another sonic gun, until the Death Riders swarmed over them.

She drew her pocket pyro and ignited it. Byron did the same, and they went to work cutting through Willoughby's chains. The bindings sloughed to the floor.

Then came the unmistakable sound of a fifty-caliber gun cracking off a series of shots. The troopers by the sonic gun erupted in a crimson mist, heads flung back, mowed down in an arc of bullets, their mounted gun tearing and shredding as if it were aluminum.

Willoughby mumbled something incoherent. She bent down, coaxing him to sit up. He groaned as he cradled his head.

"Can you run?" she asked him.

He let out a soft laugh, running his tongue over the open cut on his lip. "I can damn well try."

She peered out. The deck to their left was clear, where just a handful of bodies were strewn about a growing pool of blood. To their right was the Death Rider with the epaulettes, sprinting up the stairs toward the helm.

They hurried to the nearest railing as H124 pulled a rope out of her toolbag. Below them the ubiquitous trash sloshed on the swelling waves, bobbing along the empty hoverboats. She tied a makeshift harness around Willoughby's hips and torso and directed him over the railing, lowering him down to one of the boats with Byron's help. The second he touched down, she vaulted over the rail, taking hold of the rope, and descended quickly, Byron following suit.

Once on board, Byron struggled with the ignition wires, and she whipped the rope free from the railing.

The engine roared to life. As Byron swung away from the ship, she could see Olivia surrounded by Death Riders on the fourth deck, the man with the skull epaulettes approaching her. She held out her hands, not in a pleading way, but as if she still had all the power and was merely negotiating. She pointed up, in the direction of the asteroid that would soon hit.

The man crossed his arms, listening.

H124 checked her PRD. Thirty-five minutes until impact. She brought up the comm window and called Gordon. His face appeared, grim in the cockpit of the helicopter. "We're ready," she told him.

"That CIWS is not making things easy," he said. "The helicopter's been hit, but I don't know how bad it is yet. How far away can you get from that thing?"

They sped around the side of the ship, the lift fan behind them roaring so loudly she could barely hear him. She spotted the platform with the CIWS, its rapid-fire system swiveling and following the path of the helicopter.

"Take us in the opposite direction from that!" she shouted to Byron above the din, pointing to the weapon.

He nodded and wheeled the boat around, speeding away from the ship. Willoughby groaned. He collapsed in the bottom of the boat, the blood seeping from a wound in his side.

She held on to him as they bounced along the waves. She heard the dull beating of the helicopter's rotor and looked up to see Gordon approaching from the right, angling away from the ship to pick them up. About four miles out, Gordon's path converged with theirs, and he began to lower over them. A ladder unfurled from the open door, dropping right into the boat.

She tugged on Willoughby, forcing him to stand. "You have to climb! I'll be right behind you!"

He looked up, his vision reduced to a tiny crack over one of his swollen eyelids. She steered his bloody hands to the rungs, helping him climb the first steps. She got on behind him, guiding him up. He winced through the pain, until at last they reached the helicopter. Byron scrambled inside after them.

"All in?" Gordon asked.

"Yes!" she called.

Gordon reeled in the ladder, then hit the control to shut the helicopter door. The ensuing quiet made H124 feel safer already. The skilled pilot banked away, heading east toward the mainland, reaching maximum speed. The inertia slammed them back, once more sinking them into their seats. When the speed maxed out, she helped Willoughby to the back of the helicopter, where they managed to lay him out.

Once he was more safely positioned, they buckled themselves into their seats.

She checked the impact time. Twenty-four minutes.

According to the data Orion had loaded into her PRD, they had to get at least two hundred miles away or the air blast could down them and blow out the windows of the chopper. This was going to be too close.

She stared out of the window anxiously, watching the ocean speed by below. In time the white and grey of the Great Pacific Garbage Patch gave way to the more beautiful, familiar sapphire.

Seventeen minutes until impact.

The sea stretched on and on. She had no sense of how much ground they were covering unless she looked at her PRD display. The engine whined as Gordon pushed the helicopter to its limit. No one spoke.

Seven minutes till impact.

They watched in silence, gripping their seats. Willoughby groaned from the back of the helicopter.

She checked her PRD. Thirty seconds to impact. On her display, the animated fragment impacted with the sea's surface. "It's hit," she said. She ran a calculation on Orion's program, entering their current location from the impact site. "Air blast will hit us in about sixteen minutes."

She braced herself as Gordon sped on, recalling the air blast that had almost downed the plane when they'd escaped with the first piece of the blast deflection craft.

Byron reached around the back of her seat and squeezed her shoulder. She placed her hand on his. They interlaced their fingers as she shut her eyes and leaned back in the seat.

And then the air blast hit them. The tail of the helicopter lurched up violently, and they fell into a nosedive, Gordon fighting desperately for control as they went into a tailspin. The windows shuddered, just barely staying intact. As they spun downward, H124 squeezed her eyes shut to block out the view of the ocean rushing up to meet them. Byron fell back into his seat, and Willoughby cried out in terror.

Gordon managed to wrest control of the helicopter. He halted the spin, lifting them back up in the very last instant, just feet above the water. Straightening them out, he rocketed away to the east.

H124 let out a gasp of relief.

Byron hugged her around the back of her seat.

"Way to go!" she called to Gordon, who looked over his shoulder, visibly shaken but smiling that familiar smile.

She thought of the small airship she'd seen on *The Morning Star,* and wondered if anyone had reached it in time. Maybe Olivia had used it to escape. If not, she wondered what Olivia's final moments must have been like, imagining the monstrous tidal wave that would have inundated the ship, drowning the floating Death Rider city. She wondered what the asteroid fragment had looked like, streaming down in a trail of fire, breaking up in the atmosphere.

But mostly she wondered what Olivia's last thought had been. Whatever it was, it likely been cold, cruel, and calculating.

Chapter 18

Gordon touched down outside Rivet's hangar at the satellite site. Carrying Willoughby between them, H124 and Byron struggled off the helicopter. Felix, the Rover doctor, was waiting with a maglev stretcher, its copters already whirring away and ready to rush Willoughby to a medpod.

As they eased him onto the stretcher, Willoughby gripped her hand. "You were crazy to come after me." He winced as he talked, clutching his ribs. "But thank you."

"Of course. I wouldn't have left you like that."

His grip on her hand loosened as Felix commanded the maglev to follow him to a medpod. H124 watched him go.

"He'll be okay now," Byron reassured her, placing a warm hand on her shoulder. "He's in good hands."

Then Rowan rounded the corner of the hangar, running up to her. "You're safe!" He pulled her into an embrace. "I feel terrible about how we left things." He pulled away and met her eyes. "I'm so sorry for what I said. Of course you had to go after him. I only meant…"

"I know what you meant," she told him. And she did. The needs of the many *did* outweigh the needs of the few, and she wouldn't have asked anyone to risk their own lives to help her save him.

She was just thinking of how grateful she was for Gordon and Byron when Rowan leaned in closer and kissed her. She was taken aback slightly, but was hit by his familiar scent, remembered the prickling of the fresh stubble on his face.

The kiss was over as quickly as it began, leaving her unsure how to react. She noticed Byron was no longer there. She saw him making his way toward Rivet's building. He looked over his shoulder, giving her a resigned smile and a wave. She turned back to Rowan. He had saved her life in New Atlantic, been the first person to express affection for her, the first to awaken these strange new sensations.

But what had Byron said to her in Basin City? *"You've fought by my side. My pulse races at the sight of you."* He had been the one to risk everything to help her, and more than once. He'd infiltrated Delta City with her to find the piece of blast deflection craft. Fought to save her from the Repurposers. Saved her from the night stalkers in Basin City at the jeopardy of his own life. And just now he'd risked everything to help her save Willoughby.

It was Byron.

It had to be Byron. Her heart thudded at the thought of him. Her eyes were alight at the sight of him.

"I'm sorry," she said to Rowan, and turned away. She had to clear her thoughts. All of this was so new, so confusing. All of these people had been around others for their whole lives. They knew how to act, knew what was normal and what wasn't. How you went about things. But H124 had no such luxury. She could only trust her heart, which lay with the one for whom it beat.

Behind her, Gordon was preoccupied with his post-flight check on the helicopter, so she made her way into the complex through one of the cool, shadowed tunnels, her footsteps echoing off the walls. Everyone was busy elsewhere in the compound, and the place felt strangely deserted.

She sensed someone approaching in the shadows. Byron. He stopped in front of her. She halted, watching him. He spoke no words, but his eyes sparked at the sight of her. She felt a magnetic pull, a flame erupting in her core. She'd never felt such a powerful attraction to someone. A primal sensation swept over her, every nerve in her body suddenly alert and full of desire.

She was rooted to the spot, grappling with what she felt. She didn't know what was right, what was expected.

What was she to Rowan? What was he to her? She'd met him first. He'd been the first person to ever kiss her. With him, it felt different, more companionship than fire.

But this pull to Byron felt insurmountable. His eyes flashed in the darkness, and their flames were so close they touched.

Then something in her broke free. She leaned toward him. He grabbed her, and they crashed into the corridor wall. His hands roamed over her body, caressing her in ways she'd never felt before.

Their tongues met, and together they rocked back and forth, hips grinding. Then he pulled back and met her eyes, and her lips burned in longing. She tore off his green canvas jacket, casting it to the floor. Her hands roamed over his muscled chest, his flat stomach, reveling in the feel of his body. He pulled her down the corridor, into his sleeping chamber. He threw her down on the bed, stripping off her shirt, and within her she felt a surging tide.

She growled, kissing him deeply. He kissed her back, lowering his weight upon her, hips moving rhythmically against hers. She felt dizzy, dreamy. "I want you," he breathed into her ear. "I've wanted you for so long."

"I want you, Byron," she whispered back, lips tingling. Her whole being was alive, rippling with currents. She grabbed his back and shoulders.

"Halo," he breathed into her neck. "Halo."

"Byron," she whispered.

They came together, ablaze and abandoned.

* * * *

Later, feeling strangely rejuvenated, H124 went to her quarters. She freshened up, then walked to the mess hall to eat. Dirk was sitting by himself. She debated joining him. He stared out of the window, eyes hollow, jaw slack. She selected a meal of salad and nuts, then decided to sit by him. He stirred as she stood over the seat.

"Can I join you?"

He blinked, the rims around his eyes red and raw. "Of course."

She ate the first few bites in silence, not sure what to say. "How are you holding up?" she finally asked, lamely.

He leaned back in his chair. "Barely. Glad you got to Willoughby, though."

"Me, too." She ate a few more bites. "Are you thinking about Astoria? You can talk to me." She felt bad for even saying it. Even though she didn't see how she could have prevented Astoria's death, she still felt like she didn't have the right to talk about it to Dirk.

"I don't even know what I'd say," he told her. "I still can't quite believe it. I always thought if she died that I'd feel…lost somehow. I don't know… empty, like half of me had been torn away. But I don't…it's like she's still here inside of me, like I'm carrying her around *here*." He brought a fist to his chest. He talked more about their childhood and happier times. H124 was amazed by his stories of a cheerful, carefree Astoria. She couldn't even imagine that.

After dinner, she stopped by the medical office. Willoughby was out of the medpod, sitting on the edge of a bed, consuming an MRE. Though parts of his face were still a bit swollen, his crushed cheekbones had been repaired, as had the gash in his side. Other than his unkempt hair and Rover clothing, he looked like his regular self.

He smiled as she entered. "Perfect timing. I'm going stir crazy. Let's go for a walk."

"Sure you're up for it?"

Willoughby stood up, talking around the last bite of the MRE. "Absolutely." They walked into the hall in silence, Willoughby wincing only slightly. "What's the next step?" he asked.

"We go to a genebank to the south. Make sure it's intact."

"I want to come," he said. "Tired of feeling useless."

"You're hardly useless."

As they continued down the hall, Onyx stopped them. "You're not going to believe this, H."

"What is it?" H124 asked.

"We just got this feed coming out of Delta City." Onyx brought up her display, the images floating in the shadowed corridor. It showed Olivia standing aboard the intact PPC luxury ship, before the Death Riders had attacked and the fragment had fallen.

Olivia's face resolved into a mien H124 had never seen—caring, compassionate, and one hundred percent fake. "I'm out here risking my life to show you good people of Delta City why you can't listen to the anarchists that threaten to tear our fine city apart. This asteroid they keep warning you about will fall nowhere near Delta City, yet I'm jeopardizing my very existence today to show you the truth. Our specialized science teams have pored over the data and found that the asteroid will land far out here, in the vast ocean. It's harmless."

H124 stared up at Onyx. *"Our specialized science teams?"*

Onyx rolled her eyes. "I know. Complete bullshit."

The footage cut to the sky, panning up to show the incoming asteroid, searingly bright, a trail of fire and smoke streaking off as parts of it broke up in the atmosphere. It was so massive that it appeared to be falling in slow motion, drawing inexorably downward. The camera followed it down to the surface of the sea, cutting away just before it hit.

"It's about to touch down," Olivia informed the audience, though this section of footage had obviously been shot long before the impact, and most certainly before the arrival of the Death Riders. It cut back to the sea, and with a clever addition of some visual effects, showed a bright light vanishing beyond the horizon. The footage now jumped to an over-the-railing shot of the waves, revealing the sea as it rolled in, lapping gently against the ship's hull. "It's hit now," Olivia lied, "and you can see how little damage it caused." From the look of it, this footage had been shot before they'd even reached the Great Pacific Garbage Patch. "I repeat, there is nothing to fear. Go back to your regularly scheduled programming, and enjoy the new series of treats we've cooked up just for you!"

Onyx made a disgusted sound, and switched off the display. "And Delta City's back to normal. They stuck up a bunch of new simulated reality shows as inane as ever. Rowan says some people are still fleeing, but it's down to a trickle now. Even the execs have been fooled by her, and they too are staying behind."

"And where is she?" H124 asked. "Did she survive?"

"We don't know."

Uneasy, she and Willoughby left Onyx. They returned outside, walking for a bit, then joined Raven and the others to prepare for the upcoming trip to the next genebank. They packed warm snowsuits and snow goggles, and checked over their weapons and maglevs. Then she turned in for the night.

* * * *

H124 awoke to Raven prodding her arm. "Onyx found the leak. How Olivia's been listening in. And she has news. Come meet us in Rivet's lab."

As Raven left the room, H124 rolled over, still groggy, and forced herself to get up. She dressed quickly, cleaned her teeth, then headed over to meet the others. When she entered Rivet's lab, she found Raven and Onyx gathered around a worktable with Rowan and Byron. When she locked eyes with the latter, she couldn't fight the smile that worked its way to her lips. He returned it with an intense gaze. Willoughby stood off to one side, leaning against the wall, while Dirk slumped on a work stool, exhausted.

"I found the leak," Onyx told them all. "It was a line of code. When Astoria allowed Olivia access, the code got deeply embedded. I went through the access program line by line, eliminating everything, and still didn't spot it until last night. All our info has been channeling to Olivia's direct line, not to the PPC in general.

"But I've fixed it. Reversed it, actually, piggybacking off it. She'll think she's still listening in, but now we only feed her what we want her to hear. And as she's listening, we're hacked into her system, able to overhear her now." Onyx looked around the room. "Now we're the ones listening, and she's none the wiser."

H124 couldn't help but notice Onyx's use of the present tense. "So did she make it to that little airship before the fragment hit?"

"I'm not sure about that yet. But I did find this on her personal feed." Onyx brought up the display and clicked on a video.

Olivia's smug face came into view. She smoothed down her immaculately tailored scarlet suit and smiled her cheerless sneer. "After seeing images of New Atlantic's destruction, some of you are convinced that the same thing is going to happen to Delta City. I'm here to show you that this is an absolute fabrication. I've come out to this location," she went on, the wind whipping her normally perfect hair in wild tangents, "to film the last piece of the asteroid falling thousands of miles away from Delta City."

It was an alternate take of the video now streaming in Delta City. The footage continued through random, unedited cuts. Now Olivia was nowhere in sight. Instead, the scene showed the ship in ruins after the battle with the Death Riders. Battered soldiers lay on the deck, and a few straggling PPC executives stared up in horror. The camera panned up to the sky, where a cluster of downward-thrusting clouds were so brilliantly lit that H124 had to squint. This was no visual effect. The fragment wasn't even near impact when a violent airburst hit the camera. She saw the whole ship tilt, the windows shattering, people screaming for their lives. One exec slid down the deck, suit on fire. The camera fell and skittered across the deck. She caught the briefest glimpse of the Death Riders and PPC execs grabbing the railings and crying out, their garments erupting in flame.

The image grew brighter and brighter, and a series of explosions blew out the camera's microphone as the fragment broke up. On the camera's sideways image, she witnessed the PPC execs and Death Riders scrambling to get through the doors as a secondary explosion rocked the deck. The ship tilted unnaturally and the camera slid, plunging off the side of the boat and splashing into the sea. The camera's descent stopped suddenly as it became suspended on a raft of plastic. Tilted on its side, the lens depicted a scene of watery chaos. The ship capsized, the PPC execs and troopers doing all they could to cling to the railings as it sank in the mire of garbage.

The camera shook violently, and was abruptly launched into the sky, along with chunks of seawater and reams of garbage. Something struck the lens, and the camera went black.

"Why would she go out there? Why not fake the whole thing?"

Willoughby regarded her. "She probably thought if she *could* get footage of it hitting, it would be a milestone for ratings. She probably didn't realize how devastating the impact would be in the water."

"Obviously it backfired on her," Raven said.

"So she really thought she could convince people that the asteroid fell in a different place?" H124 asked.

"She was probably hoping people would stay in Delta City," Willoughby added. "She'd get the A14 and launch the blast deflection craft, and she could keep her little domain intact and maintain her rule."

H124 shuttled the footage back to the beginning and watched it again. "I wonder if there were any survivors."

"Let's hope not," Byron said.

Onyx lowered the display. "Seems like a huge risk to take. I would have just fudged some visual effects."

Willoughby touched his temple as the truth dawned on him. "Wait… she didn't just want to convince the *citizens* it was fake. She wanted her fellow execs to believe it. They wouldn't be fooled by special effects. But Olivia knew the impact wouldn't be harmless. By bringing them out there to film it, *telling* them it would be harmless, she sealed their fate. That must be why she had the personal airship. She had her own escape plan, but probably told them they were far enough from danger. Then she'd be able to get out of there scot-free, and all the competing execs would die." He shook his head. "Insidious."

H124 couldn't believe she and this woman shared the same blood.

Rowan leaned on the table. "I'm going back to Delta City and the surrounding Badlander camps. We've located an ancient bomb shelter to the east that can hold far more people than we thought possible." He brought up his PRD display, revealing the shelter's interior. "It's called Greenbrier. It was meant to shelter politicians, heads of state. For a while they turned it into a museum. Then they put it to use again, expanding it even more. It's got everything." The images showed kitchens, movie theaters, bowling alleys, recreation rooms, sleeping facilities, fancy dining rooms. "I'm going to try to move as many people there as I can. Chadwick and I are also going to restart the pirate broadcasts. He's built another mobile transmitter." H124 remembered the Silver Beast, the transmitter that moved like a living creature, able to cut into feeds inside Delta City and disrupt broadcasts. Its creator, Chadwick, had helped them infiltrate Delta City.

Raven consulted his PRD. "We've got six and a half days until impact, and one more genebank to visit. It's the farthest one yet, in Antarctica."

He brought up a map, rotating the globe so they could see the underside of the earth. "Here. The southernmost continent."

The mere sight of the exotic location stirred her. And now she saw why they needed snowsuits.

"We don't know what condition we're going to find it in, so we're bringing supplies in case we need to repair damage. It'll be our last stop before we all seek final shelter. Then comes the impact."

H124 looked to Rowan. "Will we be joining you in Greenbrier?"

He nodded. "I hope so."

The meeting soon dissolved, and H124 helped load the *Argo* with supplies in preparation for departure. She was carrying some long-range rifles out of the armory when Onyx called to her from down the hall.

She turned. Onyx hurried to catch up. "I just intercepted this series of transmissions." She pulled up a list of communiqués on her PRD. They were all from Olivia, all sent recently.

H124 met Onyx's gaze. "She survived."

"It gets worse." She played a few of the video feeds. The first were a series Olivia had prepared for fellow Delta City PPC execs, informing them that the asteroid fragment that fell in the Pacific Ocean had been the one predicted to hit Delta City, so all was fine now. At first H124 thought her grandmother might still be clinging to the plan to somehow get the A14 and divert the asteroid. But as she read Olivia's next coded communiqué, she realized it was far more devious than that.

In it, Olivia informed Melbourne City that she was heading there to take over its programming. Once Delta City was destroyed, Melbourne City would be the new seat of PPC power, and with all the Delta City execs dead, Olivia would rule the roost.

"She's planning a coup," H124 groaned. "She's convinced all those people to stay there so that they'll be killed and she can take over as head."

"She'll be the reigning PPC exec on the planet," Onyx agreed.

"So she's not planning to retrieve the A14 anymore."

"It doesn't look that way."

H124 was stunned. She wondered if the continued pirate broadcasts would eventually overpower Olivia's machinations in time to get the rest of the people out of Delta City.

"Thank you for letting me know."

"Of course." The hacker smiled. "Good luck out there."

"Thanks."

"Hágoónee'," Onyx said in Navajo.

"Hágoónee'," H124 answered. She'd been picking up bits of the language from listening to Onyx and Raven, and "hello" and "goodbye" had been the first two words she'd learned.

Chapter 19

The journey to the southern continent was a long one, but the *Argo*, able to stay aloft for weeks, didn't have to land once. They sailed south, passing over dry, barren land. Jagged mountain peaks rose and fell beneath them, often snowy and visible through banks of clouds. At other times there were only miles of flat plains, stretching on forever.

In one spot a series of step pyramids rose out of the brown soil, arranged in a square pattern, with dusty roads leading off in every direction. The site looked ancient. She wondered who had lived there, and how long ago.

She watched their progress on her PRD, zooming out on the map. The land grew narrower as they headed south, with vast oceans opening up to either side. Then the shores of another continent came into view, and once more they sailed over a vast landmass.

They frequently passed over the ruined remains of PPC megacities, the buildings crumbling and toppled, the shield walls weathering away. All around these sites lay destruction, the land beyond dead. In more than a few of them she could see channels meandering out, evidence of old rivers of human waste like those that streamed from Delta City.

They slept and ate, talked and played cards. Onyx had joined them in case her skills were needed. They all took turns spelling off Winslow. Dirk taught H124 *Go Fish*, the game he and Astoria had played in the weather shelter after their harrowing experience in Delta City and the Death Rider arena. It felt so long ago now, almost another life. As Dirk dealt the cards, sadness crept into his eyes. He blinked rapidly.

"Want to play a different game?" she asked him.

He rubbed his face on his shoulder rather roughly. "No. Let's play this one. I like to think of her. It makes me feel connected to her." After he dealt the hand, he spread the remaining cards in a fishing pool in the center of the table. "It's like her spirit is here with me."

They sailed on, heading ever southward, crossing an ocean. Then a coastline came into view, a few large icebergs floating off a rocky shore. The *Argo* crept over the ice-coated land. Nothing prepared her for the sheer immensity of the ivory landscape below. She pressed against the glass, marveling at the bright scenery. In the distance rose saw-toothed peaks, where bare rock stuck out in jagged arêtes on their steep sides. The *Argo* motored towards them, its engines humming through the cabin. Like the genebanks in Greenland and Siberia, she knew this one had also been built into the side of a mountain, deep underground, taking advantage of the natural cold temperatures to keep the samples intact.

Though the sun remained strangely low on the horizon, the sky, dotted with a few wispy clouds, stood so blue against the white snow that her eyes started to tear. She donned her goggles and peered back down. She viewed the brilliant vista, taking in the sculpted edges of ice and windswept rock.

As they neared the genebank, Winslow pulled the *Argo* to a stop, hovering in the same spot. "We may have a problem."

Raven rose from his seat. "What is it?"

"Someone beat us here."

Everyone clustered around Winslow. She'd brought up a display that zoomed in on the genebank, still several miles away across the snowy terrain.

Staring at the display, H124 was eager to spot its entrance. Then she found it and froze.

A tall, grey tower, nearly identical to the one they'd visited in Greenland, jutted out near the base of one of the mountains. But the sight of the immense spire wasn't what made her blood freeze.

A PPC airship waited near the entrance, its shining silver surface flashing in the sun. Winslow zoomed in. Objects littered the snow nearby, discarded as they'd been at the first genebank they'd visited.

Soldiers emerged from the entrance, carrying maglevs loaded with items. They dumped them unceremoniously into the snow, then vanished inside again. Moments later they appeared with a large shelving unit, casting it haphazardly on the ground.

Winslow pivoted the view. Several other groups of soldiers busied themselves with luxurious furniture from the airship, bringing it inside the genebank—a bed, a tremendous armoire, a plush couch.

The PPC wasn't just destroying this genebank—they were moving in.

"It's just a single airship," Byron observed. "I don't see a dropship."

"What are they doing here?" H124 asked. "How could they know about this place?"

Raven eyed Onyx. "Could they still be listening in?"

"No way. But they could have gotten the information a while ago, when Astoria originally let them in."

Dirk looked out the window, clenching his jaw. Astoria had given the PPC access to the Rover computer systems to save his life, and she knew he still felt guilty about it.

"Wait—I see more movement down there. An exec is coming out," Winslow told them.

A man in an immaculately tailored grey suit emerged, blinking in the bright Antarctic sun. "Give me the nocs," Willoughby said. He zoomed in on the man.

"That's Caster, a junior exec from Delta City." A slender woman joined the man, dressed in a blue suit that blazed against the white terrain. "And that's Fino, a producer I've worked with in the past."

They ordered the troopers around, gesturing angrily when one of them dropped a massive canopied four-poster bed. The troopers hurried inside with it.

"What are they doing?" H124 asked.

Raven pulled out his own nocs, studying the ground around the entrance. "They're throwing out the DNA samples to make room for their own stuff."

H124 joined him, zooming in on the suited pair, watching as troopers carried in bulky settees, mahogany desks, and stained-glass lamps.

Raven lowered the nocs. "They must think they can ride out the big impact inside the vault. We've got to get them out of there."

"Will more PPC people arrive?" Winslow asked.

Willoughby pursed his lips, considering. "I doubt it. They wouldn't want other people to know about the location and risk having a mob down here, with PPC execs vying for space and resources. They're probably hoping to wait out the impact, then move up to Melbourne City."

Where Olivia was heading, H124 thought. She'd told them of Olivia's plan to take over the PPC in Melbourne City. "Maybe she spared these two execs so she'd have support people."

Willoughby lowered the nocs. "Makes sense. They're both on Olivia's immediate staff. Been with her for years. Both are absolute sycophants. Looks like they don't have a lot of troopers with them, not in a ship that size. Probably just a protection detail." Willoughby leaned over the controls, zooming in on the soldiers' uniforms.

H124 noticed the tattered state of the black uniforms: sleeve stitching pulled away, threadbare pants with the knees worn through, face shields dented, scuffed helmets scored and scratched, all as if they'd been through countless battles.

"It's a DisPos unit," Willoughby breathed, wincing.

"What's that?" H124 asked.

"The PPC uses them for tasks where the soldiers are disposable. They kill them at the end of the mission. Usually they're prisoners or troopers who disobeyed orders, or even soldiers who annoyed an exec a single time." He looked away from the display, meeting her gaze. "Under those helmets, they're likely wearing cranial webs."

"What are those?"

"Metal nets fitted to the skull, full of electrodes. If the troopers don't follow orders, the nets deliver an excruciating dose of electricity. It's agonizing. Each time they disobey, the shock gets worse, until eventually it becomes lethal. The PPC lies to the troopers, telling them that once they complete whatever task they've been ordered to do, they'll remove the web, and the troopers can resume their normal duties. Or if they were a prisoner, they'll have some time taken off their sentence. So they go along with it, not realizing what's in store for them after they do the PPC's bidding."

H124 rubbed her arm. "That's terrible."

Willoughby nodded."

Byron came forward, his Henry repeating rifle in hand. "So when the PPC sees us, they're going to order that DisPos unit to fight to the death."

Willoughby winced. "That's my guess."

He cocked the rifle. "Then we'd better be ready."

"How do you want to play this?" Dirk asked, studying the grouping of troopers on the screen. He glanced around at H124 and the others. "Obviously a frontal assault won't work. We're outnumbered."

Byron nodded, leaning over the display. "This will require stealth." He looked out of the window, scanning the terrain. "There." He pointed to the ridge that lay between them and the vault. "Drop us off there, and we'll snipe them from that ridge. Even the odds."

Despite everything the PPC had put them through, H124's stomach turned at the thought of sniping unwilling soldiers in cold blood. But they had to think of the bigger picture—to secure that genebank. She also knew the soldiers wouldn't hesitate to kill them in the same fashion.

"Okay," she said reluctantly.

They donned the white snowsuits, with thick mittens over liner gloves and crampons on their boots. They didn't want to leave Winslow alone with the *Argo*, so only Byron, Dirk, and H124 elected to go on the initial outing. Armed with long-range rifles and pistols, they piled out of the *Argo* as it set down gently on the snow. Her boots crunched the compact drifts, and a bracing wind tugged at her parka hood. Her eyes teared in the cold. She donned her goggles, lowering her hood briefly. It was enough for the cold to penetrate to her eardrums, now stinging and throbbing. She replaced her hood quickly.

Moving stealthily on the far side of the ridge, keeping out of sight, the *Argo* motored off slowly, ready to circle the genebank and gather more intel.

The three climbed to the top of the ridge. The going was slow, and even with the crampons they slid often, losing their forward momentum to gravity.

More freezing gusts assaulted her, so she zipped her parka all the way up, shielding her face even more. The thick mittens felt awkward as she held the long-range rifle. She didn't know how she'd have the dexterity to aim and fire properly, but without them, her hands would surely be frostbitten.

Beside her Dirk scrambled, one mittened hand in front of him as he climbed, the other gripping his rifle. Byron did the same as they made slow progress up the ridge.

At the very top she gripped the exposed rocks and hefted herself up, hooking her elbows on the far side and lying flat in the snow. Already she could feel the cold through her suit, but as yet, it wasn't unbearable.

As Dirk and Byron lay down on either side of her, she pulled out her diginocs. They were a little over two miles from the genebank now. She zoomed in on troop movements by the entrance. A flash of red drew her eye to the left. H124 sucked in a breath. A woman stood there in a crimson suit, arms crossed, her silver hair flapping lightly in the wind. Olivia.

A group of DisPos troopers stood around her in a semicircle. As she addressed them, they each peeled away, seeing to some order or another. When they'd all gone, H124 was shocked to see the man standing next to Olivia. It was the head Death Rider from the PPC ocean liner attack, his skull epaulettes decorating his jacket, his immense stature towering over Olivia.

H124 swept the area, looking for more Death Riders and spotting three, then five more, moving among the DisPos unit, carrying furniture and equipment.

She could picture Olivia making a truce with him on the ship. *"Don't kill me and you can wait out the asteroid impact with me. I know of a place."* She remembered Olivia pointing up to the sky, indicating the impending asteroid impact.

"Do you see what I'm seeing?" Dirk asked, puzzled.

"If you mean a bunch of Death Riders, then yes," Byron answered.

"It doesn't look like the PPC are their prisoners, or the other way around." Byron lowered his nocs.

H124 zoomed in on the main Death Rider's face. When Olivia wasn't looking, he peered down at her with blatant disgust, but he made no move against her. He stood with his arms crossed, looking out at the others imperiously, occasionally shouting orders to his subordinates.

She counted seven Death Riders in all, four men and three women, all with human body parts as fashion accessories—ribs, necklaces of teeth and finger bones. From her belt, one woman wore a battle axe that flashed in the sunlight. The haft appeared to be a human femur.

Among the DisPos unit, H124 spotted a small collection of regular PPC troops. One of them approached Olivia and spoke, and she pointed to the airship, gesturing with her hands, as if describing some object. The soldier nodded and hurried toward the ship, emerging moments later with some kind of elaborate wooden box. She nodded at him and he rushed inside, no doubt delivering it to whatever room Olivia had selected as her private residence where she would wait out the impact.

H124 studied her grandmother's face. The woman stood with her hands on her hips, wearing a smug, conniving expression. When Epaulettes wasn't looking at her, she likewise gave him a disgusted appraisal. Clearly these two would betray each other at the first opportunity, but for now they were unenthusiastic allies. Olivia gave out a few more orders, then disappeared inside the genebank.

H124 made a quick scan of the present weapons. The DisPos soldiers carried only flash bursters and batons. She didn't see any energy rifles or sonic weapons among their tattered group. The few PPC soldiers carried flash bursters and energy rifles on their backs, and as usual, the Death Riders were armed with a range of deadly weaponry, from shotguns to pistols, cattle prods, and swords. One woman had throwing knives strapped to her thighs.

"What's the plan?" Dirk asked.

"I say we take out the Death Riders first," Byron said. "Then the regular troopers, then the DisPos. And if we get a clear shot at any of the PPC execs, get rid of them for good." Byron glanced at her. "Unless you..." his voice trailed, off but she didn't need him to finish. She knew what he meant. Unless she had a reservation about killing Olivia. She did, once, when Astoria had stood over the woman, revolver pointed at Olivia's head. H124 had hesitated then. And it had cost them all dearly. Sanctuary City lay in smoldering ruins. Willoughby had been tortured and almost repurposed.

She would show no mercy now. She nodded to Byron, and he gave her a sympathetic look, then gazed back down at the enemy.

"Once we start firing, it's going to be a mad house," Byron warned. "And look at this slope." He pointed to the far side of the ridge that angled down to the genebank. If soldiers wanted to ascend the ridge to attack them, they'd have a much easier time climbing than they'd had on the far steeper side facing away from the genebank. "We can still pick them off if they try to come up here, but only as long as they don't vastly outnumber us."

Her PRD beeped. She opened the comm channel. Willoughby appeared, his expression grave. "We're on the far side of the genebank now. Let us know if you need some kind of distraction. Maybe we can lure some of them over this way. Divide and conquer."

"Thanks," she told him.

"All right. Here goes," Byron said, and he readied to take the first shot. "I'm going for the big one first."

Peering into his scope, steadying the barrel of the long rifle on a rock, Byron aimed for Epaulettes. He fired. Through her own scope, H124 watched a spray of viscous red erupt from the gigantic man's neck. Astonished, he slapped a hand to the pulsing jets he collapsed in the snow. Two nearby Death Riders instantly dropped the equipment they were carrying and rushed to his side, dragging him inside the airship. A second round from Dirk hit him in the leg.

"If that airship takes off, we're going to have a hard time getting out of here," she pointed out. She scanned the crowd for anyone dressed as a PPC airship pilot, then spotted one on the right side of the genebank, talking to a weapons officer. She could pick off both of them in short order if she was any good with the rifle. She'd never used a scope like this before, and they were so far away that wind and distance would play a vital role in making the shot. She studied the scope's readout, the rifle's built-in anemometer apprising her of the wind speed and direction. The reticle accommodated for these factors, and a laser told her exactly how far away she was from her targets. With these automated assists, she hoped she could make the shots. The rifle also served as a dual weapon, being mounted with a grenade launcher. It only held two grenades, but she'd stuffed a few more in her parka pockets.

Dirk squeezed off two more rounds, hitting one of the Death Riders in the side as he helped their commander to the airship, but missing the second one entirely. "Damn!" Then they were out of sight, up the ramp and into the airship. "You know that thing has a medpod," Dirk said through clenched teeth.

Chaos erupted. With the crack of the shots reaching them two miles away, troopers turned in confusion, trying to figure out where the sniping was coming from. The weapons officer pointed to the airship, gesturing for the pilot to come with him. H124 held her breath as he walked in front of the pilot. She fired just as their heads lined up, one in front of the other. The round struck the weapons officer in the skull, spraying the pilot behind him with blood. But the pilot wasn't hit. He started running for the airship, and again she held her breath, leading the target. The scope readjusted for distance and angle, and she waited for him to run into the shot. As soon as the targeting system flashed red she fired, striking him in the chest. He staggered, falling to his knees. He brought a hand to his chest, and it came away slick and red. He struggled to his feet, gasping, limping for the airship ramp. She tightened her chest and took another shot, this time hitting him in the side of the head. He collapsed like a sack of grain.

With the cacophony of shots echoing off the ridges and genebank, the troopers still couldn't quite pinpoint their location. They spun, guns drawn. H124 shifted her scope to the entrance just as Olivia reappeared and then vanished back through it, her face panicked.

One of the PPC soldiers happened to be looking in the right direction when Byron's rifle went off, cutting down a Death Rider. The soldier pointed up the ridge, pinpointing their location. Everyone scattered below, some running inside the genebank, others racing for cover in the airship. The DisPos soldiers took up shielded locations along the genebank entrance, flash bursters drawn, pressed into recessed sections. Three PPC soldiers emerged from the airship, pushing a sonic gun. They began setting it up. Byron took aim and shot one of them. The target collapsed in the snow. The other two hunkered down behind it. Dirk took a shot, the round pinging off the gun and going wild.

H124 wondered if Epaulettes was inside the medpod, making a plan for when he emerged.

The two soldiers by the sonic gun managed to find enough cover to get it online, then aimed it at the top of the ridge.

"What's the range on that thing?" H124 asked.

"Not exactly sure," came Byron's reply.

Dirk left his perch and slid a few feet down onto the protected side of the ridge. "Better take cover!"

She and Byron did the same, just as a blast of rock came raining down over them.

Byron smiled mirthlessly. "Guess we know the range now."

H124 scrambled back up to the ridge, threw herself down, and quickly took aim at the two soldiers. She hit one, whose exposed arm was just barely visible behind the sonic gun. He clasped his hand over the wound, and she could see the blood pulsing out. She'd hit an artery. The soldier next to him shoved him aside, and readied to fire. H124 slid back down to where Dirk and Byron waited.

Another hail of rocks. Again she sprinted to the top, collapsed, and took aim. But the remaining soldier wasn't exposing any part of his body. "Damn!"

She switched to the grenade launcher mode, the scope readjusting to accommodate the different ammunition. She only had a second before he fired again. Before the scope was fully calibrated, she pressed the trigger and slid back down. They heard a dull whump far below as the grenade hit, and no sonic blast came in reply this time, no rocks falling over their heads.

The three scrambled to the top of the ridge, discerning the remains of the sonic weapon lying in scattered rubble across the snow. A red splotch of lumps told them where the PPC soldiers had been.

Her PRD beeped. She lifted it. Raven's face filled the floating display. "We've found something strange. Looks like the this genebank is armed."

"What? Why would it need to be armed?"

"Someone's been doing repairs. Updating it, just like in Greenland. This is the largest genebank we've found yet. Someone wanted it protected. Right now someone inside the genebank is trying to bring the weapon system online."

"Olivia?"

"We think so. Onyx is trying to block her. If we can get control of that system…"

"Keep us posted!" H124 told him.

A retinue of PPC soldiers emerged with long-range rifles and took up protected stations around the airship. As the first one took aim, Dirk picked him off. She and Byron took out two more.

The DisPos soldiers remained pressed against the entrance or flattened behind snowbanks, still lacking weapons that could reach H124 and the others. Either they didn't have enough long-range munitions to go around, or the PPC was hesitant to arm them lethally.

H124 swept her scope up the sides of the entrance, spotting two guns mounted at the top of the entrance tower.

She returned to sniping the PPC soldiers who had rifles, and managed to hit one in the leg. But the others were too well-guarded behind the airship. Bullets chipped away at the rock by H124; one drove into the snow, sending up a plume of white.

A gust tore at her parka hood and threatened to roll them right off the ridge. She had to plant her boots between two rocks to steady herself. The wind tugged at the barrel of her rifle, threatening to tear it loose from her grasp. These were not ideal shooting conditions.

Then she heard a dull thrum. The airship weapon was warming up. It would take out the entire ridge, and them with it.

Chapter 20

"Can they fire that thing when they're not airborne?" she asked Byron. "I've never seen it done before, but that doesn't mean it's not possible." "What do we do?" She was just about to turn and flee down the ridge when the snowy ground on both sides of the genebank entrance started to rise up. Two mounds grew skyward, dry snow cascading off them in the wind.

As the mounds grew in height and more snow sloughed off, she made out shapes beneath them. Several DisPos soldiers moved away from them.

Transparent glass shields at the top of each snow tower slid away, revealing two massive cannon turrets. They had only seconds before the airship's weapon would have sufficient power to fire, and they didn't know if Olivia or Onyx controlled those turrets.

The turrets swiveled, centering on the airship. Brilliant lights flashed out of both of them, then more came from the two guns mounted atop the entrance. The pulses hit the airship, igniting its skin of tiny solar panels. As the ship erupted in flames, PPC soldiers and Death Riders streamed from its belly. She didn't see Epaulettes at first. Maybe he was still in the medpod when the ship caught.

Then she saw him, limping out, hanging onto the shoulders of two comrades.

Obviously, the medpod hadn't been able to finish. She couldn't see a neck wound anymore, but the hole in his leg seeped blood onto the snow.

The guns swiveled, but they didn't fire on the DisPos soldiers who'd taken shelter beside the genebank. It was apparent Onyx didn't want to risk damaging the vault.

As the remaining PPC soldiers scattered, fleeing to the safety of the entrance, H124 saw Olivia appear again. She blocked the doorway, arms crossed. Her inferiors pointed outside, gesturing toward the cannon, but she remained a stone. She pointed to the ridge. She yelled something, still not exposed enough for H124 to get a clear shot. H124 watched as the PRDs on all the DisPos soldiers lit up simultaneously. One looked reluctantly up the ridge to their location. The soldiers at the door, still gripping their long-range rifles, turned and faced them. They gestured to the DisPos soldiers, pointing to H124's location, clearly ordering a charge.

Some of the DisPos responded, lining into formation behind the troopers, but several hesitated, still standing against the entrance.

Moments later, all three grabbed their heads and collapsed into the snow.

"They're shocking them," Byron told her.

The three DisPos troopers staggered to their feet, arming their flash bursters, and reluctantly joined the fray. It was ridiculous to send them up there with only this weapon. They'd have to make it all the way to the top of the ridge before they would be able to hit H124 and the others.

But Olivia didn't care. They were disposable, after all, just meat vehicles to throw at the enemy in the hopes of overwhelming H124's location.

With a collective roar, the soldiers raced toward them, charging up the gentler side of the ridge. H124 took up position and picked off the PPC troopers in the front, targeting rows farther and farther back as the front ones fell. Rifles fired in return, their rounds pinging and cracking off the nearby rock. One struck only an inch to Byron's left, but the troopers couldn't aim well enough as they ran.

The cannon swiveled and began launching on the advancing soldiers. Some fell pitifully, tumbling down the hill. But there were too many of them. In time they overwhelmed their location at the top of the ridge. H124 slid down the back side, careening down in the snow until she reached level ground. She spun, bringing her pistol to bear and slinging her rifle across her shoulders. She had to rip off her mitten, relying only on the thin glove beneath to guard her hands from the bitter cold. She hit a PPC trooper. Dirk nailed a few more. She ran in an attempt to keep out of range of the flash bursters.

A DisPos soldier pulled out a baton, turning on Byron. He tried to get off a shot, but she struck his Henry repeating rifle, sending it flying. She advanced on him, and he stepped backward, tripping in the snow.

Suddenly aware of a PPC solider mere feet away, H124 spun and fired, blasting him in the torso. Bleeding, he grasped his chest, and fell back.

Only one PPC soldier remained now. The rest looked to be DisPos, racing feverishly toward them to avoid a lethal shock. Though she couldn't see any of their faces through their helmets, she imagined they were as desperate as she was.

The PPC soldier advanced on her, leveling his rifle. She took aim, but he ducked and rolled, rising up again and letting off a shot. She dove to the side just before he pulled the trigger, landing hard on the cold ground. It took a moment to shift her weight and bring up her gun, but she did so just as he was preparing to fire again. This time the bullet hit his arm. He dropped his rifle, gripped his humerus, and watched the blood stream out between his fingers.

The DisPos soldiers streamed onward, circumventing him. She glanced back to Byron. The same DisPos solider stood before him, delivering a savage kick to his head. Byron staggered back, and she was on him in an instant, aiming a blistering blow to his throat, but he managed to parry, and her fist landed on his jaw, snapping his head back. He went down in the snow on his back, and the soldier leapt on him, twisting his arm around to dislocate it, ready to kill him with a palm to his throat.

H124 leveled the gun on her, her finger moving to the cold metal trigger. Then Dirk grabbed her hand, and wrenched it upward. The gun went off in the air. "Don't!" he shouted. "Don't you see?" His face was desperate, emotional.

She didn't see. But now the wave of DisPos soldiers had closed in on them, aiming their flash bursters, some opting for their batons. She couldn't see any of their faces behind the opaque face shields, but imagined some of them were relishing the act of cornering their prey.

And then they all fell prone to the ground, completely immobile.

She stared down at the fallen bodies, and already Dirk was running over to Byron. The DisPos trooper who'd attacked him lay sprawled across his body, face down in the snow. "What the hell?" Byron breathed.

H124's PRD beeped. Onyx's face filled the comm display. "I shut down their cranial webs, but it won't last long. You need to pull the nets off quickly."

H124 dove into the snow, whipping off the closest trooper's worn helmet. On his shaved skull clung a metal net filled with electrodes. Needles went down into his skin. Carefully H124 peeled it off. Then she went to the next trooper and the next, shucking off the webs. But Dirk and Byron remained by the trooper who had so savagely attacked Byron. When she'd removed the last net from a trooper, she jogged over to them. Dirk was bent down by the fallen soldier.

Hearing H124 approach, he looked over his shoulder, wearing a huge grin. She hadn't seen him beam that much in a long time. "I knew I recognized that fighting style," he said.

Perplexed, she came around his side and gazed down at the fallen trooper. It was Astoria.

Chapter 21

H124 couldn't take her eyes off her fallen friend. They'd shaved her black-and-red mohawk, and her hair was shorn all the way to the scalp. Astoria's eyes fluttered as she propped herself up on an elbow, groaning. Her eyes fell on Dirk, and her brow creased in confusion. "What the..." she began to say.

Dirk bent and hugged his sister, clinging fervently to her. Over his shoulder, Astoria stared up at Byron and H124.

With their help, she stood groggily. She took a long look at H124, then extended her hand. H124 shook it, knowing better than to pull the warrior into a hug, no matter how much she wanted to.

Astoria sized up Byron next, then gripped his shoulder as she swayed in a wave of dizziness. "Damn thing." She shook her head. "I sort of recognized you. Something deep down was telling me that if I fought you hard enough, I'd somehow break free of the thing." She kicked the cranial web where it lay in the snow.

"How did you..." H124 managed. "How did you survive?"

Astoria gripped her forehead. "I didn't think I had. The explosion on the rooftop took out most of those soldiers. Some of us lived though. Olivia found me in a coma." She went silent. "Then she..." She shook her head, unwilling to finish. She stared back at the cranial web with disgust.

Others troopers struggled to sit up, cradling their heads, some groaning in pain.

Byron stepped forward. "We've removed the nets," he told them. "You're once again your own masters. The PPC no longer controls you." He allowed them to absorb their new reality. "If you're willing to go on your way or join us, then our fight with you is done here."

Several struggled to their feet, their faces worn and scarred, deep circles lining their eyes. Olivia had obviously been working them to exhaustion. Many were gaunt with sunken cheeks, clearly malnourished.

"And where could we go to in this godforsaken place?" one asked, gesturing around at the barren white expanse.

"Then I suggest you join us, and we go kill this damn PPC faction once and for all," Byron told them.

Astoria gripped Dirk's shoulder, ready to pass out. The others swayed on their feet. Without the pain of the cranial web driving them on, these soldiers were spent.

H124's PRD beeped, so she brought up her comm window. Willoughby looked concerned. "You all okay?"

"Yes. We've had some amazing news." She told Willoughby about Astoria, showing her on the display.

"Now we just have to take out Olivia and her crew of sycophants," Willoughby said over the comm link.

Needing to form a plan, they climbed the ridge again, some of the DisPos soldiers coming with them, others sitting down in the snow, exhausted.

Astoria held onto Dirk's shoulder, struggling to make it up the steep incline. The deep hollows under her eyes and the sharpness of her cheekbones told H124 that she hadn't eaten a proper meal in weeks. Her arm trembled. Soon Byron joined them, Astoria leaning on both of them to make it to the top.

When they reached the jagged rocks at the crest of the ridge, they stared down at the damage that lay between them and the genebank entrance. The remains of the airship smoldered, the solar skin completely tattered and melted, the luxurious contents of the cargo hold burned black and giving off an acrid, black smoke.

Corpses of soldiers and Death Riders lay in the snow, with smears of red staining the pure white.

Beyond, the entrance to the genebank was closed. The cannon swiveled, Onyx keeping an eye on everything through its remote cameras.

"What do we do now?" Dirk asked, catching his breath from the climb.

H124 opened a comm link to Onyx. When the hacker's face appeared, she asked, "Any chance you can open the main doors for us?"

She watched as Onyx entered commands on her floating keyboard. "Looks like I can override the inner lock they've engaged. Let me know when you're close so they won't have the chance to counter my commands."

"Will do." H124 signed off.

She looked at the others in turn. Astoria hung on Dirk's shoulder. Byron checked his long-range rifle's targeting system. Then he checked his Henry repeater. On the other side of H124 stood two DisPos soldiers who had made the climb back up, a man and a woman. The man, likely in his sixties, was battle-worn, his thick, mahogany neck scarred as if he'd survived having his throat slashed. His dark eyes focused on the genebank entrance. The woman was younger, probably just a few years older than H124 herself. A jagged scar ran from her cheek to the back of her neck, and part of her ear was missing. Tattoos on her pale, shaved skull spiraled in elaborate designs.

"We're going to have to infiltrate the genebank on foot. Root them out," Byron told them.

The man nodded, his grizzled face a mask of grim determination. He gritted his teeth. "I will have revenge."

The woman turned to H124. "As will I," she growled, the scar pulling at her mouth as she clenched her teeth.

She stuck a mittened hand out. "I'm H124."

The woman shook it. "Scarlet."

She held the same hand out to the grizzled veteran. He gripped her in a tight handshake. "Garrett."

Scarlet eyed Astoria. "You know these people?"

Astoria patted Dirk's shoulder. "This one's my brother." She nodded toward Byron. "This one's an old friend." She gestured toward H124. "And this one's a pain in the ass."

Scarlet's expression grew wary. "You Badlanders?"

"Some of us," Astoria told her.

Scarlet glanced at the snow. "I came from a Badlander camp in the southwest. Hot there."

"Did the PPC capture you there?" H124 asked.

Scarlet crossed her arms. "I sabotaged one of their transmitters. They moved on my camp, killed everyone. I escaped, but they picked me up out in the desert. I couldn't find water, so I collapsed. Woke up in a prison cell."

"What about you?" H124 asked Garrett.

He cleared his throat. "I was no captive. I actually used to guard Olivia, the PPC cream of the crop. For years I protected her, escorted her through the city. Then one night she got news that someone she thought was dead was actually alive. I didn't hear the specifics. But she broke down. I mean, sobbed. I moved to help her." He went silent, staring back at the entrance. "Offered to listen." He narrowed his eyes. "I guess she doesn't like people seeing her cry. She ordered a group of soldiers to her quarters and they arrested me, dragging me to prison. I couldn't believe it. I'd served her faithfully for years. When I saw they were going to fit me with a cranial web, I was incredulous. I tried to fight them, but they hit me with a flash burster. When I woke up, they'd shaved my head and attached the damn thing, and I was on a dropship sent to wipe out a Badlander camp."

H124 wondered if that had been the night Olivia learned *she* was alive.

Scarlet stared back where their webs still lay in the snow at the bottom of the ridge. "Those things are terrible. You can't speak. Can't talk to each other. Can't voice an opinion. You get an order and all you can do is obey or die."

"How long did you have yours?" H124 asked her.

"Two years. Two years I've been fighting to the death for a regime I despise." She studied the closed entrance of the genebank. "But that stops today. I'm going to kill as many of them as I can."

H124 nodded, then checked her rifle and revolver. Glancing around at the others, she said, "Let's go."

They half-walked, half-slid down the more gradual side of the ridge. Moving at a crouch, maneuvering from one place of cover to another, they kept watch for any PPC soldiers who had remained outside. But the place looked deserted, with everyone hiding beyond the doors.

When they got within ten feet, H124 gave the signal to Onyx to open the doors. She heard a loud, metallic clank, then pushed on the door. It opened a crack. She waved everyone forward, slipping into the genebank.

Beyond, the place lay shadowed and dark, with only a few lights in the foyer illuminating a pathway to the stairs and elevator.

The layout was very similar to the other genebanks they'd visited.

They swept the first room, finding no one on the top floor. Pausing at the top of the stairs, H124 listened, tightly gripping her Glock 9mm. They had to be careful about using weapons in here. Energy propulsions could short out delicate equipment, and bullets could destroy liquid nitrogen tanks.

They started down the stairwell, stopping at each landing to listen for any hint of movement below.

Only silence greeted them. The stairs wound down into the earth, the air there holding at a constant temperature, warmer than outside.

At the bottom of the stairs they reached three doors, all of them closed. H124 tested the handles, finding them all locked.

Dirk went to work on the first one, prying off the cover plate of the locking mechanism and exposing its wires. The tech was old, but not as old as the vault. Still, it was nowhere near as new as the guns mounted outside. Someone had been here, updating the genebank where needed.

With a touch of two wires, the door lock clicked. H124 tested the handle, which gave. She swung the door wide and stepped back, anticipating a rain of fire to reach them on the landing. But no shots came.

She crept into the room. Scarlet and Garrett trailed close behind, armed with weapons gleaned from dead Death Riders. Dirk and Byron came next, with Astoria taking up the rear, moving backward to cover their six.

Like in Greenland, the control units and fittings for the liquid nitrogen tanks had been updated. They passed utilitarian shelves full of samples, both seeds and animal DNA. The grey shelves reached all the way to the ceiling, ledge after ledge of genetic material. The room was massive, and it was only the first. The extent of this genebank was far bigger than all the others they'd visited combined.

No sign of the PPC's presence made itself known in the room. No destroyed shelves, no PPC belongings. They moved through the entire room and its network of connecting tunnels and chambers, but turned up nothing. All of the samples looked intact, the liquid nitrogen tanks functioning properly. Olivia and the others must have been moving into another part of the facility.

They returned to the base of the stairs and the other two doorways. Dirk was in the middle of rewiring the second lock when the door suddenly swung open and an arc of electricity snaked out. It connected to the metal railing on the stairs. H124 and the others pressed themselves against the walls, waiting. But no one emerged. Then Byron darted into the open doorway, blasting a deafening shot from his Henry. H124 heard a man scream in pain. She ducked low, taking up position behind Byron. A Death Rider lay writhing in agony, a hole in his chest. No one else was in sight. The man ceased moving, and his arms slumped to the floor.

Byron advanced, H124 behind him, Dirk taking up the third position. Some of the shelves had been stripped and moved near the door for removal.

Movement caught H124's eye to the right, where a flash of blue moved between shelves.

Astoria caught the motion, too, and kicked over the shelf between them. Fino lay in wait. The exec gasped, covering her face with her hands. Astoria gritted her teeth and let out a roar, unleashing a steady stream of lethal electricity from her energy rifle. It hit the woman, melting her features away, setting her clothes on fire. Astoria kept the stream going until the woman's flesh liquefied and slumped off her fallen frame.

"Astoria," Dirk said gently. "Don't deplete your rifle's battery."

Only then did Astoria let up. As they filed past the dead Death Rider, Garrett gave his body a savage kick. Free from their bonds, they wreaked vengeance.

Up ahead, more movement among the shelves caught H124's attention. She spotted Olivia in her red business suit, sneaking alongside her other junior exec, Caster. The shelves back here were still full of undamaged samples, so Astoria's approach wouldn't work. H124 didn't want to hit anything important. She couldn't tell if Olivia or Caster was armed.

As they rounded a shelf, Astoria fired off a shot that hit Caster in the back. He went down, his skin crackling. Olivia raced on.

Suddenly the report of a shotgun blast filled the room. The broad epaulette-wearing Death Rider dove into view, running out from behind a liquid nitrogen tank. The blast went wide, catching both H124 and Byron with a few stray pellets. She felt her arm sting as one struck near her shoulder. Diving down, she aimed her 9mm, but the Death Rider was too fast. He rolled out of sight, moving through the shelves. She and Byron gave pursuit, while Dirk and the others circled back around a different aisle, hoping to trap Olivia.

They crept down the aisles, glancing between each shelf, hoping to catch sight of him, but for such a huge man, he was invisible. Behind them they heard something break. They spun, only to find an empty aisle. He was toying with them.

She and Byron kept going. Epaulettes leapt into view again at the end of the aisle. H124 dove, raising her pistol and firing toward him, not taking the time to aim carefully. The round struck him in the upper thigh. He cried out, firing his shotgun. Byron dashed between two shelving units, and Epaulettes missed them both this time.

The Death Rider took off, limping as fast as he could, blood dripping on the floor. H124 scrambled to her feet and gave chase, Byron close in tow. She rounded the corner, watching the Death Rider disappear into a neighboring room. She reached the doorway, cautious, pressing herself against the wall, and dared a quick peek. This room had been completely emptied of its original contents. An elaborate four-poster bed, towering wooden armoire, mahogany desk, and velvet chaise lounge filled the room now. She recognized the same furniture from Olivia's quarters in Delta City.

She pointed to the armoire, the only visible hiding place in the room, then noticed a second doorway leading off the room to the left. Byron fired a shot through the armoire. The door swung open, revealing a number of expertly tailored suits, but no Death Rider.

They hastened to the next door.

This led to a short hallway and another room. They'd be easy targets in the hallway; they'd have to move fast. Blood droplets ran the length of the corridor. Running at a squat, they raced to the next doorway, again pressing against the frame and moving out of sight.

Byron dared a glance inside, then hugged the wall. "Blood trails to the next room," he whispered.

They moved into the next chamber, which had also been emptied of its genebank contents. Another exec had planned to call this room their own. A canopied bed and polished desk had been moved inside.

The blood trail led them to a hallway at the opposite end. Here the corridor branched, leading to a set of emergency fire escape stairs, and to another set of storage rooms.

The blood brought them into one of the storage rooms, so they followed it cautiously, guns drawn.

They passed a closed door on their left, opposite the stairwell. But the blood led them past it.

The storeroom still held all its contents, the shelves storing scores of products made from endangered species parts. This time H124 saw what an elephant foot umbrella stand looked like. She felt sick. She held her breath, following the glistening red drops. They passed into an adjacent storeroom.

Shouts rang out behind them. They spun as a cacophonous shotgun blast echoed down the corridor.

The door opposite the stairs burst open, and the Death Rider appeared, Olivia in tow. They raced up the stairs. Somehow he'd doubled back on them, likely running through the connected room as they crept along.

H124 and Byron raced back the way they'd come, meeting Dirk and the others at the bottom of the stairwell. H124 turned and ran up the stairs, but already Olivia and the Death Rider were out of sight, rounding landings above them.

She took the stairs two at a time, keeping to the far wall in case the injured man decided to fire his shotgun down over the railing. Natural daylight spilled into the stairwell as a doorway above banged open and shut again.

H124 raced up the stairs, legs burning, her breath coming in gasps.

She reached the doorway, an emergency fire exit, and reached for the handle. Flinging it open and darting back out of the way, she narrowly escaped a shotgun blast. Pellets peppered the opposite wall.

The deep thrum of an airship engine filled the small space, so she dared a look outside to see one landing in the snow, its ramp descending.

The thing looked ancient, battered and rusted in parts, its hull patched in numerous places. Red and black paintings covered the pilot's cabin, a skull with eyes of fire, its dangling spine made of gleaming knives. As the ramp came down, two Death Riders came into view, one gripping a rifle, the other a battle axe. Epaulettes gestured for them to return inside. He shoved Olivia ahead of him as H124 and the others emerged from the stairwell, blinking in the bright white landscape.

She and Astoria fired off shots, but already the pair had disappeared inside, and the ramp closed. The genebank cannon swiveled and fired at the airship, landing a couple good shots in the hull. Then the ship blasted off, moving out of range so quickly the cannon had only hit home twice.

Winslow hailed H124 over the comm channel. "Sorry we had to keep out of sight. That airship looked like something the Death Riders had salvaged. I managed to fire a tracker at the ship though, before it moved away. They were coming in from the north, probably intending to land and help take over the vault."

H124 frowned at Byron. "Olivia's obviously aligned with them. She probably negotiated to save her own life in exchange for a safe place to wait out the asteroid impact."

"Wouldn't they just have killed her once she got them here?"

Dirk pursed his lips. "Probably."

The sound of the retreating airship now faded completely. "Do you think they'll be back?" she asked.

"Guess it depends if they have a backup plan," said Byron. "Somewhere else to go."

Raven appeared on the comm link. "Let's secure the vault. See what samples we can salvage from what they threw out in the snow."

* * * *

The *Argo* dropped Raven, Willoughby, and Onyx off by the vault entrance. Winslow remained on board, withdrawing to a safe distance. They all began picking through the discarded DNA material, using maglevs to transport them back inside. It took the rest of the day to fix the damage and replace the samples to their storage spaces.

The remaining DisPos soldiers returned to the vault, shivering from the brutal cold, a few of them helping to move the shelving. The others took shelter inside, where Raven fed them with food supplies from the *Argo*.

The dim sun hovered low on the horizon. As it dipped below, the cold grew even more brutal. Everyone took refuge inside the genebank, taking up spaces on the floor. A few of the DisPos soldiers took over the comfortable quarters of the PPC execs, sleeping three to a bed.

As H124 leaned against a wall, eating a chewy, dry MRE that was supposed to simulate something called "macaroni and cheese," her PRD beeped. She brought up the display, seeing a familiar string of numbers. The Phantom Code again.

First Sanctuary City, then the genebank at Greenland, and now here. Why these places and nowhere else? Nearby, Raven lifted his PRD, also noticing the code.

Onyx sat next to him, recording the numbers as they streamed in. When they'd finished, she compared the code to the one they'd received at Sanctuary City, then the one from Greenland.

A thoughtful expression overtook Onyx. "Gordon and I have been puzzling over this. Most of this code is identical. There's only one place where it changes." She moved away from the others to a quiet corner. Raven joined her.

Willoughby entered the room, exhausted. He sat down by H124. "I'm sorry we didn't get Olivia," he told H124, stretching out his legs.

"Me too."

"Where is she headed?"

"According to Winslow and the tracker she attached, north toward Melbourne City."

"Maybe she's hoping the atmospheric shield there will protect them from the effects of the blast."

"Can it?" Willoughby asked.

"I don't know. She probably had her doubts, too, which is why she came here first."

"She's going to miss that chaise lounge," he laughed.

"Probably the only thing she'll miss." H124 felt stung by how different Olivia was. How could the woman be of the same flesh and blood as them? She turned to her father. "I've been meaning to ask you…what's my real name? You call me 'H.' I'd love to go by my actual name."

Willoughby grimaced, hesitating. "To tell you the truth, we never decided on one. You see, before you were born, we had planned on calling you Olivia after your grandmother. But then…well, you know…"

"Oh, god," she groaned. "I think I'll stick to H124."

He chuckled. "Figured you would."

H124 stretched out on the floor, using her jacket as a pillow. Throughout the night, she drifted in and out of sleep, her fitful dreams making her toss and turn, a fear that Olivia and the Death Riders would return to the vault and slaughter them all.

"I've cracked it!" came a cry across the room.

Groggily, H124 sat up. She had no idea what time it was. Willoughby and Dirk stirred beside her. Astoria was still sleeping, snoring through an open mouth.

"You're not going to believe this," Onyx's voice came again. H124 and Willoughby hurried over, Dirk following reluctantly after a backward glance at his sleeping sister.

Onyx's face lit up. "I know why this code only came into places like the genebanks and Sanctuary City. They know about us. Thought we might eventually visit the DNA vaults."

"Who?" Dirk asked, rubbing the sleep out of his eyes.

"They're like us. Held onto science. They're the ones who've been repairing these genebanks. Trying to create a sanctuary for all the imperiled and extinct life. They've brought hundreds of species back from extinction."

"Rovers?" H124 asked.

Onyx shook her head. "No. Older. They call themselves the Binit. From what I understand, that was a local word for the first bird they ever brought back, the tawny frogmouth. They took over an entire continent after the PPC died out there from drought and food shortage. These people improved the atmospheric shield there, tore down and removed many of the buildings. Created a thriving, natural habitat. This Phantom Code," she said, looking around at them, "is an invitation to join them."

H124 leaned forward. "Why was the code different in each place?"

Onyx highlighted the disparate section of code on her display. "The directions change depending where the receiver is. Before it was directions from Sanctuary City. This time it's from Antarctica, and we've never been closer, geographically speaking. They're in Melbourne City. They call it Tathra now."

"Melbourne City?" Willoughby frowned. "But the PPC's still there. I've monitored their transmissions."

Onyx shook her head in excitement. "No. The code talks about this. The Binit people put out dummy transmissions using PPC tech. They randomly generate programming, just like the PPC does, and broadcast it, so if anyone's listening in from afar, they think Melbourne City is still up and running. But in actuality, Melbourne City fell more than a hundred years ago."

Dirk's mouth fell open. "How did you decipher this?"

Onyx grinned, loving the challenge. "The code has missing parts. It's a substitution cipher, with numbers representing letters. But some of the numbers are null strings. Blanks. I had to substitute correct answers to crack the code, things only people like us would know about. Things about geology, taxonomy of organisms, climatology, oceanography. The PPC would never be able to crack this."

"Do they know about the incoming asteroid?" H124 asked.

Onyx scrolled through the message. "I don't know. This message was created years ago. It's been being sent out automatically since then. We'd have to reach out and contact them in return."

"They might not know," Raven said.

"Wait a minute," H124 said. "Isn't Olivia headed toward Melbourne City with that airship full of Death Riders?"

Raven regarded her gravely. "We have to get up there. Warn them about the asteroid, about Olivia, about everything."

"Do we even know they're still there?" Dirk asked.

Onyx patched into Nimbus's satellite system and they began looking through stored images. She pointed to a grainy picture. "I see something at the location, but there's some kind of distortion. It does look like the city has a shield of some sort, but the satellite can't see through it. It's like it's putting out some kind of interference."

"Probably so the PPC can't see it," Raven offered.

"That's what I was thinking," she agreed. "I think they're there."

"Can we send them a message?" Raven asked. "It'll take us a while to get up there."

"We can try." Onyx backtracked the source of the signal. "What do you want to say?"

H124 thought back to her first warning broadcast on the windy top of the PPC tower in Delta City, warning the citizens to step away from their consoles and take refuge. She wondered how Rowan was faring there now, moving as many people as he could to the bomb shelters.

"Do you think you can use the same code to encrypt a message to them, maybe even embed a video?" Raven asked.

"*Aoo.* Who wants to record it?"

Willoughby stepped forward. "I will."

They began to work out a script for Onyx to encrypt. She nodded in approval as they finished it. "This way they'll know we're Rovers who cracked their code. We'll send a text version separately from the video transmission in case the video doesn't reach them. Double our chances."

"Sounds good," Willoughby said. He smoothed his hair back. It had become unruly these last few days. It was strange to see him in Rover clothing, a button-down black shirt and worn pants all made from bamboo, rather than his usual three-piece suit. Willoughby stood in front of H124's PRD recorder. "Ready when you are."

She pressed record and pointed to him.

"This is a warning," he began. "A devastating asteroid is due to hit the earth in only three and a half days. You must seek shelter. It will make impact at the following location." H124 brought up the coordinates, showing them as subtitles on the screen. "In addition, a contingent of Death Riders, led by the head of the PPC from Delta City, is inbound to your location. They are extremely dangerous and should not be trusted. We're on our way to lend any assistance you might require." He nodded at H124, and she turned off the recorder.

She played it back. "Looks good."

Onyx finished encoding the text message, and sent both of them out. "Let's hope they're listening and not just transmitting."

"It'll be light soon," Raven said, checking the time. "Let's get some sleep."

Everyone curled up again on the floor, H124 once more making a pillow of her jacket. It was freezing in the genebank, which was good for the samples, but H124 shivered all the same.

She was just drifting off when her PRD beeped. She looked down to see an incoming call from Rowan.

Moving away so she wouldn't wake the others, she entered the darkness of a neighboring room, slipping on her jacket. She brought up the window.

"H," Rowan said. "We expected to get a message saying you were on your way back." Behind him she could see an elaborate dining room, with a long table stretching at least twenty feet behind him, and framed paintings, mostly portraits and landscapes.

"We ran into some trouble."

He raised a brow.

"Olivia had brought some of her people down here, along with troopers and Death Riders."

"What?"

"She must have forged an alliance with them." She told him about Onyx hacking the cranial webs, and how Astoria was one of the DisPos units.

His mouth parted. "I can't believe it. How's Dirk?"

"Shocked but happy. Hasn't left her side."

"I'll bet. Are you coming up now, then?"

She frowned. "There's more." She told him about the signal they'd received, and how those people might not know about the asteroid. "Olivia might attack. She'll need a place to wait out the impact. So we're going up there."

"You won't make it back here in time."

"If Melbourne City still has its shield, it's possible we can weather the impact there."

"That's a big if."

"Onyx saw some kind of shield there on satellite images."

Rowan glanced around, considering. "I don't feel right staying up here while you're all risking your lives. If Olivia does attack, you're going to need help."

"She might just have the one airship," H124 told him. "And we don't know what kind of defenses these people have."

"More airships might arrive, like the one that picked her up."

He had a point.

"I'm coming down there. Going to gather as many fighters who are willing to come with me."

"You don't have to do that, Rowan. It helps knowing you're safe up there."

"If something happened to you all down there, I would never feel right about it."

"But—"

"I'm coming. Send me the coordinates."

She sent him the location to Melbourne City. She couldn't deny the fact that she felt bolstered by the thought of him arriving with reinforcements. But if the shield couldn't protect them from the effects of the impact...

"I'll send you a message when I get closer. And H..."

"Yes?"

He hesitated, appearing as if he wanted to say something, then changed his mind. "Be careful."

"I will."

She returned to her place on the floor, leaving her jacket on. Nearby Astoria slept soundly, blissfully, the first real sleep she'd had in a long time. H124 smiled, then curled up on the floor and tried to follow her into the same land of dreams.

* * * *

In the morning Raven placed a call to Winslow, who had been running the *Argo's* engines all night, circling it to keep the engines warm and rime off the skin.

"We're ready," he told her.

She nodded. "I'll be there in a few minutes."

Raven slung his pack over his shoulder. "We're moving out!" he called to everyone. The remaining DisPos soldiers regarded him curiously. "Anyone who wishes to join us is welcome to. But I should warn you that we will very likely be heading right back into another battle. You can stay here, but I don't recommend it. We can give you food, but it won't last long enough to wait out the fallout from the asteroid impact. You are welcome to take shelter on our airship until the battle is over."

Dirk slid up beside him. "How do you know we can trust them? They could sabotage the *Argo* as soon as they're on it. We don't know these people. They could be as bad as the PPC. Some of them *were* PPC, remember, former soldiers."

Astoria leaned over to her brother. "And some were like me."

The DisPos soldiers huddled together, murmuring. Garrett spoke up. "We're with you. And I, for one, will fight."

"So will I," Scarlet said. The others cast their tired gazes down. Most of them were so thin that H124 could see their bony frames beneath the tattered uniforms.

One man had taken off his jacket, and she could see his jutting shoulder blades and ribs protruding from his undershirt. She would be amazed if he had the energy to walk, let alone fight.

They heard the outside rumbling of the *Argo's* four engines, and moved to the door.

Bracing themselves for a freezing blast of air, they swung the door open. H124 witnessed the strange dawn as the sun rose just above the horizon. The oblique angle made the light strange, ethereal.

They filed up the ramp onto the *Argo.* All of the DisPos soldiers came with them. She and Raven locked the doors behind them. Then his gaze met hers. "This place will be able to withstand the effects of the impact. All that DNA. Missing pieces to our collection. I can imagine the rewilded world already." He managed a small smile, and they turned, H124's thoughts on the struggle ahead. She fought away images of the PPC destroying Tathra as they had Sanctuary City.

They had to stop them.

Chapter 22

The *Argo* headed north, sailing over the crystal white landscape. As they drew closer to the ocean, the icy terrain gave way to bare mountains, in deep browns and reds.

"It's really warming up down here," Raven said. "Look at that! Plants are growing."

H124 followed his gaze out the window, descrying patches of green dotting the plains. In the distance she saw the ocean, sparkling and blue, dazzling even under the low sun, which lay beneath a bank of clouds.

Raven leaned forward. "It's hard to believe that vast ice shelves used to spill off this continent."

"What happened to it all?" H124 asked.

"Like in Greenland, things started warming abruptly, much faster than a natural warming cycle. Huge cracks developed, and the ice shelves broke off into the sea. The flooding was disastrous."

H124 thought of the remains of the city she'd seen off the coast of New Atlantic, where buildings peeked out above the waves. An arm holding a torch, an elaborate spire.

Once they reached the open ocean, the wind tore at the *Argo* once more. It buffeted its sides, gusting against the glass windows. Huge waves surged below, with curling whitecaps. Soon ocean was all she could see.

Dirk and Astoria sat off in one corner, talking quietly. Astoria slouched, looking haggard, her cheekbones pronounced, her arms too thin. Dirk brought her food. They ate largely in silence.

When they'd been motoring for a few hours, Raven checked his PRD and conferred with Winslow. No return message had come through from Tathra.

H124 wondered if they would receive the message before Olivia got there. Then a darker thought occurred to her. They still didn't know if a shield was under that distortion on the satellite images of Melbourne City. How long ago had the message from Tathra gone out? It was on auto-repeat. Would the city even still be there? She moved over to where Willoughby sat at a table, eating a salad.

He dotted his mouth with a napkin as she sat down. "I didn't know how amazing real food tasted."

H124 recalled her own first experience eating greens, the pea she'd eaten straight off the vine in Sanctuary City. "Incredible, isn't it?"

Willoughby nodded, chewing with savor.

"What do you think Olivia will do when she reaches Tathra?"

Willoughby put his fork down. "I imagine she doesn't know the PPC isn't in power there. She probably thinks that as a high-ranking exec, she can waltz in and take over, or at least find a spot on the programming board."

"And when she finds out the PPC is gone?"

"Likely lay low, figure out her next move. But the clock is ticking for her to find shelter before the impact."

Raven approached the table, catching the end of their conversation. "The clock is ticking for all of us."

* * * *

As they drew closer, even from miles out at sea, H124 could see the shimmering atmospheric dome of Tathra. It *did* exist. The shield wasn't amber like the megacities run by the PPC. This dome was transparent, and from some angles she could barely see it. She assumed that natural light streamed through to the ground below. It didn't glow, so she imagined that at night, you could even see the stars.

It rose up, vanishing into a bank of clouds.

"If they have automated defenses," Winslow said, "this might be a short trip."

They flew along the perimeter, keeping to the coast. The environmental shield extended to the farthest edges of land. She didn't see any buildings, only natural terrain, verdant and vibrant. Winslow's transmitter told them that Olivia's ship had stopped some way out to sea along the western coast. They headed in that direction, intending to intercept her.

H124 couldn't tear her eyes away from the sights through the clear shield. They passed over steep snow-capped mountains, between whose peaks lay lush valleys with sapphire lakes, blooming wildflowers in vast meadows, and dense forests of pine.

Onyx once again sent out the warning video, along with the encrypted message. They'd gotten no response. As they covered more ground, H124 didn't see any sign of human habitation below. The land thrived, entirely natural. Beaches, mountains, forests, deserts, waterfalls, rivers…

"We're nearing Olivia's location," Winslow called out from the cockpit.

Raven joined her at the control console, standing over her shoulder. "Let's hang back. Can you put on the long-range view?"

Winslow brought up a floating display, revealing a close-up of the Death Rider ship. It hovered, holding its position a few hundred feet above the ocean surface.

H124 joined Raven. "What are they doing?"

"Scheming, most likely," said Willoughby, who'd come up behind her. "By now she's got to know the PPC doesn't exist here anymore. The asteroid is coming, and she's run out of options."

H124 thought of their own chances. By now, all the people from Badlander camps would be taking refuge in the bomb shelters, supplied with food and water, joining whomever Rowan had managed to save from Delta City.

But if they stayed to help Tathra, the *Argo* wouldn't be able to make the journey back there in time to join them. Nor would Rowan and the fighters who headed here even now.

She'd always thought this quest might be a one-way mission. Find the Rovers and stop the asteroid, or die trying. Then the plan had changed. They'd had to check and secure the vaults, make sure the samples were still viable. Ensure that the species driven extinct by society could be resurrected after the asteroid fell. But the new mission hadn't left much room for their own survival.

Down below, some remnants of the PPC megacity came into view. Many of the buildings had toppled or been dismantled, and greenery grew on everything. She pulled out her diginocs and studied the streets. Small batches of crops grew along the shores of a river. She zoomed in more, spotting movement among the upper stories of one of the taller buildings. As she adjusted the focus, she saw they were birds of prey, diving and returning to perch, swooping at incredible speeds through what was left of the urban canyon.

The people had used the remaining structures to simulate steep canyon walls. She'd read about a bird in one of her books, the peregrine falcon, whose populations grew so low due to habitat loss, that some people had started an initiative to bring them into cities to nest, where they could dive off the sides of skyscrapers to hunt. For a while it had worked, until pressures from drought, megastorms, and human population growth had proven too much and the falcons had died out.

She scanned the terrain with her nocs. Though she saw no sign of them, she wondered if the people of Tathra were down there right now. Maybe they dwelled in living buildings like the Rovers, and the structures would be too hard to spot from the air.

"Something's happening." Winslow zoomed in on the underbelly of Olivia's airship. A vehicle dropped out, then shot toward the shield. A lone Death Rider rode on the back of the small, sleek craft, his long hair streaming behind him, his face painted red, teeth bared.

"What is that?" H124 asked.

"A combat glider," Winslow answered. "A one-person flying craft. Without a pressurized cabin, they can't go too high, obviously, but they're fast and maneuverable. And armed." She pointed out the two forward guns, and a rear gun on a pivoting arm.

The Death Rider sped along the wall of the shield.

"What is he doing?" Raven asked.

"Looking for ingress?" Winslow offered.

He sped away from them, out of sight, headed in the opposite direction. They lost sight of him as he rounded the wall. "At least he went the other way," Raven said.

Just then a second and third combat glider dropped out of the underbelly. They shot off directly toward the *Argo.* "You had to say that out loud, didn't you?" Astoria mumbled. She'd come up behind them and leaned a hand on Dirk's shoulder. She still looked ragged and half-starved.

"What do we do?" H124 asked.

Winslow took them up, rising through the clouds, where they were out of sight.

A few minutes later, H124 heard the gliders rocket beneath them. "Do you think they saw us?"

"We'll find out soon enough," Winslow said. She moved them laterally, gliding above the clouds. The *Argo* was quiet. H124 clenched her jaw as they crept though the sky, moving up and away from the Death Rider airship. But now they couldn't see what it was doing, or where the gliders were.

Winslow continued to rise. "The gliders won't come up here at least. Too little oxygen."

The clouds quaked and parted before their eyes, and the *Argo's* shell vibrated with a low thrum. H124 looked out the starboard window to see clouds rushing by. Then they parted, and a sleek silver airship slid into view.

"We're spotted!" Winslow called out.

The thrumming grew louder, and H124 knew it all too well. The airship was powering up its main weapon. One blast from that thing and the *Argo* would go down in flames.

They had to fight back. H124 thought of the glass gunner pods located on either side of the ship, which until now hadn't been used. She darted toward the hatch that led to a gunner station. "Someone get the other gun!" she shouted. She hefted open the hatch, climbing down the ladder into the gunner seat.

Pivoting the gun, she targeted the airship's main weapon. Though it was a powerful armament, the exit port for the airship's blast was small and inconveniently located near the underside. She opened up the comm channel on her PRD to Winslow. "We have to get lower!"

The *Argo* dipped with sickening speed. H124's ears started to throb, the vibration from the airship's weapon so close it hurt. She peered up, swiveling the gun around, and unleashed a stream of fire at the weapon. The hits tore along the airship's hull, missing the target altogether. She'd never fired this kind of gun before, and it showed. She tried again. The *Argo* dropped more, and the angle opened up, giving her more room. Again she swiveled the gun, this time hitting home. Smoke billowed out from the airship's weapon port. The low vibration choked and sputtered, then cut to a high-pitched whine. Then the entire armament dropped off the airship's underside, plummeting down. H124 craned her neck to see it explode as it fell out of sight, shards of glowing metal raining in flaming trails.

"I got it," she said over the comm.

"Now we just have to take out the airship's guns," Byron told her. "I'm in the other gunner seat."

H124 couldn't see him past the curving underbelly of the *Argo,* but was buoyed by his presence.

Off the starboard side, the Death Rider ship turned slowly, revealing a mounted series of guns.

"Taking evasive action!" she heard Winslow yell, and the *Argo* dropped again at a sickening speed. H124 lost sight of the airship in the clouds, but she knew it couldn't be far behind. The *Argo* was no match for the airship's maneuverability. They couldn't outrun it, and certainly couldn't outgun it. The *Argo* just wasn't built for aerial combat. It was an exploration vessel.

Below them, the atmospheric shield came into view. Sunlight glimmered off parts of the otherwise invisible dome.

A blast of air hit the *Argo,* and they shot violently to one side as the Death Rider airship rocketed into view, drawing up moments before they would have collided. The bank of guns took aim, and fire erupted from the turrets' muzzles all along the flank of the ship. The roar and rattle of the guns was earsplitting. H124 gritted her teeth as she released another stream of ammunition toward the airship's gun array. A few of them exploded in flame, but the rest continued to retaliate.

"We're hit!" Winslow cried out. "We're going down! They've taken out the starboard engine!"

H124 craned her neck to see fire billowing out from the spot where one of the engines had been. Careening straight for the atmospheric shield, with no engine on that side to direct them away, H124 braced for impact. If this shield was anything like the PPC ones, they'd be incinerated. Winslow pivoted the craft, turning them a hundred and eighty degrees as they plummeted. She fired up the port engines, angling them away from the shield. But it was too late. The engines couldn't make up for the angle of descent fast enough, and now they were exposed to the guns on the left side. H124 couldn't see the airship anymore, but she could hear the bank of gunfire, then the answering report of Byron.

The edge of the shield came into view on her side. They were still too close. It rushed up beneath them.

"We've lost port engines!" Winslow shouted.

Byron continued to lay down a steady stream of fire. The *Argo* shuddered. H124 could feel heat radiating from its body, reaching her in the exposed gunner seat. Flames shot out on the other side of the glass gunner bubble, closing in on all sides as the *Argo's* skin went ablaze.

"We're losing air fast!" Winslow cried.

Now they were dead in the air, plunging downward, no engines. The atmospheric shield drew ever closer. H124 grabbed her seat, and her stomach flew up into her mouth. They had only fifty feet before they'd hit the shield. Twenty-five. Ten. Five. H124 clenched her jaw, clutching the edges of her seat as she became weightless.

Then the shield blinked off, and they passed through, still falling. She peered up through the flames around the glass of the gunner bubble to see the section of shield wink back into place. The Death Rider airship remained on the far side.

They continued to plummet. She'd be crushed if she stayed where she was. "Byron!" she shouted over the comm. "We have to get out of these!"

She grabbed the ladder and climbed up through the open hatch, struggling against the force of gravity to keep hold of the rungs. She rose up through the floor of the *Argo.*

Briefly she caught a glimpse of Raven and Astoria, strapping themselves into the seats in the main lounge. Willoughby reached out, and she managed to take hold of his hand. He reeled her in and she grabbed a seat, then its safety harness. She buckled herself in. Twisting her neck back, she saw Dirk helping Byron into a seat. He clicked his harness seconds before they hit.

Then everything went black.

Chapter 23

H124 lifted her head. Her neck throbbed from the impact.

Beside her, Willoughby unbuckled his harness and gripped his shoulder, pivoting at his waist. "Ow." He turned to her. "You okay?"

She nodded.

Slowly everyone around the cabin unbuckled their harnesses. Though banged up, none of them had serious injuries.

Smoke filled the cabin. The windows were all cracked, some shattered. The heat of the flames on the ship's exterior intensified, and the air grew stifling. Sweat beaded on H124's forehead and back as the acrid stench of burning wires and insulation greeted her nostrils.

"We need to get out of here," Winslow said from the cockpit. She unstrapped her belt and stumbled into the lounge area. The ramp came down. "Everybody off!" She waited by the door. The DisPos soldiers went through first, Garrett and Scarlet taking up the rear of their contingent.

H124 grabbed her toolbag while Raven scooped up a number of rolled up maglev sleds and his pack. Byron and the others grabbed all the weapons, and they piled out as quickly as they could.

Once outside, H124 wasn't sure what to expect. Above them, she could see that the shield remained intact. The Death Rider airship hovered up there, a small speck high in the sky, locked out for now. But someone had let the *Argo* in. She hoped they'd gotten the message. As they moved away from the smoking wreckage, she could make out some of the terrain around her.

They stood in a meadow, surrounded by trees. She caught hints of the scent of sun-warmed pine, and off to her right stood a massive granite boulder with bright orange and yellow lichen growing on its sides.

A small aircraft landed in the distance. Coughing from the smoke, H124 pulled her shirt up over her face and moved away from the burning *Argo*. Several figures piled out of the aircraft, and approached them hesitantly. Some started running through the smoke. They ran past her, men and women in fire gear, faces covered in masks, oxygen tanks strapped on their backs. Once they reached the wreckage they began dousing the flames with powerful handheld suppression units that streamed out white foam.

The smoke began to dissipate immediately.

Three other figures continued to approach them at a slower pace, then came to a halt. The tendrils of smoke parted, and she could just barely make out their faces. In the center stood a tall woman with long brown wavy hair. She looked to be about Willoughby's age, with kind blue eyes and a tanned peach face.

Flanking her were a man and woman. The former had some kind of mobile device tucked under an arm. He was a bit younger, with short blond hair worn close to his scalp and brown eyes set in a fawn face. The other woman was about his age, with dark, wavy hair. Her ochre face appeared kind, with a hint of curiosity crinkling her almond eyes.

As the last tendrils of smoke drifted away, the older woman's face came fully into view. Slackjawed, she brought a hand to her heart. Next to H124, Willoughby let out a strangled cry. He went down to his knees. He barely caught himself in the grass. H124 stooped beside him. "Are you all right?"

His eyes were fixed on the woman's face. She came forward reluctantly, then began to run, closing the distance. She threw her arms around Willoughby, kneeling in the dirt with him. He squeezed her tightly, tears streaming down his cheeks.

H124 stood up and stepped back. The two remained locked in a trembling embrace. Then Willoughby started to laugh, a shocked reflex tinged with joy. He pulled back and stared at her, cradling her cheeks. "Is it you?" he asked.

"Yes," she whispered. "When I saw that video message, saw your face, I couldn't believe it."

Willoughby laughed again, this time with pure ecstasy, and clutched her to his chest again.

H124 looked at Byron, then Astoria and Dirk, who likewise watched the scene with puzzled expressions.

Finally they stood, not once breaking contact. He slid his arm around her. He turned to H124. "H, this is Juliet. Your mother."

The words punched her in the solar plexus. She could only stare as her mind tried to make sense of it. *"What?"*

The woman came forward, finally releasing Willoughby's hand. She reached up and touched H124's hair, her chin, her cheek. Her expression wavered, then the woman brought her into a fierce embrace. H124 hugged her back tentatively. The woman pulled away, her eyes brimming with tears. "I thought I'd never see you again."

"Where have you been?" Willoughby asked her.

She wiped away her tears with long, slender fingers. "Well...here. Mostly."

"What happened?"

"After I escaped Delta City, we were attacked at the rendezvous site. Lawrence was killed."

"I went there. Found his body. Looked like Death Riders hit the place."

"It wasn't Death Riders. It was the PPC."

"What?"

"A PPC exec had been moving through the area, scouting locations for a more powerful transmitter, something that could reach other megacities. He arrived at our camp with bodyguards, looking for water. And he recognized me. He heard I'd been killed. The look on his face when he realized I was alive was pure greed. He knew he'd be able to parlay my capture into a promotion, even though Olivia meant to kill me."

She looked to H124. "He guessed you were alive, too. Said he'd see that you and Willoughby paid the price. I tried to plead with him. Told him what Olivia had been up to with the Delta City street population and the food cubes. But he didn't care. He gave orders for his bodyguards to grab me and raze the place to the ground. Lawrence shot him. A firefight broke out between his contingent of soldiers and Lawrence's people. The place caught fire in the chaos. Lawrence was killed. I managed to get out with a few of his friends. But I knew then I'd always be on the run, and if anyone found out I was alive, they'd target you two."

"Fortunately, the people I'd escaped with knew where a Rover camp was, far to the south on the gulf. We fled there, and the Rovers took us in." She took Willoughby's hand, gazing up into his eyes. "I wanted to send you a message so much. I heard through channels that you'd settled in New Atlantic. I knew you'd protect her." She looked at H124. "You were both safer without me."

H124 didn't know what to think. *Had* she been safer? She thought back to her life there, the isolation, the threat of Repurposers. But if the PPC had come for her when she was an infant, she wouldn't have stood a chance. She'd grown up anonymously, and perhaps it had saved her life. As she heard Juliet speak, H124's heart sank like a cold stone inside her chest, and reality no longer felt so real.

Juliet went on. "But the PPC patrolled the area on the gulf, sending over drones. Sometimes execs showed up in the area looking for transmitter sites. It was too risky. The Rovers there kept getting this coded message. A group of people were looking for extra help to maintain and expand this place. They called it Tathra. It means 'beautiful country.' I decided to make the journey."

"We would have gone with you," Willoughby said. H124 wondered if he was feeling the same combination of shock and joy, with the sting of hurt around the edges. Why hadn't she asked them to come with her?

"I wasn't sure if I could get a secure message to you," she told him. "We'd worked so hard to escape Delta City, to keep her safe, that I worried I'd endanger you both."

Willoughby regarded her with a tearful gaze. "I thought you were dead."

"I'm so sorry."

They shared another hug, this one of fervid apology.

A hand fell on H124's shoulder. She realized Byron had come to her side. "You okay?" he asked in a low voice.

"I don't know," H124 whispered honestly.

The two other people who'd approached with Juliet stood silently to one side, maintaining a respectful distance from the reunion. Now the man stepped forward.

Juliet pulled away from Willoughby, constantly wiping away her tears, and cleared her throat. "Oh, forgive me. This is Porter, our resident astronomer." She gestured to the woman. "And Parrish, our shield specialist."

The two nodded their heads in greeting.

Porter spoke with a deep voice. "We'd like to know more about this asteroid you mentioned in your message. While we've got some rudimentary telescopes here, we don't have the kind of facilities we'd need to track near-earth objects in any kind of detail."

H124 swallowed.

Raven stepped up. "Of course." He patted his pack. "I've got everything you need here."

Parrish reached out and shook his hand. "We need to know if our shield can withstand the blast, what the asteroid's velocity and entry angle will be."

"Is there a way to stop it?" Porter asked, and H124 felt herself go numb. There had been a way, yes. And they'd fought hard for it. She looked around at the varied greenery, the giant life-giving trees, hearing bird song fill the air.

More than ever she thought they were doing the right thing. The world deserved a chance at something like this again. A paradise for *all* living things.

When no one answered Porter's question, Juliet looked up at the hovering airship. "Let's get somewhere safe."

They boarded the small aircraft. Juliet introduced them to Donovan, who sat at the helm. H124 hadn't seen anything like the craft before. It was like a small airship, but had no visible engines or propellers. They all piled inside, and the craft took off, accelerating at such a gentle pace that she could barely tell they were moving. They flew over the landscape, H124 and Raven pressed to the windows, in awe of the terrain below.

They sailed over the canopy of a lush rainforest, where trees grew so thick she couldn't make out anything except their top stories. Birds and insects fluttered around the branches.

Fog enshrouded the nearby mountains, cascading over the crests like waterfalls of mist. They passed over a section of snowcapped peaks, avalanche chutes green and lush. On one slope, she spotted two bears digging for roots and tubers. A family of white mountain goats meandered across a snowfield, two babies cavorting playfully with each other.

They then sailed over a section of desert, spotting a bighorn sheep hopping around on barren mountain slopes, a desert fox, and a handful of camels navigating the sandy terrain. Palms dotted the vista, with water pooling at their bases. Raven pulled out his diginocs, pointing out wildlife excitedly. They zoomed in to watch a desert tortoise digging a burrow, puffed up chuckwallas sunning themselves on rocks, sidewinders weaving across the warm sands.

The flight continued. Upon a vast golden savannah she caught sight of elephants rubbing on trees, herds of zebras, wildebeest, giraffes, gazelles. A pack of African wild dogs slunk near a watering hole.

The next few minutes took them over a temperate forest with deciduous and pine trees towering over meadows of wildflowers. H124 spotted a herd of deer grazing in a field. In an area rich with eucalyptus trees, she watched kangaroos and wallabies bouncing along, and a bandicoot digging on a hillside.

Then an expansive grassland opened beneath them, very much like the recovered section that had thrived outside Sanctuary City. A sparkling river meandered through the grass. H124 was thrilled by the sight of it all.

"Oh my god," Raven breathed, pointing down. H124 followed his gaze to a herd of elephant-like animals grazing in the sun. Thick woolly fur covered their bodies, and their gleaming white tusks were tremendous, curving out from their mouths. "Mammoths!" Raven cried. Nearby, woolly rhinoceros munched on grasses. He pointed out a group of bison. "Are those Beringian bison?" he said breathlessly. "And look there!" he said, pointing out smaller elephantine creatures. "Mastodons!"

Parrish turned to follow their gazes. "We're hoping to reintroduce these animals back to their native continents as their populations stabilize and we restore their habitats."

They traversed landscape after landscape, each habitat thriving and revitalized. And this was just one continent, and one of the smallest, to boot. H124 imagined what they could do with the rest of the earth, bringing those species that had been decimated back to life, giving them a chance.

They hadn't yet told Juliet and the others that they'd had a plan to stop the asteroid, but now were letting it hit. She looked over at her mother, who was sitting near the front with Willoughby, chatting excitedly with one another. She'd never seen Willoughby so animated, so lively. It made her smile.

"Once we're at our HQ, we can talk about the asteroid's trajectory," Porter started to say, but his words cut off abruptly. The aircraft slowed to a halt near the edge of the shield. On the far side of the shield wall, ocean waves broke along the seashore. A line of wind turbines ran along the beach, turning busily.

"What is it?" H124 asked, peering out of the window. And then she saw it. The Death Rider ship had tracked their progress, still hovering on the outside of the dome above. At first H124 wasn't too concerned. They hadn't been able to penetrate the shield. "What are they doing?" asked H124, turning to Onyx. "Can you tap into Olivia's communication again?"

Onyx nodded and went to work.

But before she could bring anything up, the clouds parted. H124's stomach sank as dozens more retrofitted PPC airships came into view, gleaming painted skulls decorating their sides, makeshift cannons mounted on their exteriors. They wheeled in unison.

The Death Riders had brought in backup.

They began firing along the shoreline, where the sand exploded upward. "What are they doing?"

Parrish stared down in horror. "They're targeting the shield's power conduits!"

On the beach, wind turbines fell, crashing into the sand. Huge craters opened up in the earth, exposing smoking conduits that quickly caught fire. Black billows drifted down the beach.

"They want to take over the city to wait out the asteroid strike," Raven told them.

"The idiots!" Juliet yelled, leaning against the glass to look down. "If they take down the shield to get inside, we'll never get it back up in time before the strike. They're targeting the city's power supply."

"They've never been ones to consider consequences," Willoughby pointed out.

H124 heard a low thrumming build up, followed by an explosive boom that shook their aircraft. A shockwave hit them, sending them hurtling downward. The ground surged up beneath them as they plunged, but at the last minute, the pilot got the aircraft under control. They came to a jarring halt just feet above the ground.

The humming ceased abruptly. H124 stared up to see the dome come down in a dazzling display of light, fading all the way to the retaining wall before winking out.

The Death Rider ships moved in at once, raining fire down on them.

"The shield is down!" Juliet cried. "We're unprotected!"

All around them grass caught fire. The pilot shot up into the air, speeding them toward cover, but already the Death Rider ships gave pursuit, cannons flaring.

The invasion had begun.

Chapter 24

Willoughby turned to Juliet as the aircraft banked through the air. "What kind of defenses do you have?"

She frowned. "Not a lot. We've always relied on subterfuge for protection, convincing the PPC that Melbourne City was still active and transmitting. We've got a few mobile cannons mounted on aircraft, similar to the ones we installed at the Antarctic genebank. We have some small arms, a handful of EMP weapons. That's about it. We've never had to use them before."

H124 wondered how far out Rowan and the other Badlanders were, and how many he'd been able to muster.

Byron leaned forward in his seat. "Backup is coming. But we have to hold them off till they get here. Think we can do that?"

Juliet nodded. "We can do our best. In the meantime, we can try to get the shield back up."

Parrish leaned over, bringing up diagrams on her floating display. Her PRD looked very different from H124's. Parrish's was far sleeker and smaller, the display brighter and three dimensional, so real that H124 wanted to reach out and touch it.

"Our wind and solar power are routed through those conduits. They're scattered around the continent, feeding into the few dwelling areas we have. The interior of the continent is completely unpowered. The shield draws so much energy that all of the conduits have to work in tandem to keep it operational."

Juliet spoke up. "We could use the excavator. Dig down under the area where the PPC destroyed the cables, and splice them together right under their noses."

"We'll have to destroy the ships, too, so they can't repeat the endeavor," Parrish pointed out. "Timing is essential. If we can repair the conduits enough to bring the shield online right after the airships are destroyed, that would be perfect."

Byron turned to H124. "How much time until impact?"

She regarded her PRD. "A little over two and a half days."

"We don't have much time for error."

Raven leaned forward. "I don't get this. They must have a backup plan. Once they're inside the perimeter of Tathra, they'll want the shield back up or risk dying in a global firestorm."

H124 patched into Rowan's comm link. "How far out are you?" she asked, bracing against the fast maneuvers of the aircraft.

"Almost there. Still out over the ocean."

"We definitely need reinforcements. The PPC just took down the city's shield."

"Send me your exact coordinates."

They ended their call, and the aircraft slowed. Out her window, she could see similar Binit aircraft, all converging on the same spot. Mounted on some were pulsar cannons identical to the ones outside the Antarctic gene bank.

A dropship modified by the Death Riders dropped into view, sending the smaller Binit aircraft scattering. She heard the dropship's main weapon powering up. Immediately their aircraft took off, weaving in and out of the others. "Trying to draw its fire!" Donovan called back. "Give those cannons a chance!"

H124 strained to see out of the window, bracing herself against the sudden movements of the craft. A cannon let loose a stream of fire at the dropship as another Binit aircraft arrived, this one fitted with a different weapon. The design was very similar to the EMP gun she'd used at the missile silo. "Hold on," Donovan said, careening out of range. The EMP fired, and the Death Rider ship dropped to the left, then spun, dead metal falling through the air. It crashed to the ground, sending up dirt and catching fire.

Death Riders streamed out of the emergency exits, scattering across the field as flames consumed the ship.

"One down," Donovan said, veering back toward the other craft as another dropship lowered into view. Death Rider guns rattled from its flank, firing off a volley of deadly shots. H124 wondered how long it would take before the EMP gun would be ready to fire again.

Then something impacted their hull, driving them down. As they went into a spin, H124 clung to her seat, feeling Raven steel himself beside her.

But this time Donovan couldn't bring the craft out of its spiral. It hit the ground with explosive force, sending H124 thrusting out of her seat as the safety harness cinched down across her shoulders and lap.

"The engine's on fire!" Donovan panicked, unstrapping and climbing out of the pilot's seat. "Everyone out!"

H124 unbuckled herself and scrambled out with the others into the open. Above them the dropship fired its primary weapon, opening a colossal crater in the earth. The Binit aircraft scattered, though one was obliterated instantly in the blast. Machine parts cascaded through the air, falling down in a cloud of smoke and debris.

Binit pulsar cannon fired on the dropship in an attempt to take out its guns. "We have to find cover!" Byron yelled, taking off toward a knot of trees. They'd crashed on a savanna, with little cover except for the occasional tree cluster and some rock outcroppings. In the distance, she spotted two giraffes running for safety, their long necks and gangly legs swaying gracefully from side to side.

Pushing herself, she reached a small gathering of trees and took refuge behind a trunk.

Pulling up her PRD display, she sent Rowan their updated coordinates. Moments later, an equally beat-up dropship appeared from the opposite direction. It pulled up on the scene, rusted and dilapidated, engines sputtering and clunky. The low pulsing sound that emanated from it told H124 that its main weapon was primed and ready to go. She braced herself, but when the blast erupted from the belly of the craft, it hit the enemy dropship, its skin instantly vaporizing in a fiery inferno. What was left of the underbelly cabin turned into a searingly bright ball of liquid metal; it rained down to the earth, killing everyone on board.

Rowan's face appeared on her PRD comm channel.

"Right on time!" she said to him, bolstered.

Then two more enemy dropships fell into view. The pulsar cannon fired on one, taking out its bank of guns. H124 felt vulnerable on the ground. Off to one side, flames completely consumed the aircraft they'd been on.

The Binit cannon fired again, hitting the damaged dropship, taking out one of its engines and igniting the skin. It careened off to one side, too low to regain control, and crashed to the ground. Death Riders streamed out, heading straight for H124 and the others, weapons raised, adding battle cries to the clamor.

As Rowan's dropship lowered to the ground, the ramp extended, disgorging dozens of Badlanders onto the battlefield. She'd never been so happy to see anyone.

The Death Riders raced forward, clashing with the Badlanders. H124 withdrew her long-range rifle and took a knee, aiming toward the mass of blood-encrusted warriors. Byron did the same.

Up ahead the Badlanders tangled with the Death Riders in a chaotic dance. The sun glinted off blood-soaked battle axes while the boom of gunfire made H124's ears ring. A cloud of smoke gathered, collating from the discharge of all the weapons. The air smelled of cordite.

Above, a Death Rider airship hovered into view. She recognized it as the one Olivia had used to escape from Antarctica. She wondered if the woman was still up there. It drew lower and lower until it was only ten feet above the ground. This seemed to encourage the Death Riders, who went into a frenzy. They slashed and fought among the Badlanders, striking anyone who stood in their way.

The ramp came down from the belly of the airship. The Badlanders stared upward nervously, and some started to scatter. Then she saw something spew forth from the ramp: a black, writhing mass of creatures, alive and thrashing. They leapt eagerly from the ship, dropping into the midst of the fighting.

H124 breathed sharply. Night stalkers.

She halted as the Badlanders turned and ran toward her. The night stalkers leapt and slashed, vaulting onto the backs of fleeing warriors and tearing at their necks and arms. Screams erupted from the battlefield, mixed with the eerie ululation of the shadowed predators she remembered all too well. Then she noticed something: They were only attacking the Badlanders.

The Death Riders didn't try to escape. They remained on the battlefield, shooting the Badlanders in the back as they fled. She watched in confusion as the night stalkers weaved around any Death Riders they encountered, targeting only the Badlanders.

One with its jaws open in a snarl darted around a Death Rider and seized the Badlander he'd been fighting, knocking the woman over and tearing at her throat. A fellow Badlander hit it point-blank with a shotgun blast, but it was too late. The woman was gone, and her neck was nothing but a ragged hole.

As more night stalkers dropped down from the ship, H124 watched as they repeatedly avoided the Death Riders, still attacking only the Badlanders. Now Rowan's comrades streamed past her, and she tried in vain to spot Dirk, Astoria, or Byron in the escaping mass. She searched desperately for Rowan, but saw only the faces of strangers absconding in desperation.

A night stalker focused on a Badlander with a twin mohawk, its sleek black body prowling forward, its curved claws digging into the dirt with every step. It slunk forward, head low, then pounced. As it landed on the man's back, H124 got a closer look. Something clung to its skull. She withdrew her rifle and took careful aim as the man beneath it screamed and struggled. The beast's claws dug deep into his back, its fangs clamping down and tearing off a chunk of meat from his shoulder.

H124 fired. The round impacted the night stalker's chest. It fell into the dirt. Racing toward the Badlander, she helped him up. Torn flesh hung from his wound, and blood soaked his shoulder. "Thanks," he said, then ran past her, fleeing with his kin. H124 approached the night stalker twitching on the ground. It wore a cranial web, identical to the ones that had enslaved the DisPos soldiers.

H124 stared up into the belly of Olivia's airship. The wretched woman was controlling the creatures. H124 watched in disbelief as more of them than she thought possible burst from the ship's hold, cavorting down from the ramp, felling every Badlander they could reach.

The Badlanders streamed from the battlefield in a mass exodus, bolting toward H124. Byron caught up with her. They reached a stand of trees, and paused to catch their breath.

"Do you see Rowan?" she asked him.

Byron turned, bringing up his rifle's scope. "No. Don't see Dirk or Astoria, either. But Scarlet's out there with Garrett, inflicting some major damage."

She followed his gaze to a tangle of Death Riders savagely swinging chains and battle axes. She spotted Scarlet grabbing the end of a chain, using it to strangle its owner. The Death Rider went limp. Another foe closed in on Garrett, swinging a shotgun around and thrusting it against the man's chest. H124 was about to squeeze off a shot when Garrett kicked the gun aside, wrenched it out of the man's hands, and fired it into the Death Rider's face. His features exploded in a fine mist.

H124 opened up a comm window to Onyx. On the screen, she saw that the hacker was facing her own threats. She was aboard a different Binit aircraft, and it was banking wildly.

"Onyx! We're in a tight spot! Olivia has attached cranial webs to night stalkers. They're decimating our forces."

"*What?* She put them on night stalkers?"

"Can you hack them like you did the DisPos soldiers?"

"I can try," came the reply as another maneuver almost sent Onyx flying off her seat. She righted herself. "Give me a few minutes."

H124 raised her rifle, sniping Death Riders from her covered location. Night stalkers swarmed everywhere, taking down Badlanders so fast she didn't think they'd last another five minutes. Time crawled by. H124 struggled to find clean shots in the chaos.

Then the night stalkers all stopped attacking. Some collapsed, but most merely shook their heads in confusion. One clawed at its scalp, ripping off the cranial web. The others followed suit, tearing at the control devices, leaving gaping wounds in their heads from the electrodes. They then slunk low, looking around, catching their bearings, regarding each other.

A Death Rider raced by one, thinking himself safe. He gripped a battle axe, ready to swing it through a Badlander's head. But the night stalker clocked the warrior's movement and leapt up onto his shoulders, biting down and ripping out his neck.

The other creatures watched, then surged together, gripping the Death Riders and tearing at their flesh. In that moment H124 spotted Dirk and Astoria. She reloaded her pistol and ran toward them, picking off Death Riders along the way. A bullet whizzed past her ear, and her scalp flared up in a sudden, fierce sting. She reached up, and her hand came away bloody. But it was just a graze.

H124 joined the frenzy, fighting alongside Dirk, with Astoria throwing herself into the fray ahead. But as smoke drifted over the battle, and dirt churned up from the airship engines, it wasn't long before she couldn't see any of them. Binit aircraft dipped in and out on the outskirts of the fighting, picking up Badlanders and Binits and transporting them to safer locations while firing their pulsar cannons. She caught sight of Dirk and Astoria climbing into one of them.

Running out of pistol ammunition, H124 ran to the far edge of the fray. She needed enough distance to properly use her long-range rifle.

She raced for a group of boulders about a quarter mile away, hoping to outrun the night stalkers. She reached the granite outcropping and pressed her back against it, catching her breath. When her breathing had stilled, she lay down on the ground, using a smaller rock as a makeshift tripod. Through the rifle's scope, she sniped the Death Riders as they moved on the Badlanders. A familiar figure detached from the tangle of fighters, and H124 watched Rowan race toward her.

A night stalker broke from the madness, and gave pursuit. Rowan was no match for its speed. The second it lunged for his back H124 fired, sending it tumbling to the ground. Rowan glanced back, watching the creature go down, then spotted her position on the ground. He veered toward her.

"Thanks," he said, panting, when he reached her. "Where are the others?" He stared back at the pandemonium. Night stalkers pounced indiscriminately. One charged and sprang, landing on a Death Rider's shoulders. As the man went down in the dirt, three more creatures joined in the feast, a mass of swirling black. Torn pieces of meat flung up into her scope's view.

Another person broke from the commotion, brandishing a revolver. She ran, firing back as a night stalker gave chase. Despite the difficulty, she managed to hit the creature in the chest. H124 watched as the woman approached. Parrish. She spotted them at the rocks, and sprinted over.

H124 picked off more Death Riders through her scope. Parrish caught up to them, gasping. "I just talked to Juliet. The excavator has been destroyed. They weren't able to get the power conduits repaired."

H124 felt a pang of hopelessness. "What do we do?"

The woman's eyes went wide as the raging battle soaked in. "I...I don't know."

The sudden thrum of a PPC airship engine drew H124's eyes to the sky. Olivia's craft, having disgorged its deadly cargo, motored away. It fired its guns as it left, picking off Badlanders and Binits.

H124 watched her go. "We need to know if Olivia had a backup plan for the shield. She might have destroyed it just to be vindictive." H124 brought up a comm link to Onyx.

"Did it work?" Onyx asked her.

"Yes! The night stalkers are attacking the Death Riders now, too. Any luck getting into Olivia's PRD?"

Onyx nodded. "Just got through. I don't have all the details yet, but there's a secondary power source for the shield." Onyx was still on the Binit aircraft, now banking violently. She held on to her seat to keep from spilling out of it. Over the hacker's shoulder, H124 saw Willoughby and Juliet crowded around a display, trying to remain standing as the aircraft dipped and veered.

"I've been talking to Juliet," Onyx went on. "Apparently, when the Binits first moved here, there was no power. The PPC megacity had failed, and most of the population died out. The survivors abandoned the city. But they didn't want other people moving in. So they closed down the power grid using some kind of PPC scrambler. The power source is still intact. It's solid-state wave energy, like what we used at Sanctuary City. But without a decoder, the power conduits are set to self-destruct if anyone tries to bring them online."

"She's right," Parrish said beside H124. "Our ancestors tried a bunch of times to hack it when they first got here, and they almost blew themselves up. So instead they opted for wind and solar, building new conduits to power the improved shield. But supposedly that old power grid is still there. You can access it from a substation."

"Where is it?"

Parrish pulled up the map on H124's PRD, dropping a pin on its location. H124 noted the distance. "That's sixty-seven miles away!"

Onyx raised her voice over the gunfire. "Juliet says it's all PPC tech there. Might not be that different from what you're used to from New Atlantic. There are a number of locked doors that have theta wave receivers. You have to get through those first."

TWRs. They were H124's specialty. "I can do that. What about a decoder?"

Onyx glanced over her shoulder as the craft banked and she almost came out of her seat. Her eyes drooped, and for a second H124 thought the hacker was going to be sick. But she swallowed and pulled herself together. "They don't know. But I'm thinking Olivia must have one. It's got to be her backup plan."

"What does this thing look like?" H124 asked.

Onyx called to Juliet over her shoulder, but Juliet only shook her head in bewilderment. Willoughby came forward, struggling as the aircraft took evasive maneuvers. "H," he said, gripping Onyx's chair. "I'll bet it's an enigma decoder. High level PPC execs use them for all kinds of things— safes, vaults, locking up rooms where IPs are stored. They pick a thirty-three digit code for a scrambler. Without a decoder, they're impossible to break. But if you're high enough in the pecking order and you have one, you should be able to crack it."

"Is Olivia high enough?"

"Definitely."

"What would it look like?"

"Should be pretty small. Maybe just an inch long, half an inch wide. It should have a floating display. Might have her exec number etched on it."

"What is that?"

"43279."

"Can you get a lock on her position?" H124 asked Onyx.

The hacker's hands flew over the virtual keyboard. "She's here."

Seconds later, H124's map beeped with the new location.

"I'm going to find her." H124 signed off.

She needed a way to close that distance and fast. As she watched, another Death Rider airship lowered into view. They were arriving faster than they could repel them. The sooner she got the shield up, the more they could block out.

She scanned the battlefield for options, her sights falling on an unmanned Death Rider combat glider parked in the distance.

She turned to Rowan. "I need to get to that glider," she told him.

She was about to dash out from the cover of the rocks when Onyx called back. She brought up the comm window.

"There's a snag," the hacker told her. "Juliet just told me that their shield controls aren't designed to work with the PPC power grid. It's different tech entirely."

"What does that mean?"

"They won't be able to selectively turn the shield on or off in different parts. Once it's on, it's just on. And the power substation is miles outside the shield edge."

The realization hit her hard. "So you're saying that whoever goes out there and brings up the power to turn on the shield…"

"Won't be able to get back in."

H124 glanced over at Rowan and Parrish, who were firing at the night stalkers and Death Riders as the battle moved ever nearer their location. They hadn't heard what Onyx had said. She'd lost sight of Dirk, Astoria, and Byron. She knew they'd argue with her, but she didn't want them on the outside of the shield when it came back up. They wouldn't have time to get anywhere safe before the asteroid hit.

She looked back at Onyx. "Could one person conceivably get the power grid up and running?"

"If they had the decoder and a way to get through the TWRs."

"Where are Byron and the others? Raven?"

Onyx typed in a few commands. "Their PRDs are saying they're about fifty-two miles to the west of you, closer to the interior. Looks like they're on an aircraft heading to an armory to restock."

H124 nodded. "I'm heading out to find Olivia. Then I'll get to the power station."

A sudden blast on Onyx's side of the link blew out the audio for a moment. Onyx squeezed her eyes shut, and her PRD's camera went askew. H124 saw a fire spring up inside the craft, a panel behind Onyx sparking, igniting.

"We've been hit!" she heard Juliet say. "Get ready to abandon the ship as soon as we touch down."

The camera shuddered. With some difficulty, Onyx lifted it back up so H124 could see her face.

"I have to go," Onyx told her.

"Let me know when you're in the clear," H124 asked her.

Before she could respond, Onyx's screen went black.

Chapter 25

Worrying for Onyx and the others aboard the Binit ship, H124 crept around the boulders. She eyed the unattended combat glider, then pointed it out to Rowan. "I've got to get on that. Have to clear some distance and fast."

The battle was almost at the rocks now. Parrish took off running, gaining some distance. Byron and H124 hastened away at an angle, trying to avoid attracting the night stalkers' attention. A few Death Riders shot at them, but there was so much smoke that hitting a moving target in all the chaos was nearly impossible.

She reached the glider where it hovered just above the ground. "Ever flown one of these things before?" she asked Rowan.

He shook his head.

Undaunted, she slung a leg over it, then quickly studied the controls. Rowan jumped on the back, holding on to her waist. She moved her fingers to the handlebars. The grips twisted. She turned the right one, and the glider suddenly jumped forward. Byron almost flipped backward. She turned the other one, and it brought them to a halt. On the right and left handlebars were buttons that operated the glider's guns. The entire front of the craft turned, pivoting on a shaft that allowed her to steer. She twisted the accelerator, and they shot away from the battle. She heard a crack behind her, and checked over her shoulder to see a Death Rider training his rifle on them. She veered wildly to one side, pushing the accelerator even more.

The glider shot across the terrain. She discovered two foot pedals. One lowered them, one raised them, so she pressed down hard on the ascender pedal. They climbed into the clouds so fast that her whole body slammed down heavily into the seat. Rowan held on to her.

As they skirted away from the fight, she brought up her PRD's map, locating the glowing dot that marked Olivia's current position. It was twenty-four miles away.

H124 punched it, and they rocketed through the air. She'd hardly ever felt so giddy and free.

Flashes of light lit up the distant sky. As they drew near Olivia's location, H124 spotted three Binit aircraft mounted with pulsar cannons. They flew fast on the heels of Olivia's airship, firing relentlessly at the rear. Olivia's transport attempted to pivot, bringing it alongside the three Binit craft. Her panel of guns blasted at the Binit, but the smaller crafts, far more maneuverable, simply dropped down beneath the lumbering airship.

The Binit craft split up, arranging in a triangular pattern with the airship between them, all firing simultaneously. One of Olivia's engines caught, then a stream of fire hit the exhaust ports. The skin of the craft ignited, and the ship took an accelerating nosedive.

The Binit aircraft hit it again and again, igniting other parts of the solar-collecting skin. Olivia's plummeting airship finally hit the ground, crashing at an angle, dragging vertically along the dirt, the cabin turned on its side, everything sliding toward its nose. H124 didn't think anyone could have survived that uninjured.

The airship ground to a halt three hundred yards away. The ramp slammed down.

H124 slowed the combat glider, hanging back at a safe distance. Olivia emerged, still wearing a smug demeanor despite the pounding they'd just taken. She smoothed her silver hair back as the Death Rider with the skull epaulettes stepped out beside her. Two haggard looking men erupted from the smoldering ship behind them, taking off at a full clip to the south.

"Don't let those workers get away!" she shouted to Epaulettes. The escaping men struggled to maintain their pace as their tattered clothes hung off their thin frames. "We can't get into the substation without them!"

Epaulettes ordered two of his warriors to go after the workers. Rowan sniped the Death Riders. H124 unslung her rifle, fixing her sights on Olivia. Battle axe in hand, Epaulettes launched himself toward one of the small Binit aircraft as it flew past. He swung down hard, clipping the craft as it flew by. It teetered, though it managed to stay aloft, swinging around for another pass. He ran to meet it.

Olivia stood in front of the burning airship, exposed and alone. H124 took a knee, and even more careful aim. She hit Olivia twice, once in the thigh, once in the shoulder. Her grandmother cried out as she collapsed. H124 took off toward her.

Olivia didn't spot H124 in the frenzy until she was almost on top of her. Her grandmother struggled for a flash burster at her side, but H124 stomped on the woman's hand.

"Where's the decoder?" H124 demanded.

Olivia's hateful eyes narrowed. "I don't know what you're talking about," she enunciated, indignantly.

H124 lowered her eyes to her grandmother's wrist. Attached to her PRD was a sleek inch-long device, exactly as Willoughby had described. H124 kneeled down and tore off the woman's PRD as Olivia's grasping hands clawed desperately at H124's arm. She studied the device's surface. Etched upon it was the number 43279.

"No!" Olivia cried, trying to grab it back.

H124 stepped away, leveling her rifle at Olivia's head, finger on the trigger. Suddenly Rowan was beside her. He placed his hand on hers. "Don't," he told her. "She doesn't deserve to live. But if you're the one who kills her, it'll haunt you forever."

H124 paused. Would it? She wasn't so sure. It's not like she grew up with the woman, and the only thing she'd seen from her was pure evil.

"He's right," Olivia pleaded, sniffling, trying to get to her feet. "You don't want to live with that memory. I'm your grandmother. *Your family.* You have to help me." Olivia looked back at the smoldering airship. "My medpod is destroyed. You have to get me to another one." Blood seeped through her suit, soaking the fabric. Her tone hardened. "You shot me. It's the least you can do." Then she seemed to think better of her demands. "I'll help you get the shield back up. We can do it together. All I ever wanted was to raise you, to work with you. But that opportunity was stolen from me."

"Because you tried to kill your own daughter," H124 yelled, her throat constricting. "You robbed me of my family!"

"Don't listen to her," Rowan urged. "Let's just leave." He gripped H124's shoulder, coaxing her away. The roar of the surrounding battle reminded her that they were just as exposed as Olivia had been.

"Goodbye," she said to her grandmother, turning away.

"Wait!" Olivia called after her. "The decoder! We have to get the shield up now. There are more Death Riders on the way! I thought by now I would have gotten rid of that stupid slab of meat." A shadow fell over Olivia's face. H124 looked up to see Epaulettes standing over her grandmother. He'd heard every word.

Olivia struggled to her feet, holding out her hands, trembling. The Death Rider's eyes flashed a cruel gleam. He hefted his battle axe high above his head, and Olivia tried to stagger back, but too late. The axe parted through her head, cleaving her skull in half, splitting her all the way down to her pelvis. Satisfied with his work, the Death Rider removed the blade, pressing his foot against his butchered quarry for leverage. Olivia, or what remained of her, peeled apart, her splintered ribs and exposed organs sloughing off to the ground. Then both halves pitched backward, falling still in the grass.

Epaulettes turned slowly, setting his sights on H124. He gave a vicious sneer.

"Let's get out of here!" she shouted to Rowan.

They raced back to the glider, where the Binits and Death Riders had shifted their conflict. Three Death Riders stood by the glider, and one was about to board it.

"We can't let them take it!" H124 said. She dropped to a knee, aimed, and shot the presumptuous rider. His neck erupted in a geyser of blood, and his companions watched him slump off the machine.

H124 searched the area for alternatives, a downed Binit aircraft perhaps, but couldn't find any. With Olivia's airship down, the Binit aircraft had moved on to other targets. The glider was her only way to close the remaining forty-two miles to the power substation.

More and more Death Riders ran to the transport. Another tried to climb on, but his compatriot grabbed him by the collar, flinging him off roughly before trying to get on himself.

Rowan fired his pistol into the crowd, winging one in the shoulder, hitting another in the chest. They whirled on him, and in a unified roar took off toward him. The distraction working, he raced away from H124 and the glider, firing again and again, aiming back at the advancing killers. Then he clicked on an empty chamber.

H124 fired at the pursuing Death Riders with her rifle, killing two. More kept coming. Rowan reloaded and fired, but they were almost upon him. One raised a chainsaw over his head.

Now even more Death Riders across the way had noticed the combat glider, and started to run for it. She only had seconds to get there.

"Get to the glider!" Rowan shouted as he was overrun.

She ran, leaping onto the glider. Starting its engine, she wheeled it around just as the Death Riders reached her. She veered away from them, ducking as one threw a hatchet at her. Her mind focused only on the roar of the chainsaw as she banked toward Rowan.

But what she saw was ghastly, and her heart caught in her throat.

More than ten Death Riders had gathered around him, the chainsaw rising and plunging, with blood shooting up in arcs. She gunned straight for the group, sailing over them as they dove aside.

And then she saw Rowan, sprawled on the ground, his body limp and red. They'd decapitated him.

H124 couldn't believe it. Grief surged within her, a white-hot fire. She wheeled the glider back around, knowing she shouldn't, knowing she should head to the substation immediately, now, while she still had the chance, that Rowan had *died* for that chance, but the rage within boiled to the surface, and her fingers slid over the glider's gun controls. Speeding past the Death Riders, she pressed hard, laying down a stream of fire, blasting two in the head. The one with the chainsaw glanced the back of the gilder with his roaring monstrosity, only to bounce off and narrowly miss her.

She veered around for another pass.

This time she targeted the man with the chainsaw, who wore a mask of a human skull. He was missing an ear, sporting a puckered hole instead. H124 never felt such a rage in her core. She roared, savagely pressing down on the gun controls, speeding directly toward him and letting loose a torrent of gunfire.

His torso blew open. He fell gracelessly. She caught a last glimpse of Rowan's ruined body, and her whole body shook.

She thought of him helping her in New Atlantic. He was her first friend, the first person with whom she'd ever had any kind of real conversation. He'd helped her get out of the city, helped her at the very start of the journey that had taken her so far from where she'd come.

He couldn't be gone.

All she could do was blink away the tears, and speed toward the power substation.

Chapter 26

H124 sped onward, tears blurring her vision. When she reached the edge of the shield wall, she brought the combat glider higher, sailing over it.

A rolling set of dunes blocked her view of the ocean, but she could taste the salty tang of sea on the air.

H124 checked her location against the map, and brought the glider to a stop fifteen miles from the shield wall. She cut the engine and sat for a moment. She couldn't believe it. She fought away images of Rowan's corpse.

A deep thunder brought her eyes to the sky. For a terrifying moment, she thought Orion had been wrong, that the asteroid was already coming down, right on top of them. She searched the clouds, unable to pinpoint the source of the noise. Then she saw it—a fleet of airships in the distance, closing in on Tathra. She pulled out her diginocs, and zoomed in on the crafts. From what she could make out, it was a mixed fleet of Death Rider and PPC dropships and airships, probably ordered out to the location by Olivia.

H124 had to get the shield up and fast.

She resumed her trek to the power substation. She crested a rise and the ocean came into view, whitecaps tossing the surface. She raced along the beach. Before long a squat grey building came into view. It was covered with so many vines she almost missed it. She slowed the glider, once more checking the location. This had to be it. She dismounted.

Hurrying to the building, she brushed aside the long snaking vines to reveal a door. Part of the building's wall came away with the vegetation. The thing was crumbling into ruins. She stared out toward the sea. Somewhere out there floated the energy platforms, charging with every rise and fall of the waves. She hoped their cables ran underground, since she didn't see any snaking in from the water. It would have made sense to bury them, protect them from the elements.

She closed her eyes, reaching out with her mind, trying to connect with a TWR. But the image of Rowan came flashing into her head with such visceral force that she could only gasp in pain. She tried again, forcing her mind to be still. She reached out, exploring, sending the signal for the TWR to disengage the lock.

Then she felt something on the other side, a binary switch. She told it to turn off. The door lock clicked. She tried the handle again. This time it groaned, but it moved all the same. She pushed down hard, forcing it open.

The door swung wide. H124 coughed as a plume of stale air breathed out, smelling of dank mildew and something rotten. She pulled out her headlamp and switched it on.

As the beam penetrated the darkness, she stepped inside, finding herself on a stair landing. Hearing the drone of the incoming airships echo about the cavernous space, she started down the stairs.

She encountered a second door at the next landing. It too was locked. Again she reached out with her mind, struggling to concentrate. Her breath came rapidly, her heart pounding. She had to get through. Taking a deep breath, she called on the lock to disengage. She heard a click, and the handle turned freely.

Ahead lay a narrow walkway that ended at another door. She ran as fast she could, coughing in the musty air. This door was also locked, so again she contacted its TWR. She commanded it to disengage, but it didn't. She tried again, wondering if it had gone faulty from disuse.

Finally it clicked, and she wrenched open the door. Another set of stairs led down into darkness. Shining her light, she took them quickly, the droning of the airships no longer audible. At the bottom of the steps was another locked door.

She got through, and found herself in a cavernous room with huge machinery, switches, dials, vents, and cables twisting across the floor and up the walls. Her headlamp hardly penetrated the gloom.

She reached out with her mind, trying to sense a TWR. She could feel something, a machine in the off position. She commanded it to turn on. Nothing happened.

A dull click sounded on her third try. Something whirred, and a red light started to blink in the darkness. She had the sudden sense she'd just triggered the self-destruct, so quickly she brought out Olivia's PRD. She switched it on, pairing it with the decoder. A floating display came up, and H124 entered Olivia's PPC exec number. It took her to a screen with thirty-three blank squares. H124 remembered Willoughby saying that scramblers relied on complex, thirty-three digit codes. The decoder started flipping through numbers, trying each digit from zero to nine in each space. Numbers flickered by. The whirring grew louder. The red light started to blink faster, searing her retinas, and then a deafening klaxon rent the quiet space. She clapped her hands to her ears, willing the decoder to work faster. It locked down a number, then a second one. Numbers flew past. More were locked down. She heard the dull clank of some kind of machinery, felt a vibration through the floor.

The decoder had only twelve numbers to go. The vibrations grew more intense, as something shifted beneath her feet. Six more numbers. Four. She thought of running out of there, but she had to stay. Had to see this thing through or they were all dead. Had to get the shield up before more Death Riders got inside.

The decoder beeped. All thirty-three numbers locked in and transmitted. The klaxon silenced abruptly, and the red light switched off. The whirring under her feet persisted for another minute, as if something was moving back into place. Then the vibration stopped. She stood in the ensuing silence, breathing hard, then lowered her hands reluctantly from her ears.

She looked around, headlamp flashing over all the machinery. On the far wall, she saw a breaker box, the kind she used to see in the basements of buildings in New Atlantic. More than once she'd had to reset the power in a living pod building after the incinerator had blown out the fuses.

She walked to the box and opened the heavy metal door. There was a single switch inside. It had two settings, a one and a zero. It was switched off, pointing to the latter.

Her PRD beeped. It was Byron. She wanted to burst into tears when she saw his familiar face, but bit back the emotion. She opened the channel.

"Where are you?" he asked.

"At the power substation."

"Onyx just told me that if the power goes back up, you'll be trapped on the outside the shield."

She didn't respond.

He exhaled frantically. "What is with you and suicide missions, Halo?"

A small laugh escaped her.

"Hang on," he said. "Let me come to you."

"Then you'll be on the outside when the shield goes up."

"I don't care."

"I do."

"Just wait a minute. We can think of another way."

"Rowan's dead," she said suddenly.

"What?"

"Killed by Death Riders."

"Halo…"

"I have to do this."

"Just hold on. We can think of something else. Just give me a minute."

"There's a whole fleet of airships descending on the city. If I don't get the shield up now, they'll overpower us. There's just too many of them."

"We can fight them."

"At the cost of more lives? I have to do this."

She met his gaze, swallowing more sorrow than she thought possible. She hadn't expected it to end like this. She'd just found him. Just found Willoughby and her mother. But this was the one way she could ensure their survival.

"Halo, no."

She studied his features, remembering his scent. Then she reached out and threw the switch to the on position. She heard new sounds, things clicking into place in the walls.

"Damn it, Halo!"

"I'll call you back."

"Halo—" he started to say, but she signed off. It was hard enough to do this without seeing him.

The walls started to vibrate. She heard a dull *whump* coming from deep under her feet, like a generator trying to come back online. Then came a whirring sound picking up in RPMs before winding down again. A second *whump* sounded beneath her feet, and the walls shook a little. Dirt sifted down from the ceiling. The whirring kicked up again and sputtered. It coughed sporadically, then powered back down.

She waited. But another *whump* didn't sound. She knelt down, feeling the floor. Something hummed down there. She moved to the wall, but it felt still. She pressed her ear against it, and heard a high-pitched whine.

Then the third *whump* came, so loud that she jumped. She waited. Something rumbled under her feet, the rhythm speeding up. It sounded lopsided though, out of sync, like an unevenly worn wheel. It slowed again. Doubt crept into H124. Maybe it had been too long. The machinery beneath her silenced. Several minutes stretched by as she stood in the dark, watching the projection of her headlamp's beam on the floor.

Then another rumble came from below, and the rotating resumed. It spun faster and faster, sounding more even this time. She stared down hopefully. The hum echoed off the walls, and once more she covered her ears. The RPMs rocketed up. Lights blinked on in the room, revealing the size of the place. She saw generator after generator, all the machinery moving, groaning from so much disuse, but working.

She raced up the stairs, passing quickly through the locked doors, and burst out of the final doorway. Sunlight hit her. She couldn't see the fleet of airships anymore. The thrumming of the power station was so loud that she couldn't even listen for them.

Lights mounted outside the structure clicked on, and a topside vent burst open, a fan rotating to life.

She ran for the glider, and for a hopeful moment she thought she could make it back inside. But when she was halfway to the vehicle, a shimmering light flashed above the distant shield wall. The dome flickered and powered on in all its glorious wonder.

She'd done it.

She surveyed the entire structure, enrapt by this stunning feat of technology. She was in awe of the way it shimmered, visible only in some places. Her legs suddenly weak, she fell back into the sand.

She reached for her PRD, and turned on the comm link. She called Byron, but he didn't answer. She waited a second, then called Willoughby.

"H!" he answered. "We're standing under the shield. You did it. I can't believe you did it! Where are you?"

"I'm still at the substation."

"What?"

"I always knew this would be a one-way trip."

"But..." The words froze in his throat.

She knew exactly how he felt.

"But I..." he tried again.

They just sat there, exchanging a knowing look. Juliet came up beside him. "You did it," she said to H124.

H124 swallowed. "There was a fleet of inbound airships..."

"The shield came up before they landed. They didn't make it in."

"And the ones already there?"

"We're routing the last of them now. I can't...I can't tell you how grateful we all are. But..." Juliet turned away from the camera. "I just found her again," she heard her whisper to Willoughby.

"I know," he said, putting an arm around her. "Me too."

Juliet turned back to the camera, her jaw set. "I couldn't be prouder. Of everything you've done."

"Has Parrish run the numbers on the shield? Will it be able to withstand the effects of the asteroid impact?" H124 knew that Delta City's shield didn't stand a chance against the direct hit, but maybe Tathra's improved shield would be able to fend off some of the aftereffects of the impact.

Juliet looked over her shoulder at Parrish. The woman nodded.

"It will," her mother assured her.

H124 swallowed a painful lump.

"I'm glad I met you both," she told them. "It still feels like a dream." They watched each other for what felt like an eternity. "Is Byron there with you?" H124 finally asked.

Willoughby shook his head. "We haven't seen Byron or any of the others. We heard that Dirk and Astoria are holed up at an armory. The Binit forces there have routed the Death Riders."

H124 looked at her PRD. Sixty-four hours until the asteroid hit.

"I'm going to call them."

Her parents nodded, and she signed off. Dirk picked up a minute later. He sat with Astoria inside a darkened building, both of them drenched in sweat and dirt. Dirk had a split lip, and Astoria's forehead bled. "You two all right?" H124 asked.

"Better than ever," Dirk told her.

"How about you, Astoria?"

"Likewise," the warrior said, lending a feeble smile. "Byron told us what you did. That you're on the other side of the shield."

She didn't know what to say, so she just nodded. Then she told them about Rowan. They went silent, open-eyed with shock.

Astoria leaned forward. "I can't believe it."

Dirk closed his eyes.

They mourned in silence. Eventually Astoria looked back at H124. "About what happened on that rooftop in Delta City...you know that wasn't your fault, right? Dirk here says you've been kicking yourself over it. Don't sweat it. That was my choice."

It was the nicest thing Astoria had ever said to her.

"Thank you. That helps." She regarded them nervously. "Is Byron with you?"

"No. He's with Raven, in another section of the city."

Relief flooded over H124. "You two take care of each other."

Dirk bit his lip, and Astoria looked away. H124 signed off. She called Raven.

When he appeared on her floating display, she felt his contagious hope again. "H," he said. "How are you?"

"Alive," she told him.

"I'm in one of the de-extinction labs. We flew over here to make sure it didn't get hit. You wouldn't believe all the samples. It's all going to be amazing, H."

"I believe you."

"Parrish told me what you've done. I..." His voice trailed off. "We've been through a lot."

"Yes."

"That hurricane!"

"The worst!"

"But we made it through."

"I can't wait to see how it's all going to turn out," she said finally. But she knew she wouldn't see it. "Is Byron with you?"

Raven shook his head. "We got separated. I was rescued by a Binit aircraft. He elected to stay behind and fight."

"Sounds like Byron."

"Sure does."

"Let me know if you hear from him."

"I will."

She signed off and approached the edge of the surf. The waves rolled in and out, soothing her with their predictable rhythm. The fleet of airships thundered overhead, beating a retreat, likely trying to find another place to hole up.

At last H124 sat down on the sand. The sun sank lower as she leaned back, basking in its warmth. She got out her diginocs and studied the inside of the dome, watching a flock of birds fly by, landing in a tree. They chattered to each other. She imagined they were telling each other what kind of day they'd had. Where to find water, the best berries...

A mild thunder brought her eyes up to the sky. She sat up straighter, trying to pinpoint the location. When it grew louder, she rose to her feet, bracing herself to see an airship lower into view.

Instead a winged craft dipped beneath the clouds, heading toward her. She moved off the beach, running toward her combat glider.

The craft descended, growing ever bigger as it neared. Wheels emerged from its belly as it touched down on the beach, sending up a spray of sand.

H124 blinked in disbelief.

It was the A14.

It plowed along in the sand, sending up huge plumes of brown pebbles. She got on the glider and steered it parallel to the beach, meeting the A14 where it came slowly to a halt.

She drew up next to the craft's door. It banged open, and a ladder flipped out.

Gordon appeared in the doorway. "Need a ride?" he asked.

She burst out laughing, hardly believing it was him. "To where?"

"Thought we'd check out that big bomb shelter Rowan found. Greenbrier. They do have a bowling alley, you know."

She eyed him in astonishment. "I—"

Then Gordon stepped aside and Byron appeared, grinning down at her.

"Byron...how the hell did you—"

"This thing goes crazy fast," Byron told her. "I called Gordon right after we crashed the *Argo*. But I didn't think he could get here in time."

"So how about it?" Gordon asked her.

She jumped off the glider. "I've never bowled, you know." She bounded up the stairs, throwing her arms around both of them.

"Then let's get crackin'," Gordon said, returning to the pilot seat.

Byron ushered her in, and the stairs folded neatly back inside. He secured the door.

The inside of the craft held a dozen or so seats, all with harnesses.

"Definitely strap in, and put on those oxygen masks," Gordon told them. "This is a hell of a ride."

She fastened herself in next to Byron as Gordon taxied down the beach. She strapped on an oxygen mask.

"Here we go," Gordon called, pointing the craft's nose up. They rocketed upward at an unbelievable speed. H124 felt the air leave her lungs as incredible G-forces pressed down on her. She felt her face straining back, her lips prying away from her teeth, her vision blurring.

They shot above the clouds, where the orange setting sun bathed the interior of the A14.

H124 squeezed her eyes shut. Then it started to grow dark, and she opened them again. She gasped at what she saw. The void of space met her eyes. Billions of stars glittered around her. Pinned down by inertia and unable to crane her neck, she peered out of the corner of her eye, where she could see the curved edge of the earth far below, brown continents suspended amid oceans of blue, thin wisps of clouds scattered around it all.

"Fastest way to cover a lot of terrain," Gordon called out. "Go really high up and go really, really fast."

As they slowed at the top of an arc and she was finally able to move her head, she took in the vastness of space. In the far distance, a bright, irregularly shaped moon heaved into sight off the starboard wing, its surface mottled in the reflected sunlight.

Then she realized it wasn't a moon. It was the asteroid, hurtling toward Earth.

Gordon pointed the A14's nose down, and they screamed back into the atmosphere. Fire erupted on all sides. It sputtered out as they dipped lower, and they continued their descent at a sickening pace, following a similar path the asteroid would soon take. Then Gordon leveled off, heading for Greenbrier.

Raven's words came back to her. "The question we have to ask ourselves is do we preserve the earth now, like it is, destroyed by geo-engineering, with almost no biodiversity and a devastating regime in power, or do we give it a chance to reset, put some of all the wrong we've done back to right, and once more give wildlife and humans the chance to live and thrive?"

H124 closed her eyes. They'd done all they could.

The earth would be reborn.

A Note to the Reader

I've depicted a dark future here, one that could happen if we continue with "business as usual," burning fossil fuels, engaging in deforestation, overfishing the oceans, and not switching over to a more sustainable, green future powered by renewable energy.

But this doesn't have to happen. We don't have to keep losing the countless amazing animals we share this planet with, or endanger our own future.

We hear a lot about the dark times ahead—drought, food shortages, catastrophic storms and sea level rise, species extinction. Let's talk now about a bright future—one in which we come together, power our cities with renewables, where we are healthier and happier.

Guilt and fear are not good motivators. But if we shift the narrative from doom and gloom to be about a clean and positive future, people will be far more motivated to act when thinking of brighter days ahead.

Let's pull on the strengths of some of our human qualities. People are competitive, and this can work for a better future. Engaging people on a local level is often more effective than overwhelming them with the global situation. Let's have some local, healthy competition to make cities greener. If one city is benefitting from more renewable energy than another, that second city, not wanting to be outdone, could implement its own sustainable energy plan.

This friendly competitiveness would also work for a greener future not just between cities, but neighbors, office departments, sports teams, and more. Who recycled the most? Who biked into work the most? We could make it fun. We could make it the social norm, something we enjoy doing.

Though the topic of anthropogenic climate change has been greatly politicized in recent years, it's an issue that affects us all, and if we combat it, everyone benefits. We need to come together not as fighting factions, but as members of a society that are affected by climate change. Perhaps you are worried at the rapidity at which species are disappearing. Maybe you are an insurance policy holder whose property is subject to flooding, or a taxpayer dealing with expensive storm cleanup. Perhaps you are interested in keeping our economy healthy by creating new jobs in renewable energy fields, or you're worried about national defense.

Instead of thinking of this issue as us versus them, let's consider: Is energy efficiency a bad thing for anyone? Would cutting back on food waste or water waste negatively affect us? Would everyone benefit from cleaner air and water? Is drought a good thing for anyone? For the economy?

Many people, when looking to change their lifestyles to aid in mitigating climate change, see it as a sacrifice. But it is actually an opportunity—an opportunity to drive cleaner cars and have cleaner air that makes us healthier, an opportunity to have more energy-efficient homes and office buildings that save us money, an opportunity to enjoy a healthier, more plant-based diet, an opportunity to enjoy cleaner water and visits to pristine natural areas.

Talk to your friends, your neighbors. Encourage your politicians to support renewable energy. Show them the advantages, both financial and environmental, of shifting to more sustainable buildings and renewable energy. Talk to them about how we'd have cleaner air and water, describe the money we'd save with net-positive buildings and more energy-efficient cars and factories.

Let's imagine this bright future and make it happen.

Acknowledgments

Writing a novel is tough. Writing a series is even more so, and encouragement and support from people in my corner was invaluable. Thanks to James Abbate, who saw my vision in this series and was amazing to work with. I could not have asked for a better editor. Thanks to Martin Biro for including *The Skyfire Saga* in the new Rebel Base imprint.

Many thanks to James Akinaka, marketing whiz extraordinaire and to Alexandra Nicolajsen and Lauren Jernigan for getting the word out.

Hearing from readers is so important to me, so thank you to Sarah, Dawn, Jon, and Mary for your enthusiastic support and encouragement. You guys are the best! When writing gets tough, I forge ahead with you in mind, and it inspires me.

My father, also a novelist, and my mother, an avid reader, share my love of the written word and the natural world. Thank you for such an amazing upbringing.

Many thanks to Becky for her stalwart friendship over the years. And as always, thanks to Jason for his incredible support, encouragement, and helpful feedback. With you in my corner, my writing has truly flourished.

I am grateful to illustrator Bruce Emmett and artistic director Lou Malcangi for the stunning covers for all three books in the Skyfire saga.

Meet the Author

Alice Henderson is a writer of fiction, comics, and video game material. She was selected to attend Launchpad, a NASA-funded writing workshop aimed at bringing accurate science to fiction. Her love of wild places inspired her novel *Voracious,* which pits a lone hiker against a shapeshifting creature in the wilderness of Glacier National Park. Her novel *Fresh Meat* is set in the world of the hit TV series *Supernatural.* She also wrote the *Buffy the Vampire Slayer* novels *Night Terrors* and *Portal Through Time.* She has written short stories for numerous anthologies including *Body Horror, Werewolves & Shapeshifters,* and *Mystery Date.* While working at LucasArts, she wrote material for several *Star Wars* video games, including *Star Wars: Galactic Battlegrounds* and *Star Wars: Battle for Naboo.* She holds an interdisciplinary master's degree in folklore and geography, and is a wildlife researcher and rehabilitator. Her novel *Portal Through Time* won the Scribe Award for Best Novel.

Visit her online at www.AliceHenderson.com.

Shattered Roads

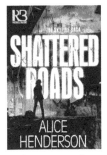

In a future laid waste by environmental catastrophe, one woman in a shielded megacity discovers a secret hidden within—and the nightmare of what lies beyond.

Her designation is H124—a menial worker in a city safeguarded against the devastating storms of the outer world. In a community where consumerism has dulled the senses, where apathy is the norm and education is a thing of the past, H124 has one job: remove the bodies of citizens when they pass away in their living pods.

Then one night, H124's routine leads her into the underground ruins of an ancient university. Buried within it is a prescient alarm set up generations ago: an extinction-level asteroid is hurtling toward Earth.

When her warning is seen as an attempt to topple the government with her knowledge of science, H124 is hunted—and sent fleeing for her life beyond the shield of her walled metropolis. In a weather-ravaged unknown, her only hope lies with the Rovers, the most dangerous faction on Earth. For they have continued to learn. And they have survived to help avert a terrifying threat: the end of the world is near.

Shattered Lands

Environmental devastation has left Earth a wasteland, but an even more nightmarish fate looms if the woman known as H124 can't stop an extinction-level asteroid from destroying the planet.

On the run from a dangerous media empire, H124 places her hope in learning more about the Rovers, the last bastion of humans to embrace science as a solution to Earth's ongoing environmental catastrophe. But with the planet under imminent threat from plummeting asteroid fragments, H124 must take on a perilous new mission: find and assemble the pieces of an ancient spacecraft capable of pushing the deadly projectiles off course.

Her journey will lead her to the hurricane-ravaged remains of the east coast, and onto the brutal streets of Murder City, where she learns a startling secret about her own past. Death Riders and night stalkers prowl the badlands, but an even greater danger lurks above as H124 fights to build the craft that is humanity's only hope for survival.

Printed in the United States
by Baker & Taylor Publisher Services